A RIPPLE IN TIME

A Historical Novel of Survival

By

VICTOR ZUGG

A Ripple In Time

© 2019 by Victor Zugg
All rights reserved.

This is a work of **fiction**. Names, characters,
businesses, places, events, and incidents are either the
products of the author's imagination or used in a
fictitious manner. Any resemblance to actual persons,
living or dead, or actual events is purely coincidental.

VictorZuggAuthor@gmail.com

ACKNOWLEDGEMENTS

Many thanks to Brandi Doane McCann (www.ebook-coverdesigns.com) for the cover design. Her creations belong in a gallery. And equal thanks to Sarah Gralnick. She's always the first to read my work. I very much appreciate her suggestions. And I'd like to express my appreciation to R. Alan Stello, Jr., Executive Director of Programming, National Society of The Colonial Dames of America in the State of South Carolina, Charleston. His knowledge of history was most helpful. They all made this book infinitely better.

CHAPTER 1

The PA system blared. "Final call for flight seventy-three with service to Charlotte, boarding at Gate Five. This is your final call. Gate Five, flight seventy-three."

Steve Mason quickened his pace along the corridor as he dodged the throngs of travelers. His hand clutched a small, black rucksack.

A lone female flight attendant with very short, dark hair was just about to pull the gangway door closed when Mason approached and got her attention with a lopsided smile. "Sorry, last-minute assignment," he said. He pulled a black wallet-sized case from his sports coat inner pocket and opened it for the attendant. A gold badge stood prominent against the black leather. Words on the badge read *United States Federal Air Marshal*.

The attendant smiled. "We were beginning to think you wouldn't make it."

"Traffic," he said, as he closed the case and returned the badge to its pocket. "Miami is lousy this time of day."

The attendant nodded as Mason stepped past her into the empty gangway. She closed the door, and they walked side-by-side.

"First class or back of the plane?" Mason asked.

"We have a couple of empty seats in first class."

"Excellent," Mason said.

"Where's Ted Wilson?" the attendant asked. "We don't see a FAM on this route very often, but when we do, it's usually Ted."

"Sick," Mason said. He stuck out his hand as they walked. "I'm Steve Mason."

She took his hand. "Karen James. I have first class for this flight, so I'll be seeing you. Let me know if you need anything."

"Will do," Mason said.

He ducked, even though his height didn't require it, as he stepped through the hatch and boarded the plane.

A younger female flight attendant, attractive, wearing her hair in a moderate stretched afro, greeted him with a smile. Her navy-blue skirt, coat, and flashy kerchief matched Karen's outfit.

He smiled at the attendant, turned right, and dipped his chin at the first empty seat, seat 3E.

An attractive younger woman with long legs and highlighted, blond hair occupied the window seat. She wore tight, designer blue jeans with a white, long-sleeve, v-neck pullover. Brown boots covered her feet.

"This one okay?"

Karen leaned toward the other attendant. "He's our FAM for this flight."

The second attendant smiled, "I'm Angie Knowles and yes, that seat will be fine."

Mason stowed his rucksack in the overhead bin and plopped into the aisle seat. "Sorry," he said to the woman next to him, as he buckled his seatbelt.

"Not a problem," she said, without looking up from the magazine lying open over her crossed legs.

Mason noted the flat tone and lack of a smile. *Oh well,* he thought. He glanced over his shoulder down the aisle at the full complement of passengers and the attendants preparing the cabin for departure. He faced front, rested his head against the seat back, and tried to relax as he ran through what his supervisor had told him over the phone.

Ted was sick and Mason was one of the few FAMs available to fill in. Normally a FAM would not be assigned to such a short domestic flight, but the threat level had been raised the day before for south Florida. Mike Reeves, his supervisor, didn't know exactly why. It was probably based on some piece of intel from one of the agencies. It couldn't be that big of a deal since Mason had heard nothing unusual on Fox or CNN. Cable news was usually the first to know. It didn't really matter. Mason, like all FAMs, was trained to handle pretty much any situation. The bad part was being rousted on his day off. But such was the life of a Federal Air Marshal. Show up and keep an eye on the passengers and the cockpit door.

The plane rocked as the last of the luggage was loaded below and the cargo doors were shut. The air pressure changed when Karen closed and secured the cabin door. Soon he felt the plane's movement as it was being pushed from the terminal and turned. The engines revved, and the plane began rolling under its own power.

The plane's PA system crackled. "Good afternoon. I'm Captain Anderson and on behalf of the flight crew I'd like to welcome you aboard. We anticipate a smooth, two-hour flight through mostly clear air. We'll be skirting the east coast. Sit back and enjoy the flight."

Mason glanced over at the woman still locked on the pages of her magazine. She was in her late thirties and athletic. He glanced at the large diamond on her ring finger, twisted his lips, and faced forward.

The plane stopped at the main runway. After a few minutes the plane turned, the engines whined, and the plane accelerated until it finally lifted.

Mason heard the rumble from below as the wheels retracted. His body pressed back into the seat as the plane continued to accelerate into a steep climb. His ears popped. Soon the plane leveled, and the engines cut back into a moderate whine. He saw Karen get up from her fold-down seat and step into the galley. She quickly reappeared and began taking drink orders. Mason's row was her first stop.

"Something to drink?" she asked, as she peered at his traveling companion.

The woman glanced up. "Thank you, no. I'm fine."

Karen nodded and smiled at Mason.

"Maybe some club soda."

Karen penned a note on a napkin and turned to the adjacent seats.

As was his routine, Mason did a mental evaluation of each of the passengers, especially when they got up to use the lavatory. Profiling, despite the negative connotation, was a necessary evil. He was always in search of the more subtle tells such as anxiety, nervousness, and anything on the edgy side of a person's demeanor. None of these passengers checked any of the boxes; they were just normal people going about their various routines as far as he could tell. There was the young woman, middle twenties, darker complexion and black hair, wearing glasses, gray pants, blue top, and leather flats. She carried maybe a couple of pounds too many, but she had a very pretty face. She wore a jade and silver bracelet. The studious type. Intelligent. And there was the extremely tall, lanky, young man. A professional basketball player maybe. Mason didn't have time to follow basketball or any kind of sports, so he had no idea if the guy was famous. The others were generally older, various ethnicities. Just people.

Karen dropped off his club soda.

Mason took a sip and returned the plastic glass to the seatback table. He closed his eyes and rested his head back. When he opened his eyes, he saw that most of the ice had melted in his glass. He took another sip and watched Karen as she passed his seat on her way forward. He glanced at the woman to his right again.

She was peering out the window. Her magazine lay closed on her lap. She seemed deep in thought.

"Business or pleasure?" Mason asked.

The woman glanced at Mason and then resumed her gaze out the window. After a few moments she shifted her body. "Neither really. Just visiting my parents."

"Charlotte?"

"Asheville."

"So, you live in Miami?" Mason asked.

The woman stared at the diamond ring on her finger. "I do. My husband runs a large real estate business." She looked at Mason. Her eyes swept his entire length hovering for a millisecond each on his closely cropped black hair, short beard, broad shoulders, gray sports coat, ringless fingers, black jeans, and finally his dark-brown, leather, lace-up service boots. "What do you do?"

"Security."

The woman nodded. "You look military."

"I was, years ago." He extended his hand. "Steve Mason."

She hesitated but finally shook his hand. "Lisa Willis."

"You told me what your husband does, what do you do?"

"That's a good question," she said. "Not much apparently." Her chin dipped but then quickly recovered. She turned her head toward Mason.

Mason nodded, not wanting to press the issue. A repressed housewife he guessed. Her job was to look pretty for the clients and support the husband's career. Ignored mostly. He could be wrong. He hoped so.

"What kind of security?" she asked.

Anonymity was the policy for the Air Marshal Service. So, his answer to that question was always the same. "I work for a government agency."

"Anything you can talk about?"

"There are many more interesting subjects," he said.

"You must travel a lot."

"It goes with the territory." He glanced at the magazine on her lap. "You have an interest in architecture?"

She picked up the magazine and thumbed the pages. "Not really. My husband would like it if I did, but I just look at the pictures." She placed the magazine in the seat pouch at her knees. "How does your wife feel about your traveling?" she asked, as she toyed absently with her diamond ring.

"My ex-wife no longer minds at all," he said. "Only lasted a year. She's back in California now."

"Children?"

"No. I guess I wasn't home enough."

Suddenly the cabin dimmed; they both turned their heads toward the window.

Dark storm clouds surrounded the plane.

Mason checked his watch. *They had been flying about an hour*.

"What's with the dark clouds?" Lisa asked. "I thought it was supposed to be clear skies."

The PA system crackled just as the plane took a dip and then immediately recovered. "Sorry ladies and gentlemen, we seemed to have run into an unexpected cell of dense air," Captain Anderson said. "We should be through this in a few minutes."

"That's really dark," Lisa said, as she continued to peer out the window. She pointed. "What's that blue haze?"

Mason leaned over.

Sure enough, the almost pitch-black clouds had a blue haze, a kind of aura.

The plane pitched again. A long streak of lightning appeared in the distance.

"Have you ever seen anything like this?"

"I haven't," Mason said. He stretched closer to the window to increase his field of view and saw that the sky was dark in all directions. He turned his head to the port windows. Same thing. Dark clouds; blue haze. It had everyone's attention. Some took pictures and videos with their cell phones.

The plane dipped again.

Mason heard the pitch of the engines rise a few octaves. The pilot was apparently trying to climb out of the storm.

Lightning flashed followed by another as the cabin filled with a blue glow.

Lisa grabbed Mason's arm and squeezed as she peered out the window. Her body trembled; her grip on his arm tightened.

He reached over and covered her hand with his own. "I'm sure we'll be through this in a few minutes."

At that moment the plane passed out of the dark mass and reentered turbulence free air. The light in the cabin returned to normal. The pitch of the engines returned to normal, and the plane resumed smooth flight.

Lisa released her grasp of Mason's arm and pulled her hand from under his. She exhaled. "Sorry."

"Not a problem," Mason said. "It was a scary moment."

Karen stopped next to Mason's seat and bent down as she peered out the window.

"That was really something," Mason said. "Ever seen anything like that?"

Karen shook her head. "Never. And neither has the captain." She stood up. "Do you need anything?"

Mason glanced at Lisa and then back to Karen. "I think we're okay here." He handed her his mostly empty club soda glass.

Karen nodded and moved off.

"Whatever it was, it's behind us," Mason said.

Lisa shifted in her seat and turned her head to Mason. "I'm really sorry about the arm. I don't care that much for flying to begin with. And that storm from hell."

"Understand completely," Mason said. "Don't worry about it. We'll be on the ground soon." They continued to chat. Mason went into great detail about a catamaran sailboat he had his eye on. He explained all the research he had done about cruising the oceans. He talked about having obtained his pilot's license, and how he was working on his instrument rating.

Lisa began to relax as she listened intently. She even interjected a question now and then.

After a half hour or so the conversation began to wilt. "Excuse me a moment," he said, as he waved at Karen headed down the aisle.

She stopped at his seat.

"Are we on time?" he asked, as he glanced at his watch.

Karen cocked her head as though she didn't know the answer. She motioned with her chin for Mason to follow.

"Be right back," he said to Lisa, as he got up and followed Karen.

She led him to the galley.

That's when he saw the lines of concern etched across her face. "What is it?"

"The pilot said we've lost most of our nav instruments."

"How is that even possible with all the redundancy?"

"I don't know, but they seem a little worried."

"Think Captain Anderson would mind a word?"

Karen held up a finger as she picked up the phone from the cradle on the galley wall. After a few moments she spoke. "The FAM would like a moment of your time." She nodded to Mason. "He's just outside the door." She hung up the phone and led Mason to the cockpit door.

The door clicked, and Mason nodded at Karen as he stepped into the cockpit and closed the door behind him.

The captain and first officer were busy turning knobs and flipping switches. A thick manual lay open on the first officer's lap.

Mason tapped the captain on the shoulder. "I'm Steve Mason, the FAM on this flight. Is there a problem?"

"It would appear there is," the first officer said. "Richard Worth." He stuck out his hand.

They shook.

Captain Anderson glanced back at Mason. "We lost VOR and GPS as soon as we came out of that storm. No signals for the last thirty minutes. It's like all the radio waypoints and satellites went down at the same time."

"And the plane is okay?" Mason asked.

"The plane is fine," Anderson said. "Actually, the instruments are fine; they're just not receiving any signals."

"And I can't raise anyone on the radio," Worth said. "It's working, there's just no one out there receiving."

"I take it you couldn't avoid that storm?" Mason asked.

"Came out of nowhere," Worth said.

"IRS is still operating and indicates we're on course," Captain Anderson said. "But it's an internal system that doesn't rely on external signals." He glanced at the overheard IRS panel, then the flight management system screen, and finally the nav display. "We should be passing over Savannah right about now."

Worth peered out through his window. "Clear skies. I see the coast." He shook his head. "Are you sure we're on course?"

Captain Anderson checked the IRS screen again. "Yep, Savannah is directly below."

The first officer raised his head and locked his eyes on the captain. "There's no Savannah down there."

Captain Anderson turned to look out his window.

Mason leaned over and took a peek. The coast was clearly visible, but there was nothing resembling a large city.

"We must be off course," Captain Anderson said.

Worth had his forehead against the window glass. "We've flown this route a million times. I can see Hilton Head, Calibogue Sound, and the inlets for the Savannah, Wilmington, and the Little Ogeechee. The landmarks are there. Only the city is missing." Worth slowly raised his head and turned to look at Captain Anderson.

The captain met his gaze. "That's impossible."

CHAPTER 2

"Should we press on or turn back?" Worth asked.

"We don't have the fuel to turn back," Anderson said. He rubbed his face with his free hand. Finally, he shook his head. "And besides, who's to say Miami is still where it's supposed to be. We press on."

"Are you going to advise the passengers?" Mason asked.

Anderson glanced back at Mason. "Of what? The city of Savannah is missing and we don't know where to find it. We'd cause a riot back there. Keep this to the three of us for now."

Mason nodded.

Worth kept an eye out of his starboard side window. "I'm seeing nothing down there, except a lot of green. No roads, towns, nothing."

"Should we drop down a little for a better look?" Mason asked.

"Without radio waypoints and communications, I think we'll maintain altitude," Anderson said. "For now."

"Columbia should be coming up soon," Mason said.

"Uh-huh, should be coming up directly below," Anderson said.

Worth was shaking his head. "I don't see a damn thing down there."

Anderson stared below. "The rivers are there, clear as a bell." He focused more intently. "But there's no Lake Murray." He glanced at Worth. "When did they build that dam?"

"Nineteen thirties I think," Mason said. "I've fished that lake."

"Well, it's not there now," Anderson said.

"What in the hell is going on?" Worth asked, as he rubbed his eyes.

"How much fuel do we have?" Mason asked.

Worth raised his head, stretched his neck, and studied the instruments. "There's enough for Charlotte plus another three hundred miles."

Anderson pinched the bridge of his nose and slowly shook his head. "We're on course. We passed over Savannah which is no longer where it's supposed to be and the same with Columbia." He turned to Worth and then back to Mason. "What am I missing? How is that possible?"

Mason shifted closer to the two pilots and knelt between their seats. "If there are no cities — "

"There are no airports and runways," Worth said.

Anderson shook his head and leaned to look out his side window. "This is crazy." He glanced at Worth. "Try the radio again, all the frequencies."

Worth twisted a knob and began asking for a radio response from anyone receiving the signal.

Anderson glanced back at Mason. "Do you have a cell phone?"

Mason nodded.

"Try it," Anderson said. "See if you can get hold of anyone."

Mason pulled his smartphone from his coat pocket, switched airplane mode off, and selected a name from his contacts. He put the phone to his ear and listened for the ring. A ring never came; there was no sound of any kind. He tried a different number and got the same response. He caught Anderson's gaze as he glanced back. Mason shook his head. "I'm getting nothing, as though there's nothing out there to get." He slid the phone back into the coat pocket. "What about that storm we went through?"

"What about it?" Anderson asked.

"It was different. Did you see the blue haze?"

Anderson nodded. "So, what are you saying?"

Mason shifted his weight to the other knee. "I don't know; it was weird."

"Nothing on the radio," Worth said. "Same as before."

Anderson glanced at the flight management display. "Charlotte should be coming up."

Worth shifted in his seat and turned his head to the window.

Mason got to his feet for a better angle. He swiveled his head back and forth and finally leaned over Anderson's left shoulder so he could see more directly down.

Anderson peered out his window for several seconds. "Mountains to the north. I can see the Catawba River, but there's no Charlotte."

"And no Lake Norman," Mason said.

"And no runway," Worth added with a grim face.

"Where do you put a 737 down when there are no runways?" Mason asked.

"Exactly," Anderson said.

Mason caught a much better angle of the ground out of Anderson's side window as he put the plane into a gentle turn to the left. All he saw were patches of mostly green.

"We need to head back to the coast," Anderson said. "We should have enough fuel to check Charleston and Wilmington. We may have to ditch."

Worth closed his eyes and dropped his chin to his chest.

Anderson reached over and patted Worth on the arm. "We might get a little wet but it'll be fine."

Mason rubbed his beard. *Son of a bitch.*

Suddenly the cockpit door opened and Karen stepped in next to Mason. "What's going on?"

Anderson and Worth stared at her for several seconds obviously lost for words. Finally, Anderson nodded at Mason.

"Not sure how to explain this," Mason said to Karen. "Savannah, Columbia, and Charlotte are no longer there."

"How'd we get off course?" Karen asked.

"We're on course," Anderson said without looking back.

"All the landmarks for the three cities are there, but the cities are gone," Mason said.

Karen cocked her head and stared into Mason's eyes. Finally, a broad smile appeared on her face. "Funny. But no, really, why are we turning?"

"He's not joking," Worth said. "The cities are gone. The airport and runways are gone."

"We're headed back to the coast," Anderson said. "We may have to ditch."

Karen stared into Mason's eyes again.

Mason nodded. "It's no joke," he said.

"You'll need to prepare the passengers," Anderson said, "but wait until I make an announcement."

"You're serious," Karen said.

"Dead serious."

Mason took in a deep breath and exhaled just as deeply. "There is no explanation. It just is. I'll be back there shortly in case you need my help."

Karen took a final look at everyone's face before she exited the cockpit.

They cruised at altitude back to the coast in the general direction of Charleston. Soon the open ocean and the coast came into view through the haze.

"I can see Sullivan's Island and the spit of land between the Cooper and Ashley rivers," Worth said.

"Anything else?" Anderson asked.

"No city, if that's what you mean. There might be something down there. Hard to tell."

"Let's check out Wilmington," Anderson said, as he turned the plane to a northeast course along the coast.

They cruised for just under twenty minutes when Anderson put the plane into a steep bank directly over the Cape Fear River.

"Nothing," Worth said.

"What about looking farther north?" Mason asked.

"We don't have the fuel for Philly or New York," Anderson said. "I'm putting this thing down off the coast of Myrtle Beach." He raised his chin at Mason. "Better return to your seat. We have about fifteen minutes to get ready."

Mason nodded, stepped out of the cockpit, and closed the door behind him.

Angie and Karen stood in the galley. Angie had tears in her eyes.

"Is this for real?" Karen asked.

Mason ushered them deeper into the galley. "We can't explain it. The cities are just not there."

Angie tried to muffle a whimper. Tears flowed.

Karen put her arm around Angie's shoulder.

"What are they going to do?"

"Ditch off the coast of Myrtle Beach," Mason said. "We have about ten minutes."

Karen turned to Angie and put both hands on her shoulders. "We need to get these people ready. I need you to be strong."

At that moment the PA system crackled with Anderson's voice. "Ladies and gentlemen, I don't know how to explain this, but we will not be able to land at Charlotte. Columbia, Charleston, and Wilmington are also not an option. Given our fuel our only option is to ditch in the open ocean."

Mason heard a combined gasp from the passengers.

Anderson continued. "We only have a few minutes to prepare. We've already started our descent. I know this is a scary time but you happen to be flying with the best flight crew in the business. Follow all directions to the letter, and you will get through this." The PA clicked off.

The rumble from the passengers grew louder. Several were out of their seats. Two men argued with a flight attendant about half way down the aisle.

Karen picked up the intercom and keyed the switch. "Ladies and gentlemen, please return to your seats. Fasten your seatbelts securely. Flotation devices can be found under each seat."

Most people did as they were told while still continuing to grumble. The two men arguing with the attendant got louder. Mason heard one of them say that he demanded to speak with the captain.

Karen headed in their direction.

Mason followed close behind. As he passed his seat, Lisa locked her eyes on Mason's. Fear was etched across her face and she was trembling. Mason stopped for a moment and grabbed her hand. "It will be okay. I need to help down the aisle, but I'll be back."

Lisa wiped a tear and nodded.

He made his way down the aisle until he caught up to Karen.

"Please return to your seat," Karen said, as she approached the two men. Both were in their forties.

"I demand to see the captain," one of the men said. He was the larger of the two and the loudest. He wore baggy shorts, flip-flops, and a green, collared pullover that read *Beach Bum* in yellow on the front. Both obviously had no intention of backing down or following Karen's order.

When Beach Bum tried to push past Karen, Mason put his left hand on the man's chest. "The flight attendant told you to take your seat."

Karen slipped past Mason and stood behind him.

"Who are you?" the man demanded in a loud voice.

Every other passenger went quiet and turned their attention to the altercation in the aisle.

Mason spoke in a low, authoritative voice as he stared into the man's eyes. "I'm the man who is going to put you in your seat if you don't go there voluntarily. Now."

"I demand to see the captain," the man said.

The other man, standing behind Beach Bum, put a finger in Mason's face. "We want to know why we're not landing in Charlotte."

"You'll be informed when the time is right," Mason said. "For now, return to your seats."

Beach Bum took hold of Mason's wrist with his right hand.

With lightning speed, Mason reached over with his right hand, grabbed hold of the man's wrist, and twisted hard.

The man winced as he was spun around finding himself with his arm behind his back.

Mason walked him toward the rear until he saw an empty seat. He directed the man to the seat and sat him down as he released the man's arm. Mason pointed to the seatbelt. "Buckle it!"

The man did as he was told.

Mason turned just as the second man eased past him and took the empty seat across the aisle from Beach Bum.

Mason stood up straight and swiveled his body around for the benefit of all the passengers. "Buckle your seatbelts," he yelled. "Ensure your neighbors' belts are buckled. Lean forward at the waist and put your face as close to your knees as possible. Don't move until the plane is down." He walked forward checking that they were following his orders.

Karen mouthed a *thank you* as he passed her.

He nodded. As he approached his seat, he bent down to view out the windows. He saw that the plane's altitude was much lower. The coast line was in view in the distance. Mason judged they were three or four miles off the coast flying parallel to the shore.

At his seat he retrieved his rucksack from the overhead bin, plopped down, and buckled his seatbelt as Lisa grabbed hold of his arm. He turned to face her. "We can't explain what is happening, but the cities are gone."

A puzzled expression appeared, replacing the fear.

"Ditching is the only option for putting this thing down," he said, as he reached over and tugged on Lisa's seat belt to ensure it was snug. "Bend over and put your head on your knees and wrap your arms behind your neck. It's going to be a rough landing." He gently placed a hand on her back and eased her into position. He checked to make sure the other first-class passengers were in the same position. He reached inside his coat and retrieved his Glock 19 from its shoulder holster. He unzipped the rucksack, rummaged around, and withdrew a gallon-sized Ziplock bag along with four extra loaded magazines.

Lisa turned her head a bit to the left at the sound. Her eyes grew large at the sight of the pistol in his hand.

He smiled. "Security."

She turned her head back so her face rested between her knees.

Mason placed the four magazines, the pistol, and two more magazines from his holster into the bag and zipped it closed. He put the items back into his rucksack, zipped it closed, and wedged the pack under the seat in front of him with his foot.

Karen put a hand on his shoulder as she hurried by.

Mason took a final look around and then bent forward at the waist. He waited for what seemed like an eternity until he finally heard the engines throttle back. The impact was worse than he expected.

CHAPTER 3

The plane's tail struck first. It initially cut a trough through the water, but the drag pivoted the nose down until it collided in a geyser of ocean spray against the waves. Shock waves reverberated along the plane's skin. The force of the impact carried the front two-thirds of the fuselage below the surface and slung the already weakened tail, including several rows of seats, into the air with such force that it separated from the rest of the plane. The vertical stabilizer slammed against the cockpit with a loud *bang*. A deafening screech followed as the tail slid over the side of the fuselage and sank in a gurgle of bubbles.

The front section of the fuselage, minus half of each wing, bobbed back to the surface with the nose deeper in the water than the jagged opening at the rear. Steam bellowed but quickly dissipated. The fuselage settled into a mass of foam and oscillated in rhythm with the waves.

Amidst the sound of screams and crying, Mason raised his torso. Those who were moving appeared to be in shock and not sure of what they should do. He saw Karen, followed closely by Angie, go to the forward hatch and begin the process of opening the door.

Mason turned to Lisa who was still bent completely over at the waist. He placed a hand on her back and immediately felt the rise and fall of her breathing. She was alive but unconscious. He took hold of her shoulder, lifted her torso to a sitting position, and began examining her body. All appeared okay except for the large knot on the right side of her forehead.

He unbuckled his belt and stood up. That's when he realized the entire tail section was gone leaving only a large, jagged opening. He saw Karen and Angie swing the hatch open and begin working to deploy the emergency slide. As the slide deployed with a sustained hiss of air, he hurried forward to the overhead bin directly behind the now open hatch. He dragged a large yellow bundle from the bin and dropped it next to the hatch opening. "We'll need this too," he said to Karen. He hurried back down the aisle. "And we'll need as much water and food as you can load into the raft," he yelled over his shoulder.

Making his way down the aisle, he yelled for the conscious passengers to check on their neighbor, get everyone able into the aisle, and man the life rafts. At the seats adjacent to the port wing emergency exit he saw an able-bodied man with thinning white hair struggling with the unconscious woman next to him. The woman's neck was obviously broken. He put a hand on the man's shoulder. "This plane is going down fast; you need to get that exit open."

The man gazed at Mason for several seconds and finally nodded.

Mason turned to the opposite seats, intending to get that emergency exit open as well, but decided the two exits would be enough. He made his way back to the large opening at the rear and scanned the open ocean. Debris littered the water in all directions along with a few floating bodies. There was no sign of the tail section.

He made his way forward getting people moving as he went. He stopped at his seat, retrieved his rucksack, and slipped his arms through the straps. He unbuckled Lisa's seat belt, took hold under both arms, and dragged her forward to the fully deployed emergency slide.

Angie was tossing liter bottles of whatever beverages she could grab into the raft tethered next to the slide.

Karen was working the combination on the cockpit door.

Mason carried Lisa out onto the emergency slide, placed her gently at the end, and was back at the cockpit just as Karen opened the door.

He turned back to the line of passengers behind him, now pressing forward toward the exit. "Calm down," he yelled. "One at a time." He pointed to a Hispanic man wearing khaki shorts and sandals. He seemed to have his wits about him. "Help the others into the rafts."

The man nodded, turned to those behind him, and began directing them through the exit.

"I'll take care of the pilots," Mason said, as he stepped past Karen. "There are people unconscious back there."

Karen hurried off without saying anything, squeezing past the people in the crowded aisle.

Mason continued into the cockpit and found it half full of water from the blown-out windows and a jagged hole in the metal skin. Neither of the pilots appeared conscious. He checked the first officer and found his chest covered in blood and a large piece of glass protruding from his neck.

Mason turned to Anderson and placed two fingers against his neck. There was a pulse. Mason quickly detached his seat harness and lifted him from the seat. Mason struggled with the odd angle and the man's weight, but was finally able to drag him out the exit and onto the emergency slide.

Mason noticed that several people were maneuvering the yellow, eight-sided raft toward the partial wing where a number of other people stood waiting for rescue.

Mason made his way back down the aisle sloshing through knee deep water. He paused at each row of seats and checked for a pulse of those who were left behind. Toward the end of the now shortened plane he found a man in a suit and tie who had apparently just regained consciousness. When he tried to move from his seat, he winced, and sat back down.

"What is it?" Mason asked.

"My leg."

Just below the man's knee, Mason felt protruding bone. "Broken," he said. He grabbed hold under the man's shoulders and dragged him into the water-filled aisle. The opening to the rear was much closer than either of the exits, so Mason dragged him through the now waist high water and into the open ocean. Mason held the man with one arm as he used the other to put distance between themselves and the fuselage which was rapidly submerging in a cascade of bubbles. A few moments later the plane was gone, and Mason found himself surrounded by various items of debris. Seabirds circled and squawked overhead. The yellow raft and the emergency slide, both full of people, sat in the water fifty yards away.

"His right leg is broken," Mason said, as he swam up to the raft and took hold.

The Hispanic man and one other grabbed the injured man and eased him into the raft.

Mason pulled himself up with both arms and flopped into the bottom among feet, knees, and several bottles of various beverages. A soft-sided pet crate containing a Chihuahua was inches from his face. The trembling dog stared at Mason through the loose-weave mesh. Mason followed the hand and arm holding the crate up to the eyes of a woman probably in her late sixties, with short, blondish hair and graying streaks. A drenched, flower-patterned, short-sleeved dress clung to her skin. She had apparently been one of the last out of the rapidly filling plane. She stared blankly at the open sea.

"We need to start paddling to shore," Mason said, as he rose up.

"Paddle with what?" the man in the *Beach Bum* t-shirt asked.

"With your hands," Mason said. "Everyone needs to work together."

The white sand beach gleamed at least two miles in the distance.

He waved at those on the emergency slide. "Head for shore," he yelled.

Karen raised a hand to acknowledge and set about getting everyone paddling including a now conscious Lisa.

Several in Mason's raft began talking and shooting questions at the same time. He finally raised a hand to quiet them. "I'll explain everything I know as soon as we reach the shore and tend to everyone's injuries. For now, we need to paddle."

Reaching the shore took longer than Mason expected. The problem was everyone trying to paddle a basically round craft. They ended up turning in circles more than they made any headway. The off-shore breeze basically did all the work. By the time they reached the shore, the sun was closing in on the southwestern horizon.

With everyone finally on solid ground, Mason beached the raft and walked over to Karen and her group. She had just finished counting heads. "How many?"

"A total of thirty-two," she said, as she shook her head. "Out of a hundred and eighty passengers and crew."

Mason took a deep breath, exhaled, and nodded. He knelt next to Lisa sitting on the edge of the emergency slide. "You okay?"

"Karen said you carried me to the raft."

Mason dipped his chin with a slight smile.

"Thank you," she said.

He put a hand on her shoulder and stood up as he scanned the passengers gathered around. Nearly everyone was drenched. Most had visible bumps, bruises, cuts, and abrasions. Several trembled even though the air temperature had to be around ninety.

Several hunched on the sand sobbing. "First of all, any chance we have a doctor or a nurse among us?"

Everyone looked around. No hands went up, but then finally a slightly overweight woman wearing a black and white sweater, gray shorts, and sneakers hesitantly took a step forward. "Nursing student," she said. She wiped tears from her cheeks.

"Excellent," Mason said. "What's your name?"

"Gail Thomas." She stepped closer to the front of the crowd.

Mason pointed at the man with the broken leg. "Sir, what is your name?"

The man, lying flat on the sand, rose up on one elbow. "Tom Green."

"Tom has a broken leg that needs to be set," Mason said. He turned to Karen. "First aid kit?"

Angie stepped forward with a red, soft-sided case. She walked over to Gail and together they knelt next to Tom.

Mason walked over to Captain Anderson still lying on the slide. "How's he doing?" he asked Karen, as he bent down and put two fingers against his neck.

"Breathing, but he hasn't woken up. He looks very pale. I think he might have internal injuries."

"Not much a nursing student can do about that," Mason said, as he unbuttoned Anderson's shirt. Deep, red bruises across his chest matched the pattern of the seat harness. Mason focused on the tree line, thick with pines, hardwoods, palms, and palmettos. He motioned for some of the passengers to gather around. "Let's move the entire slide with him on it into the shade."

The group grabbed hold and dragged the slide across the sand to a clearing a few feet inside the trees.

The woman in the flowered dress walked up with her dog on a leash. "We'd like to know what happened. And when will the emergency people be here?"

Mason took a moment to search for the right words. "I don't believe anyone will be coming."

The group gasped in unison.

Before anyone could ask another question, he continued. "I'm the federal air marshal on this flight, and I was in the cockpit when we flew over Savannah, Columbia, Charlotte, Wilmington, and Charleston. With the possible exception of Charleston, there was no infrastructure visible where those cities were supposed to be. No buildings and no airports."

"What are you saying?" Beach Bum asked. "We were off course?"

"What's your name?"

"Nathan Sims."

"Nathan, we were on course," Mason said. "We verified it with the instruments and from landmarks visible from above. There was no question about the course or our location. But we did lose all contact with the outside world when we passed out of that weird storm with the blue light. No radio contact with ground control, no GPS, and no radio beacons. It's like everything and everyone outside of the airplane just vanished."

"That can't be," the woman with the dog said. Several others agreed.

Mason stared at her for several moments.

"Mildred, Mildred Spears."

"Mildred, right now you are standing smack dab in the middle of Myrtle Beach, South Carolina."

Everyone's head turned in unison. The beach was completely deserted and desolate in both directions.

"There's no way," Nathan said, as he shook his head.

The back and forth continued for several moments until the young dark-complected woman from first class spoke up.

"So, what are you saying?"

Mason shifted his attention to her. "I can't explain it, but we now find ourselves alone. I doubt we will be able to count on anyone outside of this group."

The woman looked up and down the beach. "Myrtle Beach hasn't been this deserted for over three hundred years," the woman said.

Mason stared at her and cocked his head.

"My name is Dorothy Weiss. I'm a graduate student at UNC Charlotte. Anthropology major. Masters in anthropology and history."

"Three hundred years?" Mason asked.

"Charleston was settled around 1670. Trading posts were established up and down the coast after that. It would have been well into the eighteenth century before this area was settled, if in fact this is Myrtle Beach."

Nathan turned to Dorothy. "What are you saying?"

"Simply that if we're standing on Myrtle Beach, it hasn't been this deserted for over three hundred years."

CHAPTER 4

Mason slipped off his rucksack, removed his sopping sports coat, and took a seat on the edge of the emergency slide next to Karen. The empty black shoulder holster blended in with his black t-shirt. Tattoos covered his right arm down to the wrist which was adorned with a stainless-steel memorial bracelet. He watched as she finished checking Captain Anderson's pulse.

"Weak," she said. "And his color is worse."

"Is there anything we can do?"

"He needs a hospital," Karen said.

"If there were going to be any rescuers, they would have been here by now," he said. Mason watched the other survivors as they stood or sat in groups talking amongst themselves under the shade of the trees. "Were you able to save any food?"

"There was no food," she said. "Just a few snacks. Pretzels mostly. I focused on the water we had on board. And there are a few sodas." She scanned the passengers. "I think they're still in shock."

"We all are," he said, as he watched Nathan walk over to the raft and pick up one of the liter bottles of soda. Mason stood. "We need to ration what we have to drink," he said in a voice loud enough for everyone to hear.

They all stopped talking and turned their attention to Mason.

He pointed toward the trees. "There's plenty of fresh water out there, swamp water. But we can't drink it without sanitizing it first and we have no way to do that. The water in those bottles is all we have for now." He eyeballed Nathan as he started to turn the cap on the bottle he held in his hands.

Nathan twisted his lips, shrugged his shoulders, and dropped the bottle back into the raft.

Mason felt the bite of a sand fly on his neck. He rubbed at the spot. "Noseeums are already coming out and there will be plenty of mosquitoes tonight. There's not much we can do about it except maybe light a fire. The smoke might help."

"Are we just going to wait here?" Nathan asked in a sarcastic tone.

"For tonight," Mason said. "We'll decide what to do tomorrow." He returned to his spot on the slide next to Karen. He unzipped his rucksack, opened the Ziplock bag, and retrieved his Glock and two of the magazines. He holstered the pistol and magazines. "This is going to be a long night." He retrieved a lighter from his ruck and stood. "I'll check back."

◆◆◆

A squirrel barking in the distance and the surf breaking against the beach brought Mason to consciousness. The smoldering remnants of the previous night's fires filled the air with the odor of burnt pine. He scratched the itching on his neck and face. He examined the bug bites covering his arms and hands. *So much for the fires.* His eyelids were heavy from lack of sleep.

He scanned the scene without moving from his position next to Karen, Lisa, and Captain Anderson on the emergency slide. The other survivors were all scattered in various states of repose. Some reclined against trees, some were on top of the flipped-over, yellow life raft, and some were just curled up on the ground next to one of the three fires. Several were scratching at various parts of their bodies. He sympathized with those with bare legs and arms. He watched everyone bounce as Dorothy rolled from one side to the other.

Her eyes opened, and she slipped on her glasses. Suddenly she raised her head slightly as though she had caught sight of something in the thick stand of pines.

Mason followed her gaze until his eyes rested on three men standing in the mist and dim light of early morning. Mason focused on the men for several seconds and then slowly raised his torso to a sitting position. In unison the three men turned their heads toward Mason's movement.

These men were not like any Mason had ever seen. All three were bare-chested except for some type of necklace gathered around their necks. Their only articles of clothing were a loincloth and moccasins. Two of the men had their black hair tied in a ponytail and adorned with a couple of feathers; the other man wore his hair loose around his face. Two of the men held what appeared to be a flintlock rifle loosely in one hand at their side. The other man held a bow with a quiver of arrows attached at his hip.

Mason blinked several times and refocused. He glanced at Dorothy as she slowly rose to a sitting position mesmerized by the three figures. When Mason looked back to where the three men had been, they were gone. Without making a sound they had simply vanished leaving Mason to wonder if he had been dreaming or hallucinating.

Dorothy got up, walked over, and knelt next to Mason. "Did you see that?"

"I saw something," he said, "I think."

"No, they were real," Dorothy said.

Karen stirred. "What's going on?"

"We had visitors," Mason said. "Native Americans."

"I think it's safe to call them Indians," Dorothy said.

Karen rose up and swiveled her head in all directions.

"They're gone," Mason said. He turned his head to Dorothy. "You're the historian, what do you think?"

"If this is in fact Myrtle Beach and those men we saw are Indians—" She left the statement unfinished.

"Let's assume we just saw three Native Americans, Indians, reconnoitering our camp."

Dorothy twisted her lips as she thought for a moment. "This is just too impossible to believe."

"I get that," Mason said. "Anything else?"

Dorothy thought about it. "Given they didn't seem all that surprised to see a bunch of white people would indicate there are other white people around."

"What does that mean?" Karen asked.

Dorothy shook her head. "Three hundred years."

Mason raised an eyebrow encouraging her to continue.

"The only large settlement in this area at that time was Charleston, Charles Town."

Mason ran his fingers through his hair as he stared at the ground.

"The large English settlements were Charles Town, Boston, New York, and Philadelphia. The Spanish occupied Saint Augustine in Florida."

Karen got to a sitting position next to Mason. "Do we need to worry about Indians?"

"There were a lot of different tribes around here then," Dorothy said.

"Wait," Mason said. "So, we've accepted that we've somehow been transported three hundred years into the past."

Dorothy turned her head in a wide arc and flung both hands in the air. "A deserted Myrtle Beach and Indians. What other conclusion is there?"

"You're absolutely sure this is Myrtle Beach?" Karen asked, as she stared at Mason.

Mason exhaled. "Yes. The landmarks were all visible from the air. This is Myrtle Beach."

"Then somehow we are no longer living in our time," Dorothy said.

"You were saying about the Indians," Karen said, as she turned to Dorothy.

"The Cherokee much farther north and the Catawba to the south of them were mostly friendly except during the Yemassee War in 1715. The war for the most part ended in 1717. They traded with the settlers before and after. There were plenty of coastal tribes, such as the Kiawah. But many of those tribes dwindled from disease after contact with the colonists. By the early seventeen hundreds the Kiawah, for instance, had been reduced to a few braves."

"What were the three we saw?" Mason asked.

"I don't know," Dorothy said.

"Did they speak English back then?" Karen asked.

"Some did, they had to. Trading in skins and pelts was a giant enterprise."

"That would explain their possession of rifles," Mason said.

Mason looked around at the other survivors now starting to stir. He thought about how different everyone looked, especially their clothing, from the people in Colonial America. He peered at the tall basketball player and glanced around at Angie. "What about slaves back then?"

"Booming," she said. "Charles Town was a major player in the African slave trade. Indians too. The only blacks here would have been slaves. In fact, in the early eighteenth century African slaves outnumbered everyone else. Except the Indians."

Mason got to his feet. "I suppose we need to get everyone up and decide what we should do."

Karen twisted around and put a hand on Captain Anderson's chest.

"How's he doing?" Mason asked.

She shifted her hand on his chest and then placed two fingers against his neck. She shook her head.

Mason nodded and closed his eyes. He wondered how many more they would lose. He opened his eyes, tightened his lips, and walked over to Tom lying awake on top of the yellow raft. "How's the leg?"

"Hurts like hell," Tom said. He reached down and adjusted the splint just below the knee. "Gail and Angie did a good job but there's no way I can walk on this."

Nathan approached scratching his arm. Several others stood behind him. "I guess you're in charge. What are your orders?"

"We wait for help," Mildred said, standing there with her dog on a leash.

"There won't be any help," Mason said, "at least not the kind we're used to seeing." He told everyone about the loss of Captain Anderson and proceeded to describe what he and Dorothy had seen only a few minutes earlier. And he told everyone what Dorothy had said about the time period.

The prospect of having been transported back in time was met with total disbelief. Everyone began talking at once.

"We were off course," Nathan yelled, "simple as that. Anything else would be impossible."

Several people agreed.

Nathan turned to Mason. "Why can't you admit the plane was simply off course? Is there something you're not telling us?"

"You know everything I know," Mason said. "The facts are this. The pilot and copilot verified the position of the plane with the one instrument on board that still worked. It was an internal system based on dead reckoning. They also verified our position based on visible landmarks that cannot be disputed. I saw them as well. We are in fact standing on Myrtle Beach. And according to our history expert, Myrtle Beach hasn't been this way for three hundred years."

"Bullshit!" Nathan yelled. "We've traveled back in time. You expect us to believe that?"

"I don't care what you believe," Mason said. He swung his arm in a wide arc. "Look around. An airliner just crashed. Where are the rescue helicopters? Has anyone seen or heard any planes? This is a major air corridor. There should be contrails up there."

Everyone mumbled.

Nathan glanced skyward as he walked away whispering to another man.

"The first thing we need to do is bury the Captain," Mason said. He approached the Hispanic man standing in the crowd and extended his hand. "Mason."

The man took Mason's hand. "Manny Hernandez."

"I appreciate your help on the plane," Mason said. "And with the raft."

Manny nodded.

"Can you get a few men together and see about digging a grave for Captain Anderson?"

"I can do that," Manny said.

Mason turned back to Dorothy. "Other than simply surviving, what do we need to worry about?"

"Pretty much everything," Dorothy said.

"Give me the top three," Mason said.

Dorothy paused for a moment and then counted off with her fingers. "Most people died of disease, primarily yellow fever and smallpox. They didn't know back then that yellow fever was carried by the mosquitoes. Smallpox was brought here by the Europeans. There's also typhoid and malaria at this time here." She paused again. "Some tribes were not friendly. There were numerous assaults on the plantations around Charles Town even after the war." She tightened her lips and cocked her head. "The settlers in this era will think we're all witches. We will definitely stand out."

Mason scanned the faces of those standing around him, mostly everyone. He turned back to Dorothy. "So, what you're saying is if we stay here, we die of disease, starvation, or the Indians. If we try to enter the Charles Town settlement or any settlement, we will probably be burned at the stake." He shook his head.

Dorothy did a subtle flip of her hands to acknowledge Mason's logic.

"Most of these people have not been vaccinated for yellow fever, and they stopped giving the smallpox vaccine routinely decades ago."

Dorothy nodded.

Mason paused for several moments pinching between his eyes. He raised his eyes to the crowd. "Okay, first things first. We need food and water. Anyone skilled at setting snares?"

Manny, who was digging in the sand with a stick at the edge of the trees along with two other men, stopped and raised his hand. "Air Force survival school. I can set a snare, and I can find potable water."

"Excellent," Mason said.

He perused the others. "We should probably take a skills inventory." He focused on the tall black man and raised his chin.

"Travis Turner," the man said. "Attorney."

Mason smirked and then queried the others in the group. He came up with an assortment of occupations but none would be of much use unless they decided to open a school or an accounting firm. "Languages? Spanish?" Several people raised their hands including Manny.

A slender man in his late thirties, wearing tight, tapered black pants, and loafers, holding a leather jacket raised his hand. "French," he said with an accent.

"Charles Town was an English settlement with people from England and the West Indies," Dorothy said. "There were also some Scots, French, and a few Dutch, along with the Africans. Also, pirating was rampant up and down the coast."

Mason stared at her for several moments before finally nodding. "Our first concerns are for water, shelter, and food, in that order. Let's get to work."

By late afternoon the group had assembled three large lean-to shelters composed of poles, limbs, sticks, and brush they found loose on the ground. Mason arranged the shelters in an arc with their backs to the ocean. He wanted to be facing the forest in case more visitors arrived. They had also set several snares in the forest around the camp using cordage adapted from the raft. And they had dug a latrine shielded from view by thick brush. It was a start.

CHAPTER 5

With Mason's time in the army and as an air marshal, he was used to long hours without sleep. No sleep is one thing, but the constant barrage of relentless mosquitoes and sand flies was something else. The lean-to and the smoke from the three fires did pretty much nothing to help for the second night. Once again, he might have gotten an hour's sleep, maybe two. He rubbed his face with both hands, pinched the bridge of his nose, and got to his feet. He found Manny reclined against the same tree as the night before swatting at mosquitoes. Mason kicked at the bottom of Manny's sandals to get his attention. "You said you could find water?"

"Shouldn't be a problem," Manny said, as he stood. "We dig a hole, let the ground water seep in, filter, and drink."

"Charcoal for a filter?"

Manny nodded. "Alternating layers of charcoal and sand. We'll need to cut more pieces from the raft to fashion some kind of tube."

Mason nodded and handed him the tactical knife. He gazed at the others and pointed to the man whose wife died on the plane. "That's Bobby March. I think he could use some distraction."

"Okay," Manny said. "I think we should check the snares first."

Mason nodded. As he turned to step off, he caught a movement in the corner of his eye. The movement turned out to be the three natives he and Dorothy had seen the previous morning. Only this time, they brought friends. Mason counted a total of eight natives. Four of them were bare-chested wearing a loincloth and moccasins, but three were wearing long-sleeve, buckskin shirts, breeches, and leggings. The eighth man wore pretty much the same except his shirt was of white cotton or linen. Among them they carried four flintlocks and four bows.

Dorothy walked up and stood next to Mason.

"What do you think?" Mason asked.

"I think if they wanted to kill us, we would already be dead," Dorothy said. "They're curious, probably wondering what we have to trade."

Three of the Indians, led by the one in the white shirt, stepped closer.

Mason turned to address them. "Do you speak English?"

Without answering, the native in the white shirt simply gazed around at the survivors all gathered loosely behind Mason and Dorothy. He seemed to pay particular attention to certain articles of clothing, usually the bright colors, and any jewelry. The native's gaze turned back to Mason.

Mason watched the man's eyes trace the full length of Mason's attire paying particular attention to the pistol in his shoulder holster and the watch on his left wrist. Mason leaned toward Dorothy. "Any other thoughts?"

"Very curious and definitely interested in trading."

"What do you think would be safe to trade?"

"I wouldn't give them anything electronic like a cell phone," she whispered. "The word would get back to the settlers and we'd be branded as witches for sure. I think the same is true of watches. In fact, we should bury anything electronic or mechanical. Pieces of jewelry should be safe enough."

Mason nodded. "First chance we get, anything linking us to the future goes in a hole," he whispered. "That includes the raft and emergency slide."

The native walked past Mason and over to the bright yellow raft. He ran his hand along the rubberized fabric. He walked over to the deflated emergency slide and did the same.

"We come from very far away," Mason said, "our ship sank." He used hand motions to illustrate what he was trying to communicate.

The native again said nothing as he walked back to rejoin the other natives.

Mason raised an eyebrow at Dorothy.

"I don't know," Dorothy said. "Maybe we don't have anything they want."

"What would they have wanted back then?" Mason asked.

"Things they can use," Dorothy said, "guns, metal cooking pots and utensils, cloth."

"The same things we need," Manny said.

"What about the jewelry we have?"

"Maybe," Dorothy replied. "It doesn't hurt to ask."

Mason approached the group of Indians who were talking among themselves in a language he didn't recognize. He removed the shiny, silver colored, stainless steel killed-in-action bracelet from his right wrist. He extended it to the native in the white shirt who turned around and faced Mason.

The Indian took the bracelet, examined it closely, and held it out for the other natives to see. They began mumbling. They ran their fingers over the inscription which read *Steve Brown, USA, 82nd Airborne, Operation Iraqi Freedom.* The native shook his head back and forth and went to hand the bracelet back to Mason.

One of the other natives, one wearing a buckskin shirt, said something. The first native handed him the bracelet.

Mason stepped up to him, took the bracelet, and placed it on the man's right wrist.

The native fondled the bracelet, held his arm up in the air so everyone could see, and said something to the others. He finally nodded in agreement and started to remove a necklace made of shells from around his neck.

Mason held up a hand and shook his head to stop him. He fingered the sleeve of the man's buckskin shirt and nodded his head up and down.

The native looked down at the front of his shirt, which was stained and in less than ideal condition, and back up at Mason. He nodded, removed his shirt, and handed it to Mason.

Mason took the shirt and smiled.

As the group of natives turned to leave, Mason put a hand up to stop them.

They turned back to face Mason.

"You come back tomorrow," Mason said, again using his hands to explain his meaning.

The natives turned without even a nod and disappeared into the trees.

"Maybe we've made a friend." Mason examined the buckskin shirt in his hand. He raised it to his face, took a whiff, and jerked his head back as he wrinkled his nose.

"Maybe some of that swamp water will improve the smell," Manny said.

Mason raised his chin and smirked.

Nathan, the beach bum, stepped up to Mason. "I think we should just move on to Charleston now, or whatever civilization is probably just down the beach." He glanced behind him. "I'm not alone with that way of thinking."

Mason saw several nods.

"I still can't believe we've somehow gone back in time," Nathan continued. "We were just off course. I'm sure a town awaits us just down there." He pointed to the southwest. "Plus, we're getting eaten by the bugs."

"How do you explain the natives?" Dorothy asked.

Nathan threw his hands in the air. "Some local rednecks dressed up to mess with us. Is that harder to believe than all of us being transported back in time?"

Mason turned his head to Dorothy for a response.

Travis, the tall attorney, spoke up. "Maybe he's right. Maybe we should head out. There could be help within walking distance."

"The evidence is clear to me," Dorothy said. "There is no help within walking distance. You might as well accept the reality. We're not in Kansas anymore. There might be some small, individual farms, maybe some hunters' cabins, maybe a small trading post within walking distance, but they would barely have enough food to feed themselves."

Nathan huffed. "We're back to that again."

Mason turned in a slow arc. His eyes stopped on Lisa for a moment. Her face and chest were dotted with red blotches from the bug bits, and her hair was disheveled. "Look, I know the situation is rough, and I do think we should eventually head for Charles Town. But we can't make it without food and water. Plus, I think we need to blend in a little better. We can't go walking in there dressed like this. We can trade to outfit a small group of us and hopefully slip into the settlement unnoticed. Once we're inside, we acquire the clothes necessary so we can all blend in."

Nathan stomped a foot in the sand. "Like I said before, bullshit."

"How long?" Mildred asked, holding her dog in her arms.

Mason focused on Mildred. "Like I said, we need food, water, and time to get to know the area and the surrounding people. I can't give a specific time."

"That brings up another issue," Nathan said. "Who put you in charge?"

Manny stepped up. "That's a stupid question. Look around. Do you see anyone better qualified?"

"I manage a construction company," Nathan said.

"I'm sure you have plenty of skills that will be valuable to us," Mason said. "For now, we need to focus on food, water, and establishing some alliances." He locked eyes on Nathan. "And we could use better shelters." He turned to Travis. "That's how we're going to survive this."

Manny motioned to Bobby. "Can you give me a hand checking the snares and digging a water hole?"

Bobby, looking depressed, hesitated but slowly got to his feet. "Sure."

Mason raised his chin and eyed several others. "We could use a second latrine." He motioned toward the trees. "It needs to be fairly deep like the other one. And we need to scavenge the area for anything that looks edible. There should be pecans, hickory nuts, and various types of berries in this area. And watch out for snakes."

One of the passengers, a slightly overweight middle-aged man, stepped forward and motioned with his hand. "I can help with that. I'm familiar with southern wild edibles. My father taught me as a kid."

Mason smiled. *Now we're getting somewhere.*

Karen stepped up to Mason and took hold of the buckskin shirt. "Let me see if I can get some of the dirt and odor out of this."

Mason raised his chin. "Thank you," he said, as he let Karen take the garment.

"Lisa mentioned you were in the military. What exactly did you do?" Karen asked.

"Delta force. Eight years."

Karen cocked her head to one side.

"It's an army special forces outfit primarily responsible for combating terrorism."

Karen tightened her lips with a slight smirk and nodded. "Might come in handy." She started to walk away but stopped and stepped back up to Mason. "Even if we were dressed in clothes of this period, we would still stick out like sore thumbs," she said in a low voice.

"I know," he said. "We just need something to work toward."

Over the next several days the survivors scavenged the area for anything edible. A hundred yards into the forest they found a stream of clear water. It was narrow but in spots it was up to two-feet deep. Rather than digging a hole for ground water, Manny ran the stream water through his makeshift filters of sand and charcoal. The stream also provided fresh water for bathing.

Every morning the natives visited. As it turned out, two of the natives could speak a bit of English including the one with Mason's bracelet. Sometimes they brought items to trade, but often they just showed up to help the survivors learn how to gather food. They obviously realized the predicament because they willingly traded what would have been a very valuable European axe, a large metal cooking pot, and ten pounds of rice for several items of jewelry, including Dorothy's turquoise bracelet.

Once they had the cooking pot, Manny was able to boil the filtered water for added protection and keep the plastic water and soda bottles full.

With the axe, the Sabal Palmetto tree, or Cabbage Palm, which was plentiful in coastal South Carolina, became a favorite food source. It took an axe to harvest the meaty core since the tree had to be cut down. Getting down to the edible part took considerable work, but it was worth it. A couple of large palm hearts could feed the entire group of survivors. The hearts could be eaten raw or boiled with game meat and whatever else they could find for a stew. The palms had other uses as well. They wove the palm fronds into sleeping mats and carved the woody stems into various utensils, including spoons.

Nathan, despite being pissed off most of the time, was able to replace the lean-to shelters with more conventional four-sided huts with domed roofs fashioned from poles. Mason figured he took on the task to showcase his skills and thus nominate himself as leader should it ever come to a vote.

The natives helped with the design of the huts and showed the survivors how to harvest tree bark to cover the outside walls and the roof.

Before turning in each night, the survivors lit a temporary fire inside each hut and burned green pine needles. The thick smoke drove out most of the mosquitoes and sand flies. It worked so well that on the fifth night Mason was actually able to get five hours of sleep.

Tom Green's broken leg was a little less painful by then, and it appeared he had avoided infection.

They dug a new latrine every couple of days. The lack of toilet paper took some getting used to. Leaves or moss were the best alternatives.

The natives showed the survivors how to fashion spears suitable for spearfishing.

Lisa, Angie, and Bobby spent most of their days trying to catch fish at a small inlet about a mile down the beach.

Another group of five people, including Mildred and her dog, took on the responsibility for most of the food preparation.

The survivors did find a number of wild edibles, nuts and berries mostly. They snared a few small animals and caught an occasional fish. Despite their good fortune, Mason estimated each person was living on less than a thousand calories per day.

Even so, everything was clicking along better than could be expected, until the fever set in.

CHAPTER 6

Mason wasn't an expert on tropical diseases, but he did know the symptoms of yellow fever. Several members of the group started showing some of those symptoms on days seven and eight. By the morning of day nine there were five people, including Lisa and the attorney, with varying degrees of the symptoms—fever, yellowed skin, headache, muscle ache, nausea, dizziness, and lethargy. The eyes of one of the survivors had turned red which was an indication of internal bleeding. They were sick.

"Is there anything we can do?" Mason asked Gail, the nursing student, as they stood outside one of the huts.

"All I know is that yellow fever is caused by a virus," she said. "Even if we were back in our time, the only thing we could do is treat the symptoms. Keep them from getting dehydrated, keep the fevers down with cold compresses, and try to make them as comfortable as possible."

"What's their prognosis?"

"From what I understand, most people recover after a few days. But in some, it can lead to organ damage and death. It's not contagious between people."

"Will there be more people sick?" Mason asked.

"Probably," Gail replied. "It depends on a person's individual immune system and, of course, if they've been vaccinated."

"Most Americans likely have not been vaccinated," Mason said, "unless maybe if they travel a lot." He scanned the other survivors, most of whom were busy with some task. "I've been vaccinated. I'm at the end of the ten-year period, but I should be okay. Likewise, for Manny. He's active duty Air Force. I'm guessing Karen and Angie have gotten the vaccine. But that's it as far as I know."

"Everyone else would be susceptible," Gail said. "Including me."

Mason closed his eyes, took in a deep breath, and exhaled. "Do the best you can."

The sound of retching emanated from inside the hut.

"I should probably see what I can do," Gail said, as she took a final glance at Mason.

Mason watched as she disappeared into the hut. He couldn't help but wonder if staying put was the right course of action. Maybe Nathan was right.

He glanced at Tom Green who reclined against a tree. He was rubbing a piece of wood against a rock. He had become pretty good at fashioning wooden spoons. He was in less pain with his leg, but it would still be weeks before he could do anything more than hobble.

Mason contemplated the natives they had encountered. Dorothy thought they were a small group of Catawba Indians who had moved south. According to her, the Catawba as a tribe were fiercely opposed to the colonists during the Yemassee War. Later the tribe would forge alliances with the colonists through trade. They even sided with them against the British during the Revolution. But without knowing the current year it was impossible to know the state of affairs. One thing was clear. For whatever the reason, these natives seemed to have taken a liking to Mason and the survivors. It is probable they would not have survived this long if not for their help.

One thing that seemed curious to Mason was that the natives did not seem to question the strange clothes and the rubber rafts. But there were probably a great many things the natives didn't understand about the colonists of Charles Town and the life they lived. They probably just chalked up the strangeness of the survivors to just another aspect of foreign life.

On the morning of the tenth day the group of natives gave Mason a buckskin pouch which contained various leaves and twigs. Through broken English and sign language, the natives explained that the mixture should be boiled and the liquid consumed by the sick members of the survivor group. Gail had no idea what the concoction would do for a virus but thought it probably couldn't hurt. After all, the natives had dealt with a variety of such diseases for centuries.

She prepared the leaves and twigs as instructed, let it cool, and encouraged her patients to consume some of the dark liquid. It didn't seem to have an immediate effect, good or bad, but by the next morning the treatment had apparently resulted in lowered fevers and less muscle pain. It didn't cure the malady, but it did make them feel better. After a few days all the sick seemed to be well on the road to recovery, except one. A middle-aged woman, the one who had the red eyes, continually got worse. She began vomiting blood the day before she finally died. The survivors dug a second grave next to Captain Anderson.

By the end of the third week the camp was back on a routine that consisted mostly of hunting, fishing, gathering, scouting, and generally making the camp more livable. It wasn't much of a life, but at least it was a life.

◆◆◆

On a bright morning the beginning of the fourth week, two natives showed up like clockwork. One of them still wore Mason's killed-in-action bracelet. He went by the name Mato. But rather than trade or pitch in with camp chores, Mato, using broken English and hand motions, wanted Mason to follow them into the forest. Mason motioned for Manny and Dorothy to tag along. They had no idea where they were being led, but the trio followed the two braves down a well-worn trail through the thick brush. About four miles deep into the marsh they emerged into a clearing and into what was apparently Mato's village.

Mason counted twenty huts very similar to the ones the natives helped build at the survivors' camp. Each hut was about ten square feet, domed in shape, and constructed of poles lashed together with strips of deer hide and covered with tree bark, mainly birch. The huts were arranged in a loose circle around two much larger huts. The bustling village sat next to another clear running stream.

Nearly everyone seemed focused on some task. Women were busy weaving baskets, working with clay for pottery, or preparing food; the men worked on the huts, crafted tools, spears, and bows, and performed various other duties. Mason watched as two men carried a deer carcass into camp on a pole. Children scurried about. A group played some kind of game that involved sticks and a ball weaved of tree bark. But all of that came to a stop when Mason, Dorothy, and Manny stepped into view.

Dorothy still wore her gray pants, blue top over a black shirt, and sandals, worn and stained as they were. Her clothes hung looser than they did three weeks earlier. She had lost weight as did all the other survivors including Mason. Manny still wore his khaki shorts, a yellow polo shirt, and sandals, again well-worn and stained.

Several of the village women immediately gathered around Dorothy and began fingering her blue top and gray pants as they mumbled incoherently. They were intrigued by the polyester cloth.

Soon the three of them were surrounded by the villagers as they gaped, poked, and prodded. An older gentleman seemed particularly fascinated with Mason.

"My home," Mato said, as he swung his arm in a wide arc. "Yeh is-WAH h'reh."

Dorothy leaned toward Mason. "Assuming these are Catawba, that name was given to them by the colonists because they were first encountered along the Catawba River. Apparently, they have a different name for themselves. And this has to be one of their smaller villages. The main tribe is much larger and much farther north."

Mason nodded as the mass of shuffling feet ushered the three of them toward an open area in front of one of the large, center huts. Everyone grew quiet as three elders emerged from the hut. All three were dressed in fancier attire consisting of buckskin shirts with plenty of fringe, breeches, and leggings. Feathers, beads, shells, and paint were very much on display.

Mason assumed they did not dress this way every day but had done so to make an impression on the survivors. They succeeded. They appeared very majestic in their regalia.

The three elders approached Mason, Manny, and Dorothy and went through the same close inspection of Manny and Dorothy's clothes, and the glasses perched on Dorothy's nose.

Mato leaned closer to Mason. He nodded at the oldest of the three gentlemen. "Our chief," he said. "Enapay."

Mason thought of extending his hand but decided he should wait and follow Enapay's lead.

Enapay did not offer to shake hands, but he did come across as extremely cordial. He motioned for Mason and Manny to follow as he turned to reenter the hut.

Dorothy took a step to follow but was quickly surrounded by a number of women, all mumbling as they directed her to a smaller hut off to one side of the central court.

Mason glanced at her with a raised eyebrow as they separated.

"I'll be okay," Dorothy said. "Be sure to accept anything they offer."

Mason nodded his understanding.

Several other braves, including Mato, joined the march into the hut.

Mason and Manny remained standing until the three elders had taken their seat around a small cooking fire. Mason watched the fire's smoke rise and exit through a small hole in the roof.

Mato pointed to two spots opposite the elders for Mason and Manny to take a seat.

As it turned out, the three elders spoke about as much English as Mato so communicating wasn't a big problem. The oldest elder directed a young brave to hand out wooden bowls to everyone. He did so and ladled some kind of thin stew into each of the bowls from a clay pot hanging over a fire.

Based on the smell and a quick glance, Mason deduced that the stew was composed of fish, corn and rice. He waited until the three elders tipped their bowls to their mouths and then he did the same. Considering the mixture was devoid of salt or any other spice, it was actually pretty good. The mild, white fish was a little chewy, but it all went down easy enough.

Between gulps, Enapay kept an eye on Mason and Manny. He would occasionally lean to an adjacent elder and whisper something, followed by nods and grunts from all three.

Mason could only imagine what they were thinking. Certainly, Mato had already described the survivors, their camp, and the strange clothes and possessions, such as the two rafts. Mato had never directly questioned any of the strange sights, probably due to politeness, but Mason was fairly sure that Enapay would not hold back with his questions.

With the bowls empty, the attending brave immediately refilled each with about a cup of a warm, dark liquid.

After Enapay took a sip, Mason followed suit. The brew had a silky texture with a hint of caramel sweetness along with a bold, nutty and grassy flavor. It had to be some kind of tea since it did not have the burn of alcohol. After a few sips, Mason felt a jolt much like the reaction he got when he drank espresso. The drink had to be loaded with caffeine.

Enapay finished his tea, sat the bowl to the side, and gazed at Mason.

"Where you from?"

Mason sat his empty bowl next to his leg. "My people come from a land very far away and unknown to the Catawba. Our boat sank on our way to New York."

Enapay leaned over as one of the elders whispered in his ear. He straightened up and alternated his gaze back and forth between Mason and Manny. "More like you come here soon?"

Mason smiled slightly. "I can assure you, there won't be any others like us."

"When you go back your land?" Enapay asked.

"I don't know," Mason said. "We may not be able to return to our land."

The questions and answers went on for another hour. Mason learned that, in fact, Charles Town was a few days travel to the southwest and that a party would make a journey there in a couple of months, sometime in September. They usually made the trip twice each year to trade deer skins for tools and rice.

The elders eventually went quiet and rose signaling the end of the meeting. They invited Mason and Manny to return and said they would be welcomed anytime.

Mato led the two survivors from the hut and into the central courtyard. All the natives had returned to their various tasks leaving the central area mostly unoccupied.

Mason darted his eyes back and forth in search of Dorothy but did not see her among those in view. "Where is our friend?" he asked Mato.

Mato pointed with his chin at a group of women sitting in front of a hut directly across the courtyard. He began walking in that direction.

Mason and Manny followed. It wasn't until they reached the group of women that Mason realized Dorothy had been sitting with the women with her back to the courtyard. Her gray pants, blue top, black shirt, and sandals had been replaced with a buckskin dress with one strap tied over her left shoulder and moccasins. She stood as the three men approached. The length of her fairly form fitting dress stopped just above her knees. Her glasses still perched on her nose.

"What happened to you?" Manny asked.

"They insisted," Dorothy said.

Manny inspected the new outfit. "It looks good. What did you trade?"

"Nothing," she said. "It was a gift."

"What about your clothes?" Manny asked.

"They needed to be burned," she said. "This is fine." She ran her hands up and down the length of her dress. "Much more functional."

Mason cocked his head and smiled. He then turned to Mato. "We should probably head back."

Mato nodded. "Just follow trail."

Mason extended his hand.

Mato gazed at the hand for a moment and then took it in his own.

"Thank you," Mason said. "We will see you soon."

Mato nodded.

❖❖❖

The next morning Mato and four other braves showed up at the camp just as the first rays of light filtered through the trees. All five of them held a bow, arrows, and spears. Mato carried an extra bow, quiver of arrows, and three spears. "We hunt for hexaka and khukhuse," he said, as he handed Mason the extra bow and three spears. "You come. Bring three more."

Mason cocked his head with a confused look.

Mato put his index fingers up next to his head to represent antlers.

Manny walked up at about that time. "I think they want us to go hunting with them for dear. Don't know what the other animal would be."

"Pig," Mato said.

Mason took the bow and arrows offered by Mato and surveyed the camp. Most were still asleep but Travis and Nathan were up. Mason motioned for the two of them to come over. "We're going hunting," Mason said.

Travis looked at Nathan and then Mason. "Us?"

Mason handed the two of them and Manny a spear. "Yep." He could tell Nathan was searching his brain for an excuse not to go, but he knew better than to turn down Mato's invitation. Mason turned to Mato. "We're ready." Mason motioned to Karen that the four of them were going with Mato as he stepped off behind the braves. Mason turned his head to Nathan and Travis. "No talking. No noise."

Their eyes scanned up and down the length of their spear taking in the multi-colored paint bands and the stone points.

"We're supposed to throw these at something?" Travis whispered to Mason.

"You may want to just jab with it if an animal gets close enough," Manny said with a smile.

Travis examined his spear; his eyes fixated on the stone point. He finally shook his head and began scanning the surrounding forest.

After an hour of walking, they entered a thick marsh with soggy ground. Mato motioned for everyone to slow down as he became particular about where he placed each foot. He worked his way several yards into the scrub.

Mason stepped carefully behind the three braves in front of him.

At the sound of a twig snap off to the right, Mato immediately lowered to a crouch and stopped. Everyone stopped behind him and knelt.

Mason heard another *snap* in the distance from behind. He twisted his torso in the direction of the noise. There was a *thump* and Mason watched as the trailing brave suddenly stiffened and collapsed to the ground. An arrow protruded from his chest.

CHAPTER 7

Mason grabbed Travis by the sleeve of his plaid shirt, jerked him to the cover of a large oak tree, and pushed him to the ground. "Take cover," he said in a raised voice to Nathan and Manny still standing in the open.

Manny took hold of Nathan's arm and pulled him down behind a thick bush.

Mason swiveled his head in all directions and saw that Mato and the remaining braves were behind cover. A few seconds later, Mato joined Mason behind the tree.

He motioned to remain quiet and stay put. He then moved off to the right and soon became invisible among the brush and trees.

The other braves had also disappeared into the brush.

Mason thought of his Glock 9mm pistol tucked in its holster under his buckskin shirt. He had already made up his mind that he would not use the weapon unless it was necessary, to save his life or the life of one of the survivors. To use the weapon in the presence of anyone except a survivor would result in a lot of questions. Word would get around of its unbelievable firepower compared to the flintlocks of the time. And soon Mason would be a target for everyone wanting the power of the pistol. But would he use the weapon to save someone who had become a friend? Someone like Mato? He honestly did not know. He hoped it did not come to that.

He tightened his grip on the bow in his left hand. With his right he pulled an arrow from the quiver and strung the sinew string into the arrow's carved nock. He rested the arrow's shaft against the bow's leather-wrapped grip and his left index knuckle. With his right index and middle finger on each side of the arrow's nock, he pulled on the string to test the strength. He was surprised at the force needed to draw the bow. As a kid he had owned and had shot a bow. He even hunted with a friend's compound bow a time or two. He knew how to handle one, but he was far from an expert.

Mason scanned the forest in all directions. He heard the rustle of leaves and saw Manny low crawl over to his position.

"What is going on?" Manny asked in a barely audible whisper.

Mason shrugged his shoulders. "Rival tribe maybe," he replied in an equally low whisper. "There's a lot we don't know about this time period."

"Where does that leave us?" Nathan asked.

"We always knew we were in a serious situation," Mason said. "It just got more serious." He glanced at

Travis' face partially buried in the leaves and pine needles and saw his lower lip quivering. It was hard to imagine dying in a place like this, but they had already lost a hundred and fifty people. Most of those were on day one. Dying from an ancient Native American arrow suddenly wasn't that hard to envision.

Mason heard a couple of whoops and hollers from somewhere in the distance and then all went quiet again. He wondered if he should stay put as directed or reconnoiter the area. He had just decided to remain where he was when he heard something thrashing in the brush some distance off to the right. It sounded like a wild boar barreling through except the sound wasn't moving. It was stationary fifty to seventy-five yards away, in the direction Mato had gone.

"You guys hang here," he whispered to Manny.

Manny cocked his head. His eyes flashed wide.

"Just stay low and out of sight," Mason said. "No sounds." He glanced at Travis still buried in the leaves and at Nathan behind his bush a few feet away. He faced Manny and held his gaze for several seconds.

"We'll be here," Manny whispered.

Mason nodded, rose to a low crouch, and stepped off in the direction of the noise. He moved quickly and quietly from cover to cover.

As he got closer, he began to hear grunts and groans intermingled with the thrashing. A few yards more and he began to see flashes of red and yellow through the foliage. A few more yards and he could clearly see two men engaged in mortal combat.

Mato, his back on the ground, struggled to hold another native at bay.

The foreign native was something Mason had never seen, even in the movies. He wore only a loincloth. His upper body and legs were painted in patterns of red, yellow, and white. His face from just under his nose to the top of his head was painted or stained a bright red. A patch of what looked like long-haired fur of some kind, dyed an equally bright red, covered the very top and partially down the back of his head. The fur stood straight up.

Mato held a knife in his right hand, but it was restrained with the native's left hand around Mato's wrist. The native held a colorful battle club in his right hand, restrained by Mato's grasp of the man's wrist. With the heavier and taller native on top, he used his weight to Mato's disadvantage. Mason could tell Mato was tiring and would lose the fight if no one came to his aid.

With no one else in sight, Mason took a few quiet steps to his right which would give him a clearer shot and a better angle at the native's back. While still behind partial cover, he raised the bow, drew the arrow to its full length, took a second to aim, and let loose.

The arrow struck with a dull *thud*. The foreign native immediately arched his back.

In that second of weakness, Mato whipped himself over taking the man down to his side. He jerked his knife hand free and slammed the knife deep into the man's chest just below his left arm pit. The native dropped the battle club and went limp.

Mato jerked his head up as Mason stepped into the small clearing. Mato sheathed his knife without wiping the blood and retrieved his bow lying on the ground nearby. Without saying a word, he glanced around as he pulled Mason back into the denser scrub. He knelt as he pulled Mason down to his knees. Mato placed a hand on Mason's shoulder.

He realized in that moment that something had changed between himself and Mato. Since he had no idea how he should respond, he just nodded.

Mato motioned for Mason to follow as he rose and stepped off in a crouch back toward where Mason had left Manny, Nathan, and Travis.

The three survivors were where Mason had left them along with Mato's three remaining braves. Everyone rose to their feet as Mato and Mason approached.

"Tashunka?" Mato grunted to one of his braves.

The brave shook his head and said a few words that Mason couldn't understand. He figured the brave was elaborating on their friend's death.

"Who were those guys?" Travis asked, still visibly shaken.

"Lenni-Lenape," Mato said. "Five-Nations from north. Raiding party."

Mason had no idea who or what constituted the Five-Nations, but he nodded as though he did.

"Are they gone?" Nathan asked.

Mato swept his extended arm in a wide arc. "Still here."

"I think he means they are still in the area but scattered," Mason said. He turned to Mato. "Do we need to worry about them?"

Mato dipped his chin one time indicating the affirmative. "We take Tashunka to village. You follow."

"I think we should return to our camp. If those warriors are in the area, they might stumble on our people."

Mato grunted at his three braves.

One of them, the largest of the three, retrieved the lifeless body of their friend, threw him over his shoulder, and then fell in between the other two braves as they all stepped off toward the northwest.

Mato lingered for a moment. He pointed to his own eyes and ears.

"We'll be okay," Mason said. "Sorry about Tashunka."

Mato turned and started off to catch the other braves.

When the Indians were out of sight, Mason swung his gaze to each of the three men staring at him. "I'll take point," he said to Manny. "You bring up the rear but stay close and keep your eyes and ears on your six and the flanks." He turned to Nathan and Travis. "Put your feet where I put mine. And don't make a sound on our way back."

The two men nodded.

Mason held up his bow and motioned to the spear in each of their hands. "Don't hesitate to use those if the need arises."

The two men's expressions turned even more serious as they each nodded.

Mason started off toward the southwest with Nathan, Travis, and Manny in tow.

◆◆◆

"How can you tell us to stay calm when there's a band of savages that might be approaching as we speak?" Mildred asked.

Standing in the midst of the survivors, Mason turned to Mildred. "If we panic, we'll make mistakes."

"Unfortunately, it may not matter what we do," Tom Green said from his reclined position on a palmetto mat. He adjusted his splinted leg. "I'm stating the obvious here, but we don't have the means to repel any sort of attack. A couple of braves would do it."

Everyone looked around at each other and mumbled.

"Mason is armed," Manny said. "And the rest of us are not helpless."

Mason glanced at Manny and nodded. "He's right. We're not helpless. We need to take a proactive stance."

"What does that mean?" Nathan asked. "With everything else we're dealing with, we're supposed to fight a war with the Indians." He huffed and shook his head. "We should get the hell out of this place."

"For one thing," Mason said, ignoring Nathan, "we need a twenty-four-hour watch. At least two people on duty at all times. It also wouldn't hurt to build some defensive barriers. Limbs and brush would do it, and maybe some of those cabbage palm trunks we've been cutting down." He took the spear from Manny's hand and held it up. "And we need to construct more weapons." He handed the spear back to Manny and nodded toward the spear Nathan still held in his hand. "Can you make more of those?"

Nathan examined the spear. "Sure, why not?" He peered at the spear again. "Except for the stone point."

Mason nodded. "We need to do what we can," he said, as he looked around at the faces. "Where's Lisa?"

"Lisa, Angie, and Bobby are fishing," Gail said, as she walked over and sat next to Tom. She checked the bindings on his leg.

Mason saw everyone's face look toward something behind him. He turned and saw Lisa, Angie, and Bobby walking toward camp. All three were carrying several fish.

"What's happening?" Lisa asked, as she hung her string of fish on a branch and continued into the group.

Mason went through the story again about the attack on the hunting party right up to the part about establishing a watch system and needing weapons.

"We might be able to get more bows and arrows from Mato," Manny said.

Mason lifted his chin in Manny's direction. "Tom is right, at least to a degree. It's only a matter of time until one or more unsavory characters come upon this camp. The Lenni-Lenape, as Mato referred to them, will be even more worked up than they already were. But there could be others, even the white hunters and trappers of this time."

Dorothy cleared her throat. "The Lenape were aligned with the Iroquois, a northeastern tribe that was really composed initially of five separate tribes — Mohawk, Oneida, Onondaga, Cayuga, and the Seneca nations. The English referred to them simply as the Five Nations. They'll be referred to as the Six Nations when the Tuscarora join, if they haven't already."

"Why are they way down here in South Carolina?" Karen asked.

"Branching out to new territories," Dorothy replied. "What Mason encountered this morning sounds like a small raiding party. Probably less than ten braves out for targets of opportunity."

Mason motioned to Manny. "Can you organize teams to work on defenses and weapons? And watches should start tonight."

Manny nodded.

Mason placed a hand on Dorothy's shoulder and guided her away from the main crowd. "Do you have any idea what year we're in?"

Dorothy pondered the question for a moment. "Best guess, probably late seventeenth or early eighteenth century. We don't have enough information."

Mason twisted his lips as he contemplated her information. "And the Lenape, do we need to worry about them?"

"I would say that right now, that's our biggest worry."

"Okay," Mason said, as he stretched his neck and shoulders. "We should get busy." He walked over to where Manny was talking to a group of men.

He turned to Mason. "Most of the women will continue to concentrate on our food situation." He waved his hand at the fourteen men standing in front of him. "Nathan and a few others will work on weapons. The rest of us will start setting up a perimeter."

Mason nodded. "Let's do what we can today, but tomorrow morning I think you and I should return to

Mato's village. We need more information about what we might be facing."

Manny nodded in agreement.

CHAPTER 8

Lisa woke to the sound of muffled voices outside the hut she shared with Angie, Mildred, and three other women including Karen. She opened her eyes and glanced around at the dim interior. Everyone was there except Karen and it was her voice she thought she heard outside. As Lisa stepped through the hut's opening, she saw Mason and Manny walking away from Karen and Dorothy. "Where are they off to?"

Karen and Dorothy turned in unison.

"The Indian village," Dorothy said. "Should be back in a few hours."

"In the meantime," Karen said, "we still have a camp to maintain and people to feed." She turned in an arc scanning the edge of their camp against the forest. "The men will be working on weapons and defenses; we will gather food as usual."

Angie stepped from the hut and stood next to Lisa. "Let's get a bite from the pot and head out," she said, as she stepped off in the direction of the central cooking pit.

The fire had reduced itself to simmering coals overnight, but the pot of stew hanging overhead from a tripod still emitted wafts of steam.

"It will just be you two," Karen said. "Bobby has perimeter duty. Maybe you should hang in camp today."

Lisa paused for a moment looking back. "We won't be that far away. If we see anything weird, we'll come running."

After walking the mile or so along the beach to their regular fishing spot, Lisa and Angie stopped at the water's edge and surveyed the area. Satisfied there was no one around, they turned inland along the sand to the back side of the spit of land the beach had become. The inlet opened up to a body of water about a hundred yards across. A small stream emptied into the pond on the back side from the swampy forest.

They both eyed the static fish trap a few yards into the water that Bobby and the two of them had built shortly after their arrival. The design was Bobby's idea. The trap consisted of a series of sticks stuck side-by-side into the sand and muck bottom to form a pen. The sticks protruded from the water's surface about three feet, so the ends remained above the surface even during high tide. The trap backed up to the shore which formed the rear barrier for the trap. The sides extended from the beach out into the water several yards and turned to join in the middle leaving a narrow opening. The opening angled in toward the shore making it easier for fish to swim in but more difficult to find their way out. It was a good design, well-constructed, and best of all, it worked.

Every morning the three of them found at least a few fish inside the trap. Sometimes there were many more. Fish from this trap had become the camp's main source of protein.

As usual, Lisa stripped off her jeans and her long-sleeve shirt which left her in a lacy bra and panties. This was her routine even when Bobby was around. She didn't do it at first, but as the days went by and she got to know and trust him more, she felt comfortable enough to strip rather than get her jeans wet. They took forever to dry. Bobby was always a gentleman around her and treated both she and Angie like daughters.

Angie remained in her flight attendant's navy-blue skirt even though the hem got wet as she waded into the water.

The first step each morning was to close off the trap's narrow opening with a makeshift door slid into the sand. Angie took care of that.

With the door in place, Lisa waded into the water within the trap to survey the day's catch. She saw several large fish. They were of different varieties, but all were edible according to Bobby who was an avid fisherman in his former life.

Initially they had fashioned spears and tried to jab the fish, but they found that the sharpened points just bounced off their bodies. Then they tried weaving a net of sorts from palm fronds, but found that didn't work either. The fish were too fast. They finally found that just bending over and scooping the fish onto the bank with their hands worked the best.

Angie joined Lisa inside the trap. Working together they herded the fish toward the shallower water, scooped, and repeated the process. Sometimes they were successful, sometimes not, but they kept at it until they had all the fish they needed or at least as many as they could catch.

After putting the day's catch on stringers made from strips of the yellow raft, they put the fish back in the water to keep them fresh. As was their routine, Lisa and Angie spent some time ensuring the trap was sound, reseating any sticks that had worked their way loose, and adding more sticks to any spots in the walls that threatened to open up.

As they worked, Lisa caught sight of movement from the corner of her eye in the direction of the beach. She focused expecting to see Bobby coming around the bend. The realization that it was Nathan walking toward them sent a jolt of anxiety through Lisa's body. She began wading toward her jeans and shirt which were draped over the limb of a scrawny tree on their side of the pond.

Before she could make it onto the shore, Nathan stepped in front of her. "I just came to check on you girls." His eyes gazed up and down Lisa's body.

"Where's Bobby?" Lisa asked, trying to hide the anxiety she felt.

"Back in camp," Nathan said.

"Why aren't you back in camp?" Angie asked, as she stepped up next to Lisa.

Nathan shrugged his shoulders. "Taking a break. Like I said, thought I would check on you two."

"We're fine," Angie said. "You can go back now."

Lisa started to move toward her clothes, but Nathan took a step to block her way. "I thought we could get to know each other a little." He ogled Lisa's body again.

Lisa knew perfectly well what he wanted; she just didn't know how far he would go. But she did know one thing for sure; she couldn't just stand there with her wet underwear clinging to her skin.

Suddenly, Lisa faked a move to the left but skirted to the right when he shifted his weight. She was nearly past him when an arm shot out and grabbed her around the waist. She twisted and tried to slap him in the face, but he blocked her hand with his own. She tried to wiggle free but his arm just tightened around her waist. That's when she heard a loud *whack* and felt his arm release as he sank to his knees. She looked back at Angie and saw her standing there with a large diameter limb from the fish trap in her hands.

Nathan reached up, felt the back of his head, and examined the red liquid on his fingers before falling over in the sand.

"I think you killed him," Lisa said, as she bent down.

"Nah, he's just dazed." She pointed at his face. "See, his eyes are twitching."

"What do we do now?" Lisa asked.

Angie waded into the water, replaced the limb in its spot in the fish trap, and turned back to the scene on the beach. She shrugged her shoulders as she exited the water and knelt next to Nathan. She put two fingers on his neck. "Pulse is okay." She bent closer and cocked her ear toward his mouth. "He's breathing." She stood up. "He'll wake up on his own. We should probably head back."

"And just leave him here?"

"Yeah," Angie said. "He'll need time to cool off when he wakes up."

Lisa threw her hands in the air and stood. She slipped into her jeans and shirt, grabbed the fish, and the two of them walked away.

◆◆◆

"The little bitch clocked me in the head," Nathan said, as he stood in front of Mason.

Lisa and Angie stood at his side. The rest of the survivors surrounded the four of them.

Nathan felt the back of his head and extended his fingers in Mason's direction. His fingers were colored with mostly dried blood.

Mason turned his head to Gail.

"He'll be okay, but he'll probably have a headache for a day or two.

Mason rubbed his face slowly with one hand as he gazed at Lisa and Angie.

"He was being a jerk," Angie said. "There's no telling what he would have done had I not hit him with the stick."

Lisa nodded.

Ever since the encounter on the plane he knew Nathan would be trouble. He just didn't know to what degree. Unfortunately, there wasn't much Mason could do about this particular situation. His actions toward the girls really weren't serious enough to warrant serious repercussions, other than the crack on the head he had already received. The fact was, no matter what his intentions might have been, he didn't get very far. "How far did you get with the spears?" he asked Nathan.

"What!" Nathan exclaimed. "That's it?"

"Yep," Mason said. "That's it."

Nathan's eyes bulged and his face turned red. He spun around and stormed off.

Mason turned to Lisa and Angie, took hold of their shoulders, and guided them a few steps away from the crowd. "I'll keep an eye on him. You two should do the same. And when you're away from camp, make sure you take Bobby with you."

Lisa and Angie nodded.

"For what it's worth, you did the right thing."

"Anything we need to worry about?" Karen asked, as she walked up with Dorothy.

"I'll try to keep him busy," Mason said.

"How was the trip to the village?" Dorothy asked.

Mason pointed at four bows and an equal number of quivers full of arrows next to his hut. "Mato said the Lenape's attacks are mainly directed at his tribe. Apparently, they are arch enemies or something. Their intentions toward the colonists vary. Normally peaceful, but my assistance to Mato probably complicates things a bit. We should keep our eyes open and our guard up."

Everyone scattered to go about their normal tasks.

Mason helped the crews on the perimeter defenses. In doing so he had a chance to work alongside Bobby. Bobby was probably in his middle to late fifties with thin, white hair. He was still dressed in the trousers and the white button-down shirt he wore on the plane, although now stained and grubby. The man didn't come across as particularly happy most of the time; probably still despondent over the loss of his wife. But he kept himself busy. If he wasn't out with Lisa and Angie, he was making himself useful around the camp. He had carried a few extra pounds when Mason saw him on the plane, but he'd since lost weight and seemed to be in better physical shape. Mason liked him.

"How's everything going?" Mason asked, as he grabbed hold of the limb Bobby was trying to move into place.

"Okay, I guess."

"I appreciate you helping out with the fishing," Mason said. "You guys are doing a great job keeping us supplied."

"Glad to do it," Bobby said. "Being around the girls makes me feel younger."

Mason nodded.

"So, how much of a jerk was Nathan to the girls this morning?" Bobby asked.

"According to Angie, he was a total asshole to Lisa. I guess he caught her with her pants down, so to speak."

Bobby nodded

"But hopefully the matter is over," Mason said.

Bobby glanced over to where Nathan was sitting on a log in front of his hut. "He's the type to hold a grudge."

"I know," Mason said. "I suggested the girls always have you along when they venture out."

Bobby nodded. "I think that's a good idea."

Mason eventually worked his way over to the opposite side of the camp where Manny and several others had built a section of the barrier out of thick brush. "Did they teach you how to shoot a bow in survival school?" he asked Manny.

"Not part of the course," he replied, as he continued working. "But I know how to handle a bow."

"We need to get as many people as possible up to snuff on the bows," Mason said.

Manny stood up and surveyed the camp. "There are several that have hunted." He pointed to Bobby and a couple of others. "We can start with them."

"Let's include Angie," he said, "she seems very capable."

Mason started walking toward the center of camp. "Might as well start right now."

CHAPTER 9

Mason came instantly awake at the touch of someone's fingers on his shoulder. He opened his eyes but couldn't see much in the darkness. Just a human form hunched over him.

"Manny asked me to get you," the man whispered.

Mason recognized Tito's French accent and rolled to his knees. "What's going on?"

"He thinks something's weird out beyond the perimeter," Tito said.

Mason holstered his pistol and got to his feet. "Lead the way," he whispered.

The two of them walked silently across the camp's central open area.

Red embers from the camp's fire pit penetrated the darkness.

Mason crouched lower as he approached Manny's dark hulk. "What is it?"

"It's quiet," Manny whispered.

"Yeah?"

"Too quiet. Normally there are all kinds of night noises from the forest. About twenty minutes ago they stopped."

Mason cocked his head and listened. He had to agree that it was quieter than normal. On top of that, the hairs were standing up on the back of his neck. His first thought was to rouse those that had been working with the bow and arrows and get them all positioned on the wall. He didn't know that much about Indians and had no idea if they reconnoitered or attacked at night. Probably both. He decided to err on the side of caution. He leaned his head closer to Tito. "As quietly as you can, wake up Nathan, Bobby, and Travis. Get them armed with the bows and bring them back to the wall. Stay low." He saw Tito's body rise, turn, and low trot back toward the huts. Mason saw no point in waking anyone else. They had no weapons and if an assault actually occurred, they would just become easy targets.

Just as Tito's footfalls in the sand faded in the distance, Mason heard a single bird's shrill, low in volume but high in pitch. One shrill and then quiet again. He had no idea if it was a bird or an Indian. Mato would have known, and Mason wished he was here now. Mason suddenly realized that the bird call might have been a ploy—a subtle but intentional attempt to get those awake in the camp to move forward toward the sound. Toward the wall. It was a common maneuver in combat. Feign an assault on one side and actually attack from the opposite.

Mason rose to a crouch and leaned toward Manny. "I'm going to check the beach. When our people show up, get them spread out along the wall." He didn't wait for a response before turning and low trotting toward the sound of the waves in the distance. He pulled his pistol as he passed the huts and entered the trees between the camp and the ocean. Inside the tree line he slowed, ducked lower, and made maximum use of the trees for cover as he moved. Every few feet he paused to look and listen. All he heard on this side of the camp was the surf. And all he saw was darkness and the even darker shapes of trees and brush. On the opposite tree line, facing the ocean, the light sand contrasted against the dark ocean beyond. He peered up and down the beach with the aid of the star and moon light but saw nothing out of the ordinary. As much as he wanted to rejoin the others in camp, he forced himself to remain. If there was to be an attack, he was sure it would come from this side. Mason holstered his pistol and settled in for a long night.

As the morning sun began to peek over the horizon, Mason stood and stretched his neck and shoulders. He took a final look up and down the beach and into the surrounding trees. Satisfied nothing was amiss, he began walking toward the camp, tired but happy the night was a bust. When he walked past the line of huts, he saw that most people were up and moving about. Manny, Bobby, Tito, and Travis were still manning their positions on the wall.

Manny stood as Mason approached. "Sorry about the false alarm."

"I don't think it was a false alarm," Mason said. "They were out there. Somebody was out there, maybe just testing our defenses."

"Can we maintain this level of vigilance every night?" Bobby asked, as he joined Mason and Manny.

Mason knew they didn't stand a chance against an attack from even a small band of natives. But that's not what anyone wanted to hear. "We'll make it work."

Mason caught sight of Dorothy and Karen adding wood to the central fire. He walked over.

"Did something happen last night?" Dorothy asked.

"It could have been hostile Indians testing our defenses, or maybe they were just curious, or maybe it was nothing at all. Whatever it was, we have no choice but to carry on with our routine. We need to gather food every day since we have no way to store it."

"That's not entirely true," Manny said, as he walked up.

Mason, Dorothy, and Karen turned to Manny.

"We can smoke any extra meat we get," Manny said. "We'd need a lot, something like a deer."

"Like jerky," Mason said.

"Exactly. We smoke and dry thin cuts of the meat over a fire. It should last a week in that state."

"I don't think it will last a week in our state," Dorothy said.

"Don't you need salt for that?" Karen asked.

"Not really. Salt would make it taste better. But the smoke will also add flavor to the meat."

"And the smoker?" Dorothy asked.

"Just a tripod of poles over a low fire. Hickory would be best with three or four racks at the top, spaced nine inches or so apart. The bottom rack would be about four feet from the fire. We'll need some cordage to assemble the rack; I wouldn't recommend using strips of rubber from the yellow raft. Jerky and rubber don't go well together."

"Where do we get the cordage?" Mason asked.

"Pull thin strips off the back side of dry cedar bark. Twist them together in a particular manner, and that's it. It will be a lot of work and it will take some time."

"I don't see where we have a choice," Mason said. "For one thing, travel will be much easier if we don't have to forage along the way."

Manny nodded.

"Where do we start?" Mason asked.

"There's a dead cedar I came across the other day," Manny said. "I'll get some people working on that."

"Include Nathan," Mason said.

"And Tom would be perfect for the twisting part, while his leg continues to mend," Karen said.

Manny nodded.

"I'll send Travis and Tito with Lisa, Angie, and Bobby for today's fishing," Mason said. "Armed with a couple of the bows."

Mason paused behind a small bush and took a knee. He motioned for the man behind him to do the same. Mason hadn't had a chance to spend much time with Jeremy Jackson since he only recently recovered from his bout with yellow fever. But from what he had seen of the young man, Mason thought he had great potential. In his late twenties, Jeremy was certainly one of the most physically fit in the camp which was why Mason selected him to tag along. Mason couldn't spare a bow for him, but he could help carry anything Mason was lucky enough to shoot. And Jeremy was on the quiet side, which was another reason to bring him along.

There were two ways to hunt deer: stay in one place and wait for one to walk by or stalk them. Both options worked. But Mason chose the latter because he wanted to survey the area for any indication of who might have been outside the perimeter. So far, he had seen nothing, which was what he expected. He had no doubt that a native to this area could trek in and out without leaving a sign.

As Mason rose to a crouch and stepped off, he motioned for Jeremy to follow. Mason had already explained to him how to walk in the forest without making a lot of noise, and at times he had to glance back to make sure Jeremy was still back there. He learned quickly.

Just as Mason paused behind another bush, he heard movement off to the right on the other side of a particularly dense growth of palmettos. The thicket was about thirty yards wide; easy enough for a deer to hop through but nearly impossible for a human to manage. To try would make way too much noise and would probably result in a snake bite. Without moving his feet, Mason twisted his torso until he was eye-to-eye with Jeremy. He pointed at Jeremy and to the right of the thicket. For himself he pointed to the left.

Mason eased forward as he pulled an arrow from the quiver and strung the nock. He glanced behind and watched Jeremy slink toward the right side of the thicket until he was out of sight. Ten yards farther, Mason saw movement. It was barely a twitch from one ear of a deer lying just inside the thicket. Normally deer would have been up and long gone. But this one apparently decided to lounge. As Mason raised the bow, he saw the reason — two small deer, both with white spots. Mason estimated they were four to five weeks old, probably born in June. As Mason's gaze turned back, his eyes locked with the mother deer staring straight at him. A split second later, the deer was up and out of there with its white tail standing straight up. The two fawns followed close behind.

Mason brought his bow up to aim but quickly realized it was too late. The deer were gone. Mason lowered the bow and dipped his chin to his chest. A subtle shake of his head said it all. *Dammit*. He raised his head and saw Jeremy staring at him from a few yards away.

The two walked toward each other and stopped where the deer had been lying. They gazed into the forest in the direction of where they had gone.

"These guys are not only stealthy, they're quick," Jeremy whispered.

Mason raised his chin.

CHAPTER 10

"I think we should send two hunting parties out tomorrow morning," Mason said to Manny, as the two of them stood in the center of the camp.

"So, you got nothing?" Manny asked.

"Saw a couple," Mason said, as he gazed around. "I like what you've done with the camp." Mason eyed three fire pits off to one side, away from the huts. Each was stacked with wood ready to light. Three long Hickory poles and numerous short lengths also lay next to each pit.

Manny nodded toward Nathan, Mildred, and several others bunched around an eight-foot length of cedar bark. Each person twisted and weaved lengths of the sinuous fiber. They already had several feet of cordage. "Just waiting on the cordage, then I can assemble the racks."

"How'd you get that bark off the tree in one continuous length?"

"A sharp stick," Manny said. "I cut a vertical line down the trunk with the axe and pried a little, lifted a little. Takes time but it can be done."

"How did you get Nathan to pitch in?"

Manny smirked. "I offered to kick his ass if he didn't."

"Whatever works," Mason said.

Suddenly, there was a loud *boom* from the direction of the ocean.

Everyone stopped what they were doing.

"Sounds like a ways off," Manny said, as he started jogging toward the beach.

Everyone got up, hurried off in that direction, and took cover behind bushes and trees at the very edge of the forest.

Mason squinted to focus on two dots on the horizon.

"Sailing ships," Manny said. "Looks like two masts on both ships."

Mason heard another loud *boom*, and then another. Smoke bellowed from the side of one of the ships.

"One is firing on the other," Manny said.

"Can you see any flags?"

"Too far," Manny said.

"Has to be a pirate ship firing on a merchant," Dorothy said, as she plopped down next to Mason and Manny. "Probably firing across her bow trying to get the merchant to stop. Both look like schooners. Popular among merchantmen and pirates."

"Heading north," Mason said.

"The merchant would be coming out of Charles Town headed for Philly or New York," Dorothy said.

"The merchant is heaving too," Manny said, as he pointed.

"Sometimes only the sight of the pirate's flag was enough to stop a merchant," Dorothy said. "The cargo usually wasn't worth losing the ship and its crew. I guess this merchant needed a little extra persuasion."

"Will they take the boat along with the cargo," Manny asked.

"Maybe," Dorothy said. "Depends on the ship and how much of a hurry the pirates are in. British war ships patrolled known pirate routes, so they didn't like to hang around too long."

"If they take the ship, what will happen to the merchant crew?" Lisa asked from a few feet away.

"That depends on a lot of factors," Dorothy said. "The pirates might be able to enlist some of the crew. The rest could be set out on a life boat. Jolly boats, they call them. Particularly brutal pirates killed everyone that refused to join them."

"This must be kind of exciting," Lisa said. "To actually be living in a time you've studied."

Dorothy twisted her lips. "Of course, but I'd rather be home."

"No doubt," Mason said, as he glanced at the sky. "Maybe three or four hours of sunlight left."

"They'll have what they want off that boat in less than an hour," Dorothy said.

Everyone stood silently watching as the two ships drew closer to each other until finally they stood as one dot on the horizon.

Forty-five minutes later Mason squinted. "Rowboats," he said, as he pointed at the unfolding scene.

Those in earshot of Mason perked up.

Manny took in a deep breath and exhaled. "Shit," he said, as he slapped the tree trunk next to him. "They'll be rowing to shore."

"Our shore," Mason said.

"How many rowboats?" Lisa asked.

Mason focused on the dots. "Looks like two."

"I agree," Manny said, still looking in that direction.

"What do we do?" Lisa asked.

Mason turned around and peered at the trees. "Can't see the camp through the trees if they walk past."

"As long as they stay on the beach," Manny said. "But that won't matter. They'll smell our fire."

Mason stretched his neck and shoulders. "Yeah."

"They won't be armed with guns," Dorothy said. "Knives maybe."

Mason ran the options through his mind—invite them to dinner or kill them immediately. Mason turned to Dorothy. "What are the chances we could encourage them to just move on?"

Dorothy rubbed her jaw with one hand as she continued to stare out across the water. After several long seconds she shook her head subtly side to side. "Maybe," she said. "But the crew of most ships was made up of hard men. Life didn't mean much. There's a good chance they'll take what food and water we have, maybe even kill the men if necessary, and rape the women." She glanced at Lisa and Angie. "The temptation would be great."

"Even if the ship's captain is among them?" Mason asked.

"Depends on the captain and the crew," Dorothy said. "There's no way to know."

"What was the size of the crew on a merchant ship back then?" Manny asked.

"Impossible to say," Dorothy said, "but for a schooner that size, probably less than twenty."

"Two rowboats," Mason said, "say six to ten each. We could be looking at twenty men coming ashore."

Dorothy nodded.

"We need a plan," Manny said.

◆◆◆

"I count a total of fifteen men," Mason said to Manny. They were both prone behind a bush on the tree line.

Manny shifted his head and peered. "Uh-huh."

Mason looked to his left and right at the men spread out among the trees. Nathan, Travis, Bobby, and Jeremy each held a bow with an arrow mounted and ready to be fired. Manny held the fifth bow. Mason rolled to his side, reached under his buckskin shirt, and took hold of his Glock. He shoved the gun into the band of his breeches at the small of his back.

"We all step out at the same time?" Manny asked.

"Just the men," Mason said. "With the bows." He glanced at the numerous people spread out in the brush behind him, including Lisa, Angie, and Dorothy. Each held a spear. "That should be plenty."

Mason figured the two men who were not rowing in one boat and the one in the other were the captain and mates. The best dressed among them was likely the captain. The man sat relaxed in the rear of the nearest boat and had one foot up on the gunwale. He wore white breeches, a white vest, a blue long coat, white neck scarf, and black shoes with silver buckles. His light brown hair was pulled together in the back and mostly covered with a three-point hat with gold trim. Mason estimated he was in his forties but it was hard to tell.

Mason watched as one of the oarsmen in the first boat secured his oar and leaped into the shallow water.

He pulled at the boat and planted the front in the sand. The rest of the men piled out followed closely by the men from the second boat.

Mason leaned his head closer to Manny. "Change of plans," he whispered. "Stay here. Back me up if needed."

Before Manny could protest, Mason rose to his feet and stepped from the tree line in full view of the men on the beach.

In unison, the schooner's crew all stopped what they were doing and turned to face Mason. Their captain stepped to the front.

"Please excuse the invasion," the captain said. "We seem to find ourselves in a bit of trouble."

All of his men focused on Mason.

"The name is William Darby, captain of the merchant ship Samuel." He glanced back at the ocean. "Formerly the captain of the merchant ship Samuel."

Mason nodded. The captain's accent was surprisingly less British, as in BBC British, than Mason expected. It actually sounded closer to an American accent. "I saw. I suppose you're lucky to be alive."

Captain Darby examined Mason head to toe and cocked his head. "Your English is of an accent I can't quite place."

Mason thought of his home and early childhood in Provo, Utah. It wouldn't be explored for another hundred years. "I was raised in the far east," Mason said.

Captain Darby pursed his lips, probably considering the veracity of what Mason had just said.

Mason could only imagine what Captain Darby would think if he saw what the rest of the survivors were wearing. "May I ask your intentions?"

Captain Darby glanced at his men, all still staring at Mason. "We need to make our way back to Charles Town as soon as possible. We just need to get our bearings and maybe top off on water." The captain glanced at the two small wooden barrels in each boat.

Mason knew of only two sources of fresh water in the area, the small stream feeding the pond where Lisa and Angie fished, and the small stream that ran behind the camp. Mason pointed to the north. "There's a fresh water stream about a mile to the north. It runs into a pond with a small inlet." Mason wasn't sure his references were even used in the time of Captain Darby. Did a mile mean a mile as Mason knew it? Did the English refer to a small body of water as a pond? Mason didn't know but apparently Captain Darby understood based on the nod of his chin.

One of the captain's men, probably a mate since he wasn't one of the rowers, spit on the sand. "You live around here or just passing through?"

"Passing through," Mason said. Mason saw the captain scan the tree line behind him probably wondering if Mason had friends.

"Right," the captain finally said after a long pause, "the chaps and I will be off to find that water." Without weapons the captain obviously didn't want to take a chance on pressing Mason further. He nodded at Mason, motioned to his men, and stepped back in the boat.

His men pushed the boats back out, manned the oars, and began rowing straight out over the breaking surf. Once past the surf they turned north and paralleled the beach headed toward the inlet.

Mason watched until the two boats were well under way and had traveled a hundred yards before he stepped back into the trees.

Manny stood up next to him. "Think they'll be back?"

Mason searched the trees until he locked eyes on Dorothy. He motioned Dorothy forward. "Will they be back?"

"They're headed for Charles Town," she said. "If they decide to walk instead of row, they'll be walking right through the camp."

"Let's hope they decide to row," Manny said.

Mason started toward the camp, but stopped in front of Nathan. "Still think we're in our own time period?"

Nathan didn't answer.

CHAPTER 11

The next morning, Mason, Manny, and Dorothy stood at the tree line and gazed at an empty ocean.

"Think they're still at the fishing pond?" Manny asked.

"I think we should find out," Mason replied, as he stepped in the open and started up the beach.

Manny and Dorothy followed.

"They would have taken their boats through the inlet and into the pond," Dorothy said. "We won't be able to see anything until we're on them."

Mason acknowledged her statement with a slight nod but kept his focus on the beach ahead.

Rather than walk the beach all the way to the inlet, Mason cut into the brush about two hundred yards short and led the way through the sparse foliage. He slowed and went to a crouch when he began to see a clearing ahead.

The three of them finally stepped out onto the narrow, sandy shore of the pond. There was no sign of the schooner crew or their boats.

Mason knelt beside two marks in the sand, left by the keels of the two boats. "They were here," he said, as he stood up and gazed in all directions.

Manny waded to the middle of the fish trap and stopped. "Nothing bigger than a couple of inches in here."

"Either there was nothing bigger to begin with, or they took what was there," Mason said. "I vote for the latter." He turned to Dorothy. "What do you think?"

"I think they topped off their water, took the fish, and began rowing south just after dark. We wouldn't have seen them."

"Is it possible to row against the Gulf Stream?" Manny asked.

"As long as they stayed within a mile or two of the coast, they'd be fine," Mason said.

"Without weapons they didn't want to chance it," Dorothy said. "They were as leery of us, or the potential of us, as we were of them."

As soon as they were back in camp, two hunting parties went out. Mason and Jeremy went northeast; Bobby and Nathan went northwest. All were armed with a bow and arrows. Manny remained in camp with the fifth bow to assemble the smoking racks.

This time Mason decided to sit and wait rather than stalk. He and Jeremy made their way as silently as possible to the edge of a bog thick with palmettos. The two of them separated and took their positions within eyesight of each other.

Mason loaded an arrow onto the bow and took a seat on a downed tree trunk surrounded by a few bushes. The spot provided good cover but also gave him a view of the bog. Sitting there, waiting, gave him time to think.

Even though the survivors had established a pretty good routine and were not starving, Mason was fully aware they could not remain in this camp forever. For one thing, winter was coming and none of them were equipped for the cold, even for South Carolina. For another, yellow fever would return at some point, or malaria, or dysentery, or infection. Even a simple tick could cause havoc. And for another, the food would run out. Mato and his tribe had been very generous, but Mason couldn't continue to impose. Charles Town seemed like the only option. But the brief run-in with Captain Darby reinforced in his mind how much he and the others would stand out. They were foreigners in their own land.

The sound of rustling behind him, away from the bog, brought him out of his reverie. He quietly slid off the log and pivoted at the same time to a kneeling position. He saw only bushes, so he rose until he was standing at his full height. He peered through the limbs and leaves in search of the noise. A low-hanging limb full of leaves moved. He saw a patch of brown. A deer. He or she was standing only thirty yards away.

Mason ducked his head trying to get a better view through the brush until he was finally able to see the two single spikes.

He glanced in Jeremy's direction but couldn't get eyes on him. So, he turned his attention back to the deer. It took a few seconds of searching to reacquire the animal, still nibbling on the leaves.

Mason decided to move to his right for a better shot. It would be easier to keep the bow and arrow trained on the patch of brown while he stepped. He explored the layer of leaves with the toe of his boot and worked it to the soil below before placing any weight. Then another step.

With the next step his head lined up with an opening through the brush. It was tight, but doable. There was no way he could keep moving. Either the deer would hear or smell him, or the deer would lose interest in those particular leaves and move on. The small tunnel through the brush would be his only chance.

Mason slowly raised the bow to eye level, drew string the full length of the arrow, took a second to aim, and let loose.

As Mason chewed on a piece of the roasted venison, he gazed at the three tripod racks Manny had constructed. Each was centered over a low fire. Smoke enveloped the thin cuts of meat. He turned his attention to Manny sitting nearby. "Shouldn't the smoking racks be enclosed?"

Manny swallowed the piece of meat he had been chewing. "The process would go faster, but this will work."

Mason turned his head to Dorothy. "I was wondering about Captain Darby's accent. It didn't sound all that British."

"Of course, we don't have any recordings from the eighteenth century, but there is written evidence to suggest that Americans didn't lose their British accent. It was the other way around."

Mason cocked his head.

Dorothy continued. "What we recognize today as a British accent, like we hear on BBC, was developed at the time of the industrial revolution in England. Prior to that, English speakers everywhere pronounced the 'r' in words, like *hard*. The Brits evolved the accent and began pronouncing words with a silent 'r' like *hahd*. Americans didn't get the memo."

"Why the industrial revolution?" Manny asked.

"Commoners in England began earning more money, but they still spoke in a commoner's tongue. Those with money tried to differentiate themselves with their accent. It caught on."

"Interesting," Mason said. "So, we may not stick out as much as I thought when we enter Charles Town. At least based on our accents."

Dorothy smiled. "We'll stick out. Our accent is different enough, but our word usage is the biggest thing. It has changed considerably since the early seventeen hundreds.

"So, we'll still be from the far east," Manny said.

Dorothy nodded.

Mason was about to comment when a blur followed by a *thunk* caused him to flinch. He whipped his head around and saw a vibrating arrow stuck in a tree trunk. The arrow had missed his head by an inch. He turned his head back to the forest side of the camp as he rolled to the ground behind the log he had been sitting on. "Everyone get down," he yelled. More arrows followed. Some found their target in those who were slow to react.

Mason pulled his pistol and scanned the foliage with the decreasing light of dusk. He saw flashes of red and then a clear view of a loincloth clad native with the upper half of his head painted red. *The Lenape.*

Mason saw Manny dive for his bow and arrows leaning against one of the huts. Jeremy did the same. People were moving, finding cover, as arrows continued. Mason caught sight of a middle-aged woman still sitting in the open apparently frozen by the sudden mayhem. Mason was on his way to his feet when he saw the woman keel over with an arrow protruding from her chest. At the sound of a loud *boom* Mason dropped back down behind the log.

Eight Lenape stepped into the open from the thick trees and brush on the back side of the camp. All eight were together in one area apparently having approached the camp from the northeast. Six of the natives held a bow; two held a flintlock. A large puff of smoke was dissipating from one of the weapons. Mason heard a second loud *boom* and saw a large cloud of smoke from the other weapon. Both natives began the process of reloading their rifles. Mason took that opportunity to move.

He jumped to his feet and began running to his right, lateral to the group of Indians. He didn't want to give them a stable target by running directly at them. Additionally, he wanted to pull their attack away from the other survivors. The plan worked. Two arrows came within inches, but both landed harmlessly in the sand behind him.

As both a delta force operative and an air marshal, marksmanship was a top priority. His ability to hit a target both stationary and in a tactical environment had been evaluated quarterly for years. He thus had considerable confidence when it came to firing a pistol.

Before the two Indians with flintlocks had finished reloading, Mason turned and began running directly at the group of Indians. The sudden maneuver had the desired effect. All the Indians paused in apparent disbelief that any single person would be making a direct assault.

With a two-handed grip, Mason began firing the Glock, moving from target to target in rapid succession. The first *boom* from the little gun muffled his hearing, and the following rounds just added to the lack of sensation. The projectiles found their mark, each one hitting center mass as he worked his way down the line of Indians. Several froze with their eyes locked on the small, oozing hole in their bare chest before they dropped to the ground. When Mason stopped firing, all eight of the braves were down. The one nearest Mason looked up from the blood on his chest with an expression of total confusion.

Mason continued at full bore and took cover behind a large pine at the edge of the tree line. Keeping as much of his body behind the tree as possible, he extended the pistol toward the forest in search of any other targets. He saw nothing move and heard no sounds, mostly because he was still deaf in both ears.

At the touch of a hand on his shoulder he whipped around ready to fire only to see Manny standing next to him. He saw Manny's lips moving but heard only a dull, unintelligible mumbling at first. Slowly, as his ears cleared, he began to understand what Manny was saying.

"—them all."

"What?"

"I think you got them all," Manny said.

Jeremy and Nathan began checking the bodies.

Mason made another slow sweep of the forest as he backed toward the camp. He kept his pistol pointed toward the trees.

He found Dorothy, Lisa, Karen, and Angie unscathed, but several people were on the ground. Some were bleeding; some weren't moving.

Mason holstered his pistol and knelt next to Gail who was bent over Bobby. An arrow protruded from his chest just below the rib cage, right where the liver would be. "How's he doing?"

Dorothy glanced at Mason without commenting.

Lisa dropped to both knees next to Bobby. Her eyes pleaded with Gail. "Will he be okay?" A tear ran down her cheek.

"I don't think so," Bobby said. "I can't feel my legs."

Gail took Bobby's hand and straddled his fingers around the arrow. She applied downward pressure with her own hand. "Apply that amount of pressure," she said, and then stood up. Her eyes scanned the rest of the scene.

There were ten other people sprawled about. Seven of them were not moving. The remaining three appeared to have non-life threatening wounds in the leg or arm. Each was being attended by one or more of the survivors. He followed Gail as she began walking to the next casualty.

"That arrow pierced his liver and apparently damaged his spine," Gail said. "He needs surgery in a trauma hospital."

"Is there anything you can do?" Mason asked.

"I can't even remove the arrow without causing more damage. I have no instruments, no sutures, and worst of all, no antibiotics." She stopped and turned to face Mason. Her eyes were moist. "All of these wounds will be infected soon and there's nothing I can do." She continued walking.

Mason watched her kneel next to a woman whose right shoulder was a mass of blood, apparently shattered by one of the flintlock balls. The only thing she could do was apply a compress to stem the flow of blood. She moved to the next casualties.

While she attended to a woman with an arrow protruding from her hip, Mason knelt next to an older man with white, receding hair, and a matching mustache and goatee. He had his hand over a bleeding wound on his thigh. A bloody tipped arrow was on the ground beside him. The arrow head was intact. Mason helped apply pressure.

"Doesn't look that bad," Mason said. He tried to remember the man's name. *John Tifton*. "You pulled the arrow out?"

John nodded with his jaw clinched in pain.

An Asian woman knelt next to him and ripped a strip of cloth from her blouse with trembling fingers.

She, along with her daughter and her daughter's young son, had all miraculously survived the plane crash and now an Indian attack. Asumi was her name. The daughter was Hana and her son was Koji. They had kept to themselves, and Mason hadn't had a chance to get acquainted. He spotted Hana helping one of the other wounded. He saw Koji alone in the opening of one of the huts.

Mason took the cloth from Asumi's hand and wrapped it tightly around John's wound. "I don't think it hit an artery. The bleeding should stop soon."

"Thanks," John said with his teeth clinched.

Mason patted Asumi on the shoulder and stood up surveying the camp. He scanned the carnage, including the eight dead braves, and then closed his eyes as he tightened his lips.

CHAPTER 12

Mason opened his eyes at the touch of a hand on his shoulder. He gazed at Mato standing next to him.

"You kill Lenape?"

Mason wasn't sure if it was a statement or a question, but to whichever it was, Mason nodded.

Mato stared at the dead braves, still lying where they had fallen. He paid particular attention to their gunshot wounds. His head tilted to one side as he stared into Mason's eyes. He held that gaze for several moments before turning to the four Catawba braves examining the downed Lenape. "We will bury," Mato said. Mato looked around at the camp, at the dead, and the huddles of people. "You have people to bury too."

Mason gave a simple lift of his chin. "How did you know?"

"Hear gunshots," he said. He pointed to the two flintlocks among the dead Lenape. He cocked his head.

Mason knew what he was thinking. The gunfire sounded like a lot more than two flintlocks. And how did eight warriors end up shot by people in a camp with no guns? That was a question Mason had no intention of answering. For the Catawba, there was no answer, at least not one they could understand. So instead, Mason just nodded and let it go at that.

Mato finally raised his chin. "Maybe someday you say."

"Maybe," Mason said.

Mato turned and spoke to his braves.

They proceeded to pick up the dead Lenape and carry them into the forest. It took three trips to get all the bodies and their possessions.

"We could have used those flintlocks," Jeremy said, as he stepped up next to Mason.

"And the knives and tomahawks they carried," Mason said. He glanced back and saw Manny approaching.

"About their knives," Manny said. He lifted the edge of his polo shirt revealing four knives in their scabbard tucked into his waistband. "These were the best of the lot."

"How did you know Mato would want to take all their possessions?" Jeremy asked.

"Saw it in a movie," he said. "They buried their dead with their stuff to help them in the afterlife."

"Those were probably Apache you saw in the movie," Mason said. "But it apparently applies to the Catawba as well."

Dorothy, overhearing the conversation, stepped closer. "The Catawba buried their dead in mounds along with what they might need in the hereafter."

Manny raised an eyebrow.

Mason turned to the camp. "We need to help with the wounded."

Over the next several days, the number of graves grew until they numbered twelve including Captain Anderson and the yellow fever victim. Of those wounded during the battle, only John Tifton avoided serious blood loss and the subsequent infection that took most of those who did not die outright. By day four he was back up and walking.

The loss of Bobby was a serious blow. Mason had come to rely on him around camp and with the fishing. He would be missed. All of those who died would be missed.

After being assured by Mato that there probably were no other Lenape war parties in the area, Lisa and Angie resumed their fishing. Tom Green, whose broken leg had mostly healed, accompanied them.

And the hunting parties resumed. There were three of them: Mason and Jeremy, Manny and Tito, and Nathan and Toby Wellen. Toby was a couple of inches taller than Mason and probably had him by twenty pounds. He had curly hair down to his shoulders and nearly a full beard. He was younger than Nathan but not by much. They were both in their forties. Toby also wore baggy, cargo type shorts along with a black sleeveless t-shirt. It was an odd combination to wear on an airplane, but nonetheless, here he was.

After the Lenape battle, the twenty remaining survivors grew closer. Mildred, for instance, spent most of her time with Lana Broadhurst. They were about the same age. Lana loved dogs as much as Mildred. And little Chico had become protective of them both. The dog would growl every time Mason, or pretty much anyone else, came near.

The only survivor Mason didn't know much about was Sandy Craven. She was middle-aged with blond hair to her shoulders. She spent most of her time alone in her hut. She would help out but only if asked directly.

The topic of discussion nearly every night was how they arrived in the time period, how they would survive, and how they would get back. Those were the three questions Mason thought about the most as well, mainly the surviving part, and mainly at night before he fell asleep. Should they remain where they were or head for Charles Town? If the latter, would they be accepted or burned at the stake?

◆◆◆

Nathan made it a habit to wake up before anyone, usually before the sun was up. The first order of business each day was a visit to the latrine. Then he would wake Toby and the two of them would scavenge the beach with the first rays of light for anything interesting. Except for an occasional sea turtle laying eggs in the sand, every day had been uneventful. But it also gave Nathan and Toby time to talk in private. The topic was almost always Mason's self-appointment as master and commander. If it wasn't for that pistol, which he never seemed to be without, there might be a different person in charge.

On this particular morning, Nathan was expecting another empty shoreline. And it was, except for the dory beached two hundred yards south. It appeared empty as it rocked in the gentle surf. But as they approached, Nathan caught a whiff of a foul odor that grew more and more pungent. They held their noses when two men sprawled in the bottom of the boat came into view. The eye sockets of both men were empty except for dried blood. Their skin was pulled tight to the bones in their faces. Their meager clothes were stained and thread bare. The only other items in the boat were a single oar and a wood chest.

"They've been dead for days, maybe weeks," Toby said.

"Uh-huh," Nathan said, as he stepped closer examining the wood chest. "Wonder what's in the box?" he asked, as he bent over for a closer look.

It was a sturdy chest, approximately two feet wide, a foot high, and a foot deep, with a substantial lock through a thick metal hasp. Nathan fingered the lock for a moment and then grabbed hold of a metal handle on one end. He lifted to judge the weight. "Grab the other end."

Toby, still holding his nose with one hand, bent over, took hold of the handle on the opposite side, and lifted. His large biceps and triceps flexed.

Nathan had to use both his hands to lift his side of the box. "For such a small box, this thing is heavy."

They dropped the box on the beach with a dull *thud*. Both men stood up and stared down.

"What do you think?" Nathan asked.

Toby, still holding his nose, nodded. "I agree, it's heavy."

Nathan snorted. He scanned up and down the still empty beach. "Let's move this thing into the forest."

"We could wait for help and move it to camp," Toby said.

"Don't be a dumbass," Nathan said. "I want to see what's in it first." Nathan bent down and grabbed hold of the handle with both hands. He raised his eyes to Toby.

Toby picked up his side of the box and together they waddled well into the trees and over to a thick stand of palmettos.

"In here," Nathan said, as he stepped over several large palmetto roots and shuffled farther into the fronds. They set the chest on the sand.

"What do you plan to do about that lock?" Toby asked.

Nathan stared at the lock for several seconds as he rubbed the thick stubble on his face. He bent down, took hold, and gave it a solid jerk. "The axe maybe," he said, as he stood and turned in a full circle. "Think they would hear that from camp?"

Toby shrugged his shoulders. "I don't know, but even if it's full of pirate gold, what are you going to do with it here?"

Nathan considered the chest as he twisted his lips. "Mason said we'll be traveling to Charles Town at some point, but you're right, how would we take this chest without everybody knowing."

"Exactly," Toby said. "Let's just take it to camp."

"Not before I see what's in there," Nathan said. He stared at the chest a few seconds longer and then led Toby back to the beach. "We'll let them know about the boat, but not a word about the chest."

Everyone from the camp stood around the dory, or jolly boat as Dorothy called it, and peered at the bodies. Most people held their nose.

Mason turned to Dorothy. "What do you think?"

"They've been at sea for weeks probably," Manny answered before Dorothy could speak. "Apparently without any water. They wouldn't have lasted long."

Dorothy nodded. "There are no markings on the boat or the men so I have no idea where they might have come from."

"Okay," Mason said, as he turned in an arc. "We need to bury them."

"What about the boat?" Manny asked.

"We carry it up to camp," Mason said. "We can make more oars."

Several of the men dragged the dead bodies from the boat and up into the trees.

Mason removed his boots, put them in the boat, and began walking the boat along the shallow surf toward the camp.

Manny and Jeremy waded into the water and helped guide the boat.

The rest of the people followed along the shore.

"We could row this boat to Charles Town," Manny said, "just like Captain Darby."

"It might be easier than walking," Jeremy said.

"It won't hold twenty people," Mason said.

"Not everyone needs to go," Manny said. "One or two of us could return for whoever stays behind."

Mason nodded but said nothing.

Manny peered at Mason for several moments. "What are you thinking?"

"I'm wondering if there was anything else in the boat when Nathan and Toby found it."

Manny glanced at Nathan and Toby walking with the others along the shore. "Like what?"

"I don't know," Mason said, "but the two of them are awful quiet."

It was late in the afternoon of the next day when Nathan eyed the axe leaning against one of the huts. Nathan threw a couple of pieces of wood on the central fire and nonchalantly picked up the axe as though he were going to get more wood. He motioned for Toby to follow.

The two of them walked into the forest until they were out of sight from the camp and began circling around to the west, toward where they had left the chest. They stepped as quietly as possible and checked their rear often to make sure no one followed.

"Did you see Mason in camp?" Nathan whispered.

"Yeah, he was over talking to Karen like always," Toby replied.

"Did he see us leave?"

"I don't think so," Toby said, "he didn't seem to be paying attention."

Nathan nodded as he continued to lead the way through the brush until they stepped out on the beach seventy-five yards down from the camp. After checking that the beach was deserted, he turned and began walking to where they had found the boat.

At the right spot he turned back into the forest and walked directly to the clump of palmettos. He stepped over the roots, pushed through the fronds, and stopped next to the chest, still where they had left it.

Nathan pulled his polo shirt off and the white undershirt beneath it. He wrapped the undershirt around the lock. With the shirt in place, he motioned for Toby to step back. Nathan raised the axe and slammed the hammer side against where the shackle entered the body. It took several swings but the lock finally popped open.

Nathan dropped the axe in the sand, slid the lock's shackle from the hasp, and flung the lid open. His eyes widened and his mouth hung open. He gaped at Toby and then back into the chest. He dropped to both knees, reached inside, and extracted a single silver coin from among many more. He held it up and twisted his hand until he could see the back side.

The coin was odd-shaped, more square than circular. The silver color gleamed in the light.

Nathan fingered the definition on both sides and then gazed into the chest at the other coins. He reached in and picked up another. "There must be thousands of them," he said, as he twisted his head toward Toby.

Toby knelt beside him and ran his fingers through the coins until he saw the glint of gold. He plucked that coin out and held it up to the light. "Wonder what this would be worth back in the world?"

"This chest might be worth millions," Nathan said, as he picked up and examined another coin. "Can you read any of the lettering?"

"Some are legible."

Nathan picked up several more coins and examined them closely.

Toby pitched his coin back into the chest. "Now what?"

Nathan jumped at the unmistakable sound of Mason's voice behind him. "Now you help carry that chest back to camp," Mason said.

Nathan and Toby jerked their head around to see Mason, Manny, and Jeremy standing a few feet behind them.

Nathan let the coins he held fall back into the chest. He slowly rose to his feet as he turned to face the three men.

"Yeah, whatever," Nathan said.

CHAPTER 13

"How much is all that worth?" Manny asked, as everyone stood around the open chest. Even Sandy was out of her hut.

Mason turned to Dorothy.

Dorothy knelt down next to the open chest and ran her fingers through the coins. "Most of these are Spanish dollars also known as pieces of eight. They were used as currency in America until the middle eighteen hundreds. Each was equal to an American dollar; it took three to equal a British pound. Silver and gold coins were rather rare in colonial America. There just weren't enough minted since each had to be produced by hand."

"What about the gold coins?" Mason asked.

Dorothy picked up one of the gold coins and examined it closely. Her eyes widened at the sight and her chin shook subtly back and forth. "I've never seen one of these until now," she said, as she continued to turn it over in her hand.

"What's it worth?" Mason asked.

"This is a single doubloon, also called an escudo, and it's worth thirty-two reales, four times the Spanish dollar which is eight reales, thus pieces of eight. The silver coins were often cut in to eight bits."

"So, what can you buy with a Spanish dollar?" Manny asked.

Dorothy dropped the two coins back into the chest and stood up. "That's really hard to say. Prices varied a great deal. A set of sheets, for instance, could cost three times what it cost to make a wooden bed. The sheets had to be shipped from London." She stared at the chest of coins for several moments and finally shook her head. "You could buy a steak, bread, and beer dinner for two or three pennies. A suit of clothes might cost three to ten dollars depending on the material used. Shoes could cost a dollar."

"Okay," Mason said, as he addressed the crowd, "the first thing we should do is count what's here." He eyed Nathan and Tom Green. "How about if you two help Dorothy figure out how much is here."

Dorothy, Nathan, and Tom dropped to their knees, began plucking coins from the chest, and arranging them in stacks of five on a palm frond mat.

Manny took Mason by the arm and guided him away from the crowd. "Nathan?"

Mason took in a deep breath and exhaled as he glanced back at the crowd. "He found it. And there's not much he can do with everyone watching."

Manny nodded. "You know, if you go walking into town carrying a pouch full of those coins, you'll probably end up conked on the head and left in an alley minus the money."

"Yeah, we could use someone to show us the ropes," Mason said. He thought for a moment as he stared at the chest of coins. "Mato."

"He's an Indian," Manny said.

"He's an Indian with some experience trading in Charles Town," Mason said. "And he's all we have."

Manny nodded. "And what about when whoever lost those coins comes looking for them?"

"This is a long coast line, but if the situation arises, we'll just have to deal with it. For now, let's see what we can do about oars for that boat."

Mason and Manny had just returned to camp with three stout poles, close in diameter to the one oar, when Tom approached.

"We have a count," Tom said, as he motioned to a mat covered with stacks of the silver coins. Dorothy, Nathan, and several others stood next to the mat.

Mason and Manny dropped the poles and followed Tom.

"Six thousand, eight hundred and forty-three Spanish dollars," Dorothy said. "There were only ten of the gold coins."

Mason raised his eyebrows as he stared down at the stacks. "And it's roughly the same in American dollars."

"Roughly," Dorothy said.

Manny whistled. "I bet we could buy an entire plantation with that."

"Probably not a working plantation," Dorothy said. "But bare land was actually cheap at this time. Free to a lot of people."

"We'll need to divide some of it up into small pouches," Mason said, "but for now, just put it all back in the chest."

"And who gets to keep watch on the chest?" Nathan asked.

Mason smiled. "You found it Nathan, why don't you take charge of doing that."

Manny used the axe to split one end of a pole and used a knife to carve the inside of both sides until he had what amounted to a ten-inch slot cut into the end of the pole.

Nathan and Toby worked on doing the same to the other two poles.

With the slots cut, they each dabbed pine tar into their slot and slid a wood slat, split from a log, into the sticky space. They bound the two pieces tightly together with buckskin strips.

"What we need is a boat," Nathan mumbled without looking up from his work.

"We have a boat," Toby said.

"No, a bigger boat," Nathan said, "a sailboat."

"Where do you plan to get one of those?" Toby asked.

"Charles Town," Nathan said. "Use some of the money to buy a boat."

Manny stopped what he was doing. "That's actually not a bad idea."

Nathan nodded.

Manny caught Mason's eye across the camp and motioned for him to come over.

"The oars are really coming together," Mason said, as he walked up.

Manny motioned to Nathan. "He actually came up with a good idea. We get a bigger boat in Charles Town."

Mason thought for a moment as he stared at the ground. "Can you sail a boat?"

"No, but somebody here must have some experience," Nathan said. "Doesn't have to be that big to carry all of us."

"Beats rowing the seventy-five miles back and forth," Manny said.

"I agree," Mason said, as he turned and scanned everyone in camp. He stepped back to the center. "Anyone know how to sail?" he asked in a voice loud enough for everyone to hear.

Lisa raised her hand. "Does a forty-eight-foot monohull count?"

"It does," Mason said. "Anyone else?"

John Tifton cleared his throat. "I've owned two sailboats in my life. Did some blue water cruising on the last one."

"Okay, we'll definitely keep a boat in mind when we get to Charles Town," Mason said.

"Who's making the first trip?" Nathan asked.

"Funny you should ask that," Mason said. "I was thinking you, me, Jeremy, and Dorothy, and now either Lisa or John, along with Mato and probably a couple of his braves if I can talk him into it."

"What about me?" Manny asked.

"You look too much like a Spaniard," Dorothy said, as she walked up.

"It would make it that much harder for us to slip in and slip out," Mason said. "Same goes for Travis and Angie. They might be mistaken for runaway slaves."

◆◆◆

The next morning, Mason and Jeremy were off early for another hunting trip and ended up trekking the four miles to Mato's village. They had been to the village so many times that the natives barely stirred upon their arrival. Only Mato and one other brave greeted them in the village center.

"No luck?" Mato asked, nodding at the bow in Mason's hand.

"Not so far," Mason replied. "Maybe on the way back."

Mato cocked his head as if to ask the reason for the visit.

"We found a boat on the shore," Mason said. "A rowboat large enough to hold ten people or so."

Mato acknowledged his understanding with a nod.

"Some of us would like to visit Charles Town, and I was hoping you would come along."

Mato looked around the village and back to Mason. "Another month, we go."

Mason stroked his beard a couple of times. "You could still make that trip. We just need a guide of sorts. We've never been to Charles Town."

"What you do there?"

"Get to know the place. Maybe buy some supplies."

"How many go?"

"Probably five, plus you, and we'd still have room for a couple of your braves if you want."

Mato scanned the village giving him time to think.

"I figure three days there and maybe a couple of days in town," Mason said.

"Okay," Mato said. "When you leave?"

"We can leave tomorrow morning."

Mato nodded. "I be your camp with sun."

"Thank you," Mason said, as he put a hand on Mato's shoulder.

◆◆◆

Mason and Jeremy spent the rest of the day provisioning the boat. Since Nathan and Toby had gotten a deer earlier that morning, Mason didn't feel bad about taking most of the smoked venison on hand. They also filled eight of the plastic drink bottles with filtered water and wrapped each bottle with buckskin.

Mason gave considerable thought to the clothes everyone would be wearing when they entered the town. His buckskin shirt and Dorothy's buckskin dress, even for Caucasians, were common for the period. Nathan, Jeremy, and John, on the other hand, were way out of kilter. John would be the better dressed of the two with his dark slacks and long sleeve white shirt, but as for Nathan and Jeremy, well, men didn't wear baggy, cargo shorts and t-shirts in Colonial America. Especially a shirt that read *beach bum* across the front. Nathan and Tom Green were about the same size and luckily Tom agreed to switch his white dress shirt and gray slacks for Nathan's shorts and t-shirt. Since the slacks were already split up to the knee on one leg to accommodate the splint he had worn, Mason went ahead and cut both pants legs off just below the knee making them look more like breeches.

Mason would also be carrying eight buckskin pouches, each containing a hundred of the silver Spanish dollars, in his rucksack. He had no idea how much he would need, but eight hundred dollars seemed like a hefty sum for the time. The rest of the money would remain in camp.

With everything done, he took a seat on the palm frond mat in the doorway of his hut. He retrieved the four extra pistol magazines from his rucksack, removed the two from his holster, and the one in the pistol and laid them all out on the mat. He removed the 9mm rounds from each of the magazines, disassembled the magazines, and proceeded to wipe down the parts with a piece of cloth. The four magazines that had been in the Ziplock bag were pristine, but the two from the holster and the one from his pistol were beginning to show signs of rust. He wiped all the parts down with fat from the latest deer kill paying particular attention to the rust spots. They weren't bad, but if left unattended they would worsen. He didn't know if fat would help prevent rust, but it was the best lubricant he had. He reassembled the magazines, wiped them down with a final, thin coat of fat, and reloaded the rounds, counting each one as it was inserted. He started with 106 rounds on the airplane and came up eight short in his count, the ones he had fired at the Lenape braves. Ninety-eight rounds remained. Just as he disassembled the pistol and was about to begin cleaning each part, Karen walked over and took a seat beside him.

"Promise me you won't take any chances on this trip," she said. She scanned the camp. "I doubt our little group here would last long without you."

The corners of his mouth turned up slightly. "Is that the only reason?" he asked.

She turned her head to Mason and stared at him for several long moments while she twisted her lips. "No," she finally said.

Mason nodded and smiled as he continued to work on the pistol.

"You're carrying eight hundred of our dollars," she said, as she tried to hold back a smile.

Mason blinked slowly. "Really?"

She put a hand on Mason's leg. "Really."

"Okay, I'll try my best to be careful."

"Thank you," she said. "Do you have everything you need?"

"Think so. We should be back in ten days or so, maybe less."

"And if you're not?"

"I'll find a way to get word to you," Mason said. "And by the way, take it easy on Manny while I'm gone."

"Will do. With Nathan on ice, we should be just fine."

The two of them continued chatting until well past dark. Everyone else had turned in. The central fire had burned down to coals leaving the camp blanketed in darkness.

"I suppose we should get some sleep," Karen said, as she went to get up.

Midway into her rise, Mason grasped her elbow, pulled her close, and kissed her.

Karen sunk to her knees at his side as she continued the kiss.

After several moments, they parted.

"Like I said," Karen whispered, "be careful on this trip."

Mason nodded and watched Karen rise and walk off to her hut. He focused on her ring finger and the gold band she wore. She had never mentioned being married or anything about a husband. Maybe she wore the ring to keep men at bay. Whatever the reason, her previous marital status really didn't matter at this point.

CHAPTER 14

People from the camp had just finished carrying the boat down to the water's edge when Mato and two braves arrived. Each of the three carried a heavy stack of bound deer hides which they placed inside the bow. Mato and one brave carried a flintlock rifle; the third carried a bow and a quiver of arrows. The hides and other provisions still left plenty of room for the eight passengers. With everything loaded, Jeremy pushed the boat a few feet into the water and held it waiting for everyone to climb aboard. Nathan, John, and Dorothy went first, followed by Mato and the two braves.

Mason watched everyone jockey for the various seats until finally everyone was settled. One of the braves sat in the rear rowing position leaving Mason to wonder if he had ever rowed a boat. Mason turned to Karen and Manny standing together on the beach.

"We'll be fine," Manny said, reading Mason's mind.

Mason nodded to Manny and turned to Karen.

Karen placed a hand on Mason's forearm.

"We'll be back before you know it," he said. He covered Karen's hand with his own. "Before you know it." He released his grasp, turned, and climbed aboard.

Jeremy pushed the boat farther into the water, over an incoming wave, and jumped aboard.

Mason immediately dipped his two oars into the water and began stroking as he gazed at Karen standing on the beach. He smiled and winked in her direction. He saw her wave.

The brave in the rowing seat gazed at Jeremy with a bewildered look.

Jeremy motioned for him to switch places. "Watch what we do," he said, as he took the seat and began matching Mason's strokes.

They were well out beyond the rollers when Mason began turning the boat parallel to the coast and putting more effort into each stroke. He kept an eye on Karen, the only person still on the beach, until she was a tiny dot and then no dot at all. He thought of their kiss.

"What do you think," Nathan asked. "An hour each at the oars?"

"Sounds good," Mason said. He was not able to see Mato sitting in the front of the boat to Mason's back, but he figured the warrior probably appreciated not having to carry the bundle of pelts all the way to Charles Town.

Given how fast they were passing the trees on shore, Mason estimated they were probably doing about three knots. If they could maintain that average for ten hours each day, they should arrive in the morning of the fourth day, maybe late on the third day if they picked up the pace.

Taking turns at the oars, they rowed with a strong pace until they had passed a small inlet. The sun was just beginning to touch the horizon. Mason didn't know the name of the inlet or how far they had rowed, but he felt good about the day's effort.

They rowed to shore, blocked the ocean breeze with the boat, and made a small fire.

Taking advantage of the last of the sun's rays, the brave with the bow walked the few yards to the inlet and returned with several fish. Apparently, they had been easy pickings for his bow and arrow. Just after sunset everyone began munching on roasted fish.

"Tell me about Charles Town," Mason said to Mato.

"Many people, many guns," he said. "My people trade skins and leave."

"Do you know anyone there," Dorothy asked.

"Just man who buy skins," Mato said. "He own tavern edge of town. Government say we can only trade there."

"What's his name?" Nathan asked.

"They call him Edwards."

Mason nodded as he swatted a mosquito on his cheek.

Mato pulled a small buckskin pouch from his larger pouch of belongings, dug two fingers inside, and extended his hand to Mason.

His index and middle fingers were smeared with some kind of greasy substance.

"Bear," he said, "keep mosquitoes away."

Mason used his own fingers to wipe the grease off Mato's fingers, raised the stuff closer to his face, and wrinkled his nose.

Mato and the two braves began laughing and proceeded to smear the grease on the exposed areas of their skin.

Mason smelled of the stuff again, cocked his head to the side, and smeared some on his face, neck, and arms. He motioned for Nathan, Dorothy, Jeremy, and John to do the same. "If you want to get any sleep."

They all followed suit.

◆◆◆

Karen woke to the sound of arguing. Her eyes blinked open to a brighter than usual hut and realized she had slept longer than normal. She rolled to her hands and knees, got to her feet, and stepped into the clearing. She rubbed the sleep from her eyes and focused on Manny and Toby standing toe-to-toe in the center of camp. "What is going on?"

"With Mason gone, Toby here feels he doesn't need to hunt this morning."

Toby shrugged his shoulders. "Like I said, I'm used to hunting with Nathan. We've established a rhythm, and I don't feel like breaking in a newbie."

"And I don't feel comfortable leaving you here in camp without my supervision," Manny said.

Karen stepped between the two men and turned to face Toby. "Look, Travis could use more time behind a bow. This is the perfect opportunity for him to learn."

"I don't think so," Toby said. "We have enough food for a few days. I'll wait for Nathan."

"No, you'll go out with Travis or you can go out alone," Manny said.

Toby stepped closer to Manny. "Who put you in charge, little man?"

"We don't need this right now," Karen yelled. "Get your bow and don't come back until you have something." She glared into Toby's eyes.

"Fine," he said, as he threw his hands in the air. He walked off in a huff, picked up his bow, and disappeared into the forest.

"Him and Nathan are two peas in a pod," Manny said.

"You didn't help matters," Karen said.

Manny stared at her with a shocked expression.

"You and Tito go out as usual. Travis can hang here in camp."

Manny gave a single nod and walked off. "But I'll be back early."

"Everything okay?" Lisa asked, as she and Angie walked up.

"Yeah," Karen said, calming herself. "We follow the same routine; it's just another day."

Lisa nodded and glanced at Angie. "We'll be down at the inlet with Tom."

◆◆◆

It was near noon on the fourth day when Mason spotted a strip of coast line he thought likely to be Morris Island. It formed the west bank of a wide inlet. As they neared, he was able to make out James Island. He imagined Fort Sumter positioned on a tiny island just off the point. It would be almost a hundred years before that fort would be built. Presently the point of land was home to a large flock of seagulls.

As the little boat hugged the east side of the inlet and rounded Sullivan's Island, the Charles Town colony came into view on the peninsula separating the Ashley and Cooper Rivers. The town was smaller than Mason expected, but still spectacular in its historical grandeur. He glanced at Dorothy and smiled at her mesmerized expression.

This was one of four major ports in the colonies Dorothy had said. Even in the early seventeen hundreds, it was kept busy with trade from England, the West Indies, and up and down the east coast of what would become the United States. It was hard not to be impressed at the historical significance.

Mason eyed the many masted ships lined up along the wharfs on the east side of the town, the Cooper River side. Mason counted eight wharfs, all occupied by large and small ships. Still two miles out, Mason was able to see the tiny specks of people coming and going along the wharfs, probably loading and unloading ships. He also noted the fortifications, basically a wall, around the south and east sides of the city. Even from his meager understanding of history he knew the wall actually surrounded the town, built to fend off attacks from the Indians, French, and Spanish.

When he looked left, back to James Island, he spotted a white structure in the distance, a few hundred yards north of where Fort Sumter would later be built. The structure was situated at the point of another spit of land that protruded north into Charles Town harbor.

Mason scooted closer to Dorothy and pointed at the structure.

"That would be Fort Johnson, completed in 1708. Three-sided with three bastions, if I remember correctly."

"Earthen walls?" Mason asked.

"Apparently," Dorothy said. "Modern scholars weren't sure. The original walls were replaced later with tabby, a type of concrete made from ground oyster shells," she said. "You remember the significance of Fort Sumter?"

Mason gave a single nod.

"The confederates fired their shots on Fort Sumter from Fort Johnson."

Mason raised an eyebrow and twisted his lips. He turned his attention back to Charles Town which was rapidly approaching. The tops of buildings were visible above the walls. Most appeared to be frame, but there were several made of brick.

Mato, sitting in the front of the boat, turned back and got Mason's attention. "The Edward's tavern is past ships," he said, as he pointed.

The wall along the Cooper River appeared to be made mostly of brick with bastions positioned at the corners and along the length. Canons protruded from the bastions. From what Mason could see, the south wall was composed mostly of earth. Mason figured the source of the earth was probably a moat in front of the walls. It was an impressive defensive structure that would have given even the hardiest of invaders cause to question their resolve.

As they approached the far north end of the brick wall, Mato pointed to the last wharf and an empty spot where they could tie up.

Nathan and Jeremy rowed in that direction and soon the boat bumped against the wood-planked structure. There were no people at the very end; all were closer to the foot of the dock loading a masted ship.

"This is good," Mason said. With the boat secured to the wharf, Mason moved to the bow to get everyone's attention. "Given our attire, I think John, Dorothy, and me have the best chance of blending." He considered Jeremy. "I don't think the town is ready for shorts." He turned his head to Nathan. "You're elected to stay with Jeremy." Next, he motioned to Dorothy. "You may want to lose the glasses."

She smiled and removed her glasses. She handed them to Jeremy.

"Can you see without these," Jeremy asked.

"Well enough," she said.

Mato cocked his head.

"It's a long story, my friend."

Mato gave a subtle nod. "Maybe you tell me one day."

"Maybe," Mason said, as he grabbed his rucksack and started to rise.

Nathan cleared his throat. "Won't that stand out?"

"I'll manage," Mason replied, as he stood and hefted the rucksack. He strained at the weight of the eight hundred silver coins inside. "I'll get back here as soon as possible."

Nathan gave a slight wave of his hand.

"What do we say if someone asks what we're doing here?" Jeremy asked.

Mason took a moment to scratch the back of his head. "I can't really think of an explanation for you two. Let's hope no one asks." When Jeremy nodded, Mason turned, climbed out of the boat, and stood up on the wood planks of the dock. He helped Dorothy up, gave a hand to John, and then moved out of the way as the two braves scrambled up.

Mato passed the three stacks of bound skins up to his braves and climbed out of the boat. He lifted one of the stacks to his shoulder. "This way," he said, as he started walking.

Dorothy fell in behind the three natives.

Mason watched her head jerk from one side to the other as she walked. She was like a kid entering Disney World for the first time. Mason couldn't even imagine what was going through her mind at the sights, sounds, and smells, especially the smells. The general odor wafting through the air was a combination of fresh baked bread, rotting fish, body odor, urine and feces. Dorothy had warned him, but the reality was worse than he imagined.

CHAPTER 15

The men working on the dock barely noticed as Mason and his group passed by. They were all tough men, obviously used to hardship, hard work, and hard times. They were lean, sinuous, and dressed in various levels of clothes, all of which would be worthy of Mason's rag hamper back home. Some were bare-chested with dark, sweat covered skin gleaming in the hot sun. Some wore thin, linen type shirts, but nearly all were dull, stained, and threadbare. The men's breeches were equally tattered for the most part. Some were bare-footed, some wore a light, almost slipper type of shoe, and a couple wore high, leather boots. One man turned his head, grinned, and examined Dorothy up and down. The man's most prominent feature was his rotten and missing teeth.

The group walked the length of the dock without mishap. They passed through the narrow opening in the wall and stepped onto a mostly sand, gravel, and oyster shell street that ran the full length along the back side. The street was wider than Mason expected even for a major thoroughfare. Narrow buildings on narrow lots lined the other side of the street. Most were rough frame, two-story structures; some had shops on the bottom with living quarters on top.

The street bustled with all kinds of people. There were several women, usually walking two or three together. They were dressed in ground-length dresses or skirts and long-sleeved tops with a variety of patterns and colors. Their heads were usually covered with a bonnet. The men, at least the Caucasians, were mostly dressed in knee length or full-length breeches, long-sleeved shirts rolled to the elbow, and three-point or wide-brimmed hats. There were several black men, slaves Mason presumed. Dingy breeches and shirts clung to their sweat drenched skin as they went about pulling wagons or carrying heavy loads. Of all the third world places Mason had ever found himself, this was the most foreign. And even though he spoke their language, he felt like the proverbial fish out of water.

A few yards north along the street, Mato turned left onto a narrow lane, an alley really, and proceeded confidently as he dodged others coming and going with all manner of goods.

Mason saw chickens in crates, pigs on leashes, large bundles of tobacco, and all sizes of wood barrels. One barrel was broken open allowing rice to spill onto the ground.

As on the dock, the people did not seem to pay much attention to the Mason parade, other than an occasional glance at John. He was the least authentic looking of the bunch.

Mato finally stopped in front of a rough wood, single story building. A carved, wood placard above the door simply read *tavern*. The Indian glanced at Mason and then stepped through the open doorway. Everyone followed.

The smell of stale beer, or more likely some kind of ale, is what struck Mason first. He had been in plenty of dive bars, but all shined in gleaming opulence compared to this one. The people reeked. And it was made worse by the dim, tropical sauna like condition inside. Mason felt the sweat beginning to bead around his neck.

The room was narrow but longer than Mason expected. The ceiling was low; the floor and walls were wood planked. A short bar occupied the left side of the tavern's front third, leaving room for a few tables and chairs near the door. Most were occupied.

As Mason's eyes adjusted to the relative darkness, he was able to make out more of the details. The back of the room was stacked with all manner of skins and pelts, dry goods, tools, utensils, and even bolts of cloth. Mason couldn't imagine that the town's people came here to trade. He figured its location on a back alley was set up for those less desirable types, like the Indians.

Two men stood behind the bar. One was a tall, burly character with a thick beard. He could have been a Paul Bunyan lookalike. He even wore a checkered shirt. He stood with both arms crossed; his eyes were locked on Mason and Mato as soon as they stepped through the doorway.

The other man was shorter, thinner, clean shaven, and dressed more like Mason expected a merchant to dress. He wore the standard coarse linen shirt with the long sleeves rolled to the elbow, a vest left unbuttoned, and dark breeches. He also sported a flintlock pistol tucked in his waist band. His demeanor wasn't all that pleasant with the man standing across the bar from him.

The inebriated man, barely able to stand, apparently wanted to trade an obviously well-used smoking pipe for a tankard of ale. The tavern owner, Mister Edwards presumably, wasn't interested.

"No one would want your chewed-up piece of shit for a pipe," the owner said. He glanced at the lumberjack standing slightly behind and to his side.

The lumberjack dropped his arms and took a step.

The man in front of the bar suddenly grabbed the pipe and hurried out the door without a word or even a glance back. The man's stench nearly knocked Mason over when he passed.

Mason noticed that Dorothy turned her head away and put the back of her hand to her nose as the man passed her.

"What can I do for you gents?" the owner asked, as he peered at Mato.

Mato and his two braves stepped forward and placed their stacks of skins on the bar. "Trade for two muskets, powder, shot, axe, cooking pot, four bags rice—"

"Hold up there," the owner said. He began leafing through the skins, taking his time to examine several in detail. "I can give you two bags of rice, the axe, and the pot. No guns, powder, or shot."

Mato shook his head and started to pick up one of the stacks as if he were going to leave.

The owner slammed his hand down on top of the skins forcing the stack back down to the bar. "Three bags of rice."

Mato shook his head again. "Two guns, powder, shot, axe, pot, three bags of rice."

Mason couldn't help but notice that an axe and a pot were among Mato's list of goods. Apparently, he needed to replace those he had 'traded' to Mason. He wanted to repay Mato now that he had the means, but wasn't sure if he should intervene in the negotiation between the two men. Doing so might embarrass Mato, or worse, piss off the tavern owner. Mason decided to remain quiet.

The negotiations went on for another twenty minutes. During that time Mato threatened to leave several times, but each time the owner stopped him by placing a hand on the skins. Finally, the owner closed his eyes, tightened his lips, and massaged the back of his neck. When he opened his eyes, he stared at Mato for several moments.

"Two guns, powder, shot, and two bags of rice," the owner said.

"Three bags rice," Mato said.

"Fine, anything to get this over with."

Mato pushed the three stacks of skins to the owner's side of the bar.

The owner nodded at the lumberjack "Get the man his goods," he said, with a slight smile.

The lumberjack came around the bar and disappeared into the dimly lit back. He returned a few minutes later with the guns, a small keg of what Mason presumed was powder, and a leather pouch of what was probably the shot. He laid the items on the bar, returned to the back of the tavern, and reemerged carrying three bags of rice. Mason estimated they were twenty pounds each.

Mato and the two braves picked up the items and walked out of the tavern with Mason, Dorothy, and John in tow. Mato led the way back to the boat and began handing the items to Jeremy and Nathan. With the items secured aboard, Mato turned to Mason. "We go now. If we stay here someone take."

"I'd like to spend a little time looking around," Mason said. "Maybe you could camp back at the inlet and meet here tomorrow morning."

"You stay alone?" Mato asked.

Mason eyed each of his people and turned back to Mato. "Dorothy, Nathan, me, and John will stay here tonight." He lifted his chin at Jeremy.

Jeremy finally nodded.

"Meet morning here," Mato said.

Mason put a hand on Mato's shoulder. "See you in the morning." He turned to Nathan. "You okay with staying."

"Sure," Nathan said, as he began climbing out of the boat.

Mato and his two braves climbed in. Jeremy and one of the braves manned the oars.

Those left on the wharf watched them row the boat out and down the river until they were well on their way.

"Is this really a good idea?" Nathan asked.

"We came here to see the town," Mason replied. "Let's go see the town."

◆◆◆

Going out with the river's flow was much easier than rowing against the current, so they made much better time. They crossed the channel to Shutes Folly Island and on toward Sullivan's Island at the mouth of the Ashley and Cooper Rivers.

Mato and the two braves seemed deep in thought and Jeremy saw no reason to break the silence. He used his oars to navigate the little boat around the point as they hugged the coast heading east.

Soon Mato raised an arm, pointed, and grunted in Jeremy's general direction.

Jeremy twisted his torso and neck in the direction of where Mato pointed and saw a sandbar in the distance. The sandbar formed a natural barrier between the actual coast and the open ocean.

He found the tide pool considerably deeper than he expected—four feet or so. Jeremy had no problem rowing through the water and beaching the boat's bow into the sandy shore.

Everyone hopped out while Jeremy secured the oars. He stepped out and helped pull the boat farther up onto the sand. With that done, Jeremy took a moment to scan the area in all directions. That's when he spotted a tall ship with full sails just visible on the horizon, apparently heading into the Charles Town harbor. He took a moment to admire its form and contemplate the history unfolding before his very eyes. He finally broke free of his reverie and helped the Indians transport most of their belongings from the boat and into the trees. It was a good place to camp. The ocean breeze would keep most of the mosquitoes at bay.

With pretty much everything done, Jeremy took a seat in the sand and rested his back against the trunk of a small oak. He gazed out on the water and watched the sailing ship grow larger as it approached Charles Town.

He thought about Mason, Dorothy, John, and Nathan and wondered how they were being received. He thought about the rest of the clan back on the beach in Myrtle Beach and wondered if all was well. His focus settled on Lisa in particular. Her tight jeans flashed through his mind.

"Trading ship," Mato said, as he pulled up a patch of sand next to Jeremy.

Jeremy nodded. "Have you ever been on one?"

"No, but some my people have."

Jeremy cocked his head.

"Slaves; later escape."

"I'm sorry," Jeremy said.

Mato cocked his head to one side as he stared at Jeremy, apparently not understanding the remorse displayed by a white man.

When Mato started to rise, Jeremy got up at the same time. "Fish for dinner?"

Mato smiled. "Fish for dinner." He turned and walked toward the two braves who had just finished gathering wood for a campfire.

Jeremy followed.

Mason and his compatriots walked up and down the main streets and several alleys. None of the streets were identified with a sign, but Dorothy, being thoroughly familiar with the town in this time period, was able to rattle off the major thoroughfares: Bay street along the water, paralleled by Church and Meeting Streets, intersected by Tradd, Broad, and Queen. All the main streets were mostly composed of sand and gravel, deeply rutted by wagon and cart wheels. The few sidewalks, surprisingly, were brick or stone.

The town included a number of what appeared to be churches, but they were greatly outnumbered by the taverns and houses of ill repute. It was a rowdy town, growing more so as the day meandered toward dusk and more and more ships' crewmen filled the streets. They had already bumped into a number of inebriated souls barely able to walk and stinking to levels Mason didn't think possible.

While they walked, Mason had been able to identify a trading post he intended to visit, but the more pressing concern was finding a place to spend the night.

"Where does one find lodging in this time period?" Mason whispered to Dorothy, as they continued to saunter along the sidewalks.

"I've seen two taverns so far that appear to take borders," she said, "we could try one of those."

"We need to get a place lined up, like now," Mason said, as he stopped and did a three-sixty. He pointed to a two-story, clapboard tavern they had just passed. "I wonder if they have rooms for rent." Mason took a step in that direction, but stopped when he felt a tug on his arm.

"Let me go ask," John said. "I probably look the most civilized of the four of us."

Dorothy's chin bobbed up and down.

"Okay," he said, as he wiggled a shoulder out of the rucksack straps and slung it to his front. He unzipped the main compartment, reached inside, and stopped. He raised his eyes to Dorothy. "How much for a room?"

"One of those Spanish dollars should more than cover it." She turned to John. "See if you can get two rooms for the silver piece."

Mason extracted a single piece of silver and handed it to John. Then handed him another one. "Just in case. We need a room no matter the price."

John nodded and walked off toward the tavern.

Mason watched him disappear inside the establishment and turned to Dorothy. "Period clothes would go a long way toward helping us blend in," he said. "How would one go about getting something to wear?"

"Everything was handmade," she said, "most of the time in the home. Cloth and clothes in this time were a person's biggest expense. The more elaborate articles of clothing, for those with the money, were ordered directly from London to fit. They also imported simpler articles of clothing and altered them as needed upon purchase."

Mason smoothed his beard with one hand and shook his head. "How long to have something altered?"

"Depends on who's doing the altering," Dorothy said.

Mason heard a shoe scuff on the sidewalk behind him and turned around expecting to see John returning. It wasn't John; it was probably the last person he expected to see.

CHAPTER 16

"You're the last person I would expect to see on this street," Captain William Darby said with wide eyes.

He still wore the blue coat, white waistcoat, white breeches, off-white stockings, and the white cravat around his neck, but all were considerably less rumpled than before. His white shirt had been replaced with one that included ruffles extending from the end of his coat sleeves. He also wore a manicured wig beneath his three-point hat. He stood next to a taller, fiftyish gentleman even more elegantly dressed with a gold handled walking cane.

"I could say the same thing," Mason said.

"I didn't get your name before," Darby said, as he raised his chin slightly.

"Stev— Stephen Mason. Most people call me Mason."

"Okay Mason," Darby said, "may I ask how you come to be here."

Mason glanced at the man standing next to Darby.

"I'm sorry," Darby said. "May I introduce William Rhett, planter extraordinaire, sea captain, and devourer of pirates."

Mason heard Dorothy take a deep breath and hold it. Apparently, William Rhett was someone with a historical back story.

John edged around the two men.

Mason motioned. "Let me introduce Dorothy Weiss and Nathan Sims. And this is John Tifton," he said, as John approached.

Darby turned his head to Rhett. "I last encountered Mason here just after said pirate absconded with my ship and part of my crew."

Rhett nodded. "And what brings you to our fair city?" His eyes examined up and down every part of Mason and his group.

Suddenly Mason was at a complete loss for words. Nothing he could think of came across as plausible. What was he doing here? "Came in search of a boat," he finally said.

"A boat," Darby said, "what sort of boat?"

John cleared his throat. "A small sloop would do nicely."

"And you have the money necessary to purchase such a boat?" Rhett asked.

"Depends on the price, but yes, I believe we do," Mason said.

"You have a very odd accent and manner of speaking," Rhett said. "And your clothes." His eyes reexamined Mason's black jeans. "From where do you hail?"

Darby nodded his head up and down as he faced Mason with an expression of expectation.

"It's a long story," Mason said, "but basically we've been in the Far East."

"Basically, in the Far East," Rhett repeated. He cocked his head slightly. "Very odd indeed."

"If he has the money necessary, does it matter?" Darby asked.

"I suppose it doesn't," Rhett said.

Darby turned to Mason. "I may know of a boat."

"We'd be willing to pay a finder's fee," Mason said.

Darby lifted his chin. He glanced at Rhett and then back to Mason. "Meet me here tomorrow morning, say eight."

"Thank you," Mason said. "We'll be here."

"In the meantime," Rhett said, "can I recommend a clothier."

"Please do," Mason said.

"Two streets over," Rhett said. "The only stone building on the street. Tell the proprietor I sent you."

"Thank you," Mason said.

Rhett nodded as he and Darby resumed their walk.

"Tomorrow then," Darby said, as he and Rhett walked past Mason's group.

"Tomorrow," Mason said. He watched as the two men ambled along until they were well out of ear shot. "What are the chances?" he said, as he turned to John. "What about the room?"

John pointed to the top floor. "The corner facing us. Only room left. It's small." He looked at Dorothy.

"I'll manage," Dorothy said. She turned to Mason. "I think we should visit that clothier right now."

"Agreed," Mason said. He motioned to John. "How about if you occupy the room. We'll check out the tailor and be back to the room as soon as possible."

John nodded. "Only three rooms up there. We have the one on the far right."

"Sounds like a plan," Mason said. "We'll see you in the room."

Mason, Dorothy, and Nathan parted from John, crossed the street, and began walking toward the closest alley. "Tell me about this William Rhett."

"All those things Captain Darby said. He's a plantation owner, a colonel in the militia, and a member of the Charles Town assembly. He was instrumental in building Charles Town, and he led an effort to clear this area of pirates. Nearly two years ago he captured the pirate Stede Bonnet. Rhett's home, here in Charles Town, is one of the few buildings that will survive to our time. He's married; wife's name is Sarah. And one other thing."

Mason twisted his head.

"Rhett dies in the early seventeen-twenties, which is probably not that far in the future."

"Of what?"

"He's put on trial for defamation, loses, and is fined. Around that time, he dies of a stroke. Apparently, he had, or has, a bit of a temper."

"Good to know," Mason said, as they stepped out onto a paralleling street.

A stone, two-story building stood amidst a line of frame structures a block toward the water.

"Must be the one," Mason said, as he stepped off in that direction.

Nathan pushed the door open, and the three stepped into a dimly lit room about the size of a small, modern bedroom. One wall was lined with bolts of cloth stacked to the ceiling. The only light came from a single window next to the door.

"I was about to close for the day," a man's voice said, as he stepped through a doorway from a back room.

"We have cash," Mason said, "and we're in need of new clothes."

"I should say so," the short, squatty man said, as he stepped closer. "What did you have in mind?"

"Something more civilized," Dorothy said, "but still functional. Colonel Rhett sent us."

"Ah-ha," the man said. A smile spread across his face. "In that case, will you need outfits for all three of you?"

"Yes," Mason said, "and one other man whom I can send over in the morning, or later tonight if you wish."

"In the morning will be fine," the man said. "I'm Francois."

"Glad to meet you Francois, I'm Mason. This is Dorothy Weiss and Nathan Sims. The other man is John Tifton."

Francois nodded, deep in thought, as he turned toward the bolts of clothes.

"How long will this take?" Nathan asked.

Francois faced Nathan and inspected up and down. "That depends on how quickly you need them."

"As soon as possible," Mason said.

Francois turned his attention to Mason, retrieved a tape measure from his pocket, and spun Mason around by the elbow. He ran the measure across Mason's shoulders and down one arm. He stood back and inspected Mason head to toe. "I may have something I could alter for you." He turned to Dorothy. "And for the young lady as well." He turned to Nathan. "For you I will either have to make something or order from London."

"Make it," Mason said. "And for me, I hope it is something light."

"Of course," Francois said. "Also, there is the question of payment."

"Is half now, half when it's done okay?" Mason asked.

"It is," Francois said.

"Just tell me how much."

"Shillings or dollars?" Francois asked.

"Dollars," Dorothy said. "Spanish silver."

Francois smiled.

Mason, Dorothy, and Nathan stepped into the tavern and found John sitting at a table alone with a bowl and mug.

John had just spooned food into his mouth. "How did it go?" he asked with his mouth full.

"Dorothy and I will have something in the morning," Mason said, as he sat at the table and peered into the bowl. "Nathan will take longer."

"Stew," John said after he swallowed. "Meat, potatoes, and carrots. Needs salt, but otherwise it's pretty good."

Mason motioned for Dorothy and Nathan to take a seat. He saw a tall man with slicked back, greasy hair, and rolled-up sleeves approaching.

"I told the owner there were four of us," John said. "The room includes supper along with two single, rope beds with thin, straw mattresses. And that's about it."

"We'll make do," Mason said. When the proprietor was within ear shot Mason pointed to John's bowl and mug. "Three more."

The man pivoted without missing a beat and returned the way he had come.

"So, we're coming back then?" John asked.

"Hopefully via that boat, along with all the others."

The proprietor sat three bowls of steaming stew on the table with three tankards of ale. He left without a word.

"He doesn't say much," Mason said, as he slid a bowl to Nathan and Dorothy.

"No, he doesn't," John agreed.

Nathan and Dorothy immediately started eating.

"You need to accompany me and Dorothy to the tailor first thing," Mason said to John. "See what he can do for you." He took a sip of the ale. His face contorted and one eyebrow went up.

"Yeah, but at least it's wet," John said.

"Don't drink the water," Dorothy said.

"Right," Mason said. He took another sip.

"How much for the clothes?" John asked.

"Sixteen Spanish dollars," Dorothy said. "Had to pay a premium for the rush jobs."

"Anybody have any thoughts on what that boat might cost us?" Mason asked.

"Not a clue," John said. He scraped the last of his stew into his wooden spoon and shoved it into his mouth.

Dorothy shook her head as she chewed.

Mason took another sip of his ale and looked around the room.

The other three tables in the room and the short bar were full of men mostly just drinking the ale or something stronger. As they drank, they got louder.

"How did we survive three hundred more years?" Mason mumbled. "Seems like we're always just one argument away from a full-blown war."

"Adaptation," Dorothy said. "Man is king at adapting to his environment."

Mason finally took a bite of the stew and chewed.

"So, what's the plan for tomorrow?" John asked.

"We're up with the sun," Mason said. "You, me, and Dorothy are at the tailor when he opens. Nathan needs to remain here, actually out on the street, in case Captain Darby shows up early." He turned his head to Nathan. "When we're back from the tailor, you will need to meet Jeremy at the dock and let him know what's happening. Hang there until one of us shows up. I also want Jeremy to visit the tailor sometime tomorrow."

"And if we can't afford the boat?" Nathan asked.

"I suppose we row back to Myrtle Beach."

"A couple of us could wait here," Dorothy said. "I'd recommend myself and Jeremy."

Mason cocked his head. "That's actually not a bad idea. If all of us are going to filter in here, an advanced party could pave the way."

"You're talking about staying here," Nathan said, "forever. When are we going to talk about returning to our own time?"

Mason leaned back on the bench and gazed at Nathan. "I haven't given up on returning. We passed through that time warp, or whatever it was, maybe there's a way to pass back through."

"Thirty thousand feet in the air?" Dorothy asked.

"Yeah, I don't have the answers," Mason said. "But we know approximately where it happened."

"That's all we know," John said.

Mason nodded. "One day at a time. Our first priority is survival. I think we have a better chance of doing that here than out in the swamp."

"Uh-huh," Nathan said. "Maybe we should buy a plantation while we wait for that blue cloud to show up."

"One day at a time," Mason said.

"In the meantime, where's the head?" Nathan asked, as he swiveled his head around the room.

"You won't find a bathroom in this time period," Dorothy said. "Our room upstairs should have a chamber pot."

"How does that work?" Nathan asked.

Dorothy scrunched her face. "It goes in the pot and the contents generally go out the window into the alley."

"For everything?" Nathan asked.

"Yep."

"We really need to concentrate on finding that blue cloud," Nathan said.

CHAPTER 17

Mason stepped from the back room dressed in a dark-blue, long coat with gold buttons, a beige waistcoat, and beige, matching breeches. White stocking covered his legs below the knees, and a white cravat wrapped around his neck. He still wore his lace up brown service boots and he carried a three-point black hat with gold trim.

Dorothy and John stared with mouths agape.

"The breeches are a little tight," Francois said, as he plucked a bit of lent from Mason's coat, "but I did the best I could on such short notice."

"I like it," Dorothy said. "But you wouldn't want to get an erection in those pants."

Francois gave Dorothy a stern look before turning his attention back to Mason. "Like I said, best I could do." He turned to Dorothy.

"Looks like you're next," Mason said.

Dorothy followed Francois and a young lady into the back room leaving Mason and John alone.

"You've got to be kidding me," John said. "Is this really necessary?"

"We need to blend in," Mason said. "This will help."

John stared at the breeches. "Are you wearing anything under those?"

"A very long, long-sleeve shirt. The tail extends well past my waist. And what are apparently considered underwear in this time. Thin, baggy material."

"What did he say about your boots?"

"He expressed some curiosity until I explained that the style is very popular in the Far East. But I ordered high black boots just the same. He measured my feet and said he would take care of it."

"What about your gun?"

"Rolled up in the buckskin," Mason said, as he lifted the bundle in his hand.

They both settled in to wait.

Francois and the young lady led Dorothy straight to a rough wooden bench with several articles of clothing neatly folded and stacked.

"I'll leave you in Maria's hands," Francois said, as he continued through a doorway into another room.

The stack of clothes included a number of items, several more than Dorothy thought necessary given the heat and humidity of the day.

Maria picked up the top item which turned out to be a long, white, thin shift. Maria let it unfold by its own weight. The wrinkles left by the folds indicated linen.

Dorothy was well aware that dressing in the eighteenth century was considerably more involved than in modern times, but she never expected to experience the process. She tightened her lips, let out a long exhale, and took hold of the hem of her buckskin dress. For practical reasons, she wore the buckskin with nothing underneath. Such was common for women of this period, even those in the most elegant of dresses. She was far from modest when it came to nudity, even less so now that her body was tight and muscled. But still, she hesitated for a moment before pulling the hem up over her head leaving herself fully nude.

Two women at sewing stations didn't give it a moment's notice, and Maria didn't even blink. So, Dorothy relaxed a bit and lowered her head when Maria reached up with the shift in her hands.

She draped the shift over Dorothy's head and let it drop down the length of her body to just above the knees. She motioned Dorothy to a nearby stool and picked up two knitted, black stockings. Each was embroidered with a simple design at the ankle.

Dorothy put her foot in the first and pulled it up its full length to just over her knee. She already knew these would be the first to go once she was out in the heat.

Nevertheless, she pulled the second stocking onto her other leg and looked at Maria.

Maria apparently expected Dorothy to take care of the next step in the process, but finally bent down and tied a small piece of knitted ribbon around each stocking just below each knee.

Maria motioned to Dorothy's black flats indicating it was time for the shoes.

Dorothy slipped the shoes on her feet. Luckily, they didn't look that much different from what some women of the eighteenth century wore.

Next, Maria helped Dorothy into a stiff stay that fit around her chest, over her breasts, and laced in the front. Next came a large neckerchief which Maria draped over Dorothy's shoulders and tucked into the stay at the front.

Dorothy was already feeling stifled and there were still several articles to go. She couldn't imagine wearing a full corset and gown at this point.

Maria tied a pair of pockets around Dorothy's waist so they hung at each thigh. Next came a petticoat of white linen with a bit of nicely patterned cloth at the hem. Maria pulled the petticoat over Dorothy's head and tied it around her waist. A second outer petticoat, a dark burgundy, went over the first and again tied at the waist. Both petticoats included gaps at the waist that gave access to the two pockets.

Next came a short gown, somewhat like a shirt, with elbow-length sleeves. Maria secured the front with several straight pens.

Finally, Maria tied a full-length, light linen apron around Dorothy's waist, and then stood back to admire her work.

Dorothy walked through the doorway wearing a long, dark-burgundy skirt with lots of folds down to her feet. On top she wore a simple beige shirt with a hem that extended past her waist. The sleeves stopped at the elbows. The expression on her face told Mason there was much more to the outfit, layers that would be removed at the first opportunity.

"Again, it's all I could muster on short notice," Francois said, as he entered the room.

"I like it," Mason said.

Dorothy gave a weak smile but remained quiet.

Mason reached into his rucksack and handed Francois eight silver coins. "Thank you. I think you did an amazing job given the circumstances. We'll be back in a week or so for John and Nathan's outfits, and I may have more business for you soon."

"That will be fine," Francois said. "Same payment structure as before."

"Yes, of course," Mason said, as he reached into the rucksack. He handed Francois an additional eight pieces of silver.

Francois smiled. "I will see you in a week then."

Everyone exchanged pleasantries and the three of them left the shop.

"How did people wear all this stuff in the summer heat?" Dorothy asked, as they began walking down the street.

"What was that you said before, adaptation. You'll get used to it."

She lifted the rolled up buckskin dress in her hand. "First chance, I'm changing back into this."

Mason, Dorothy, and John met Nathan, Captain Darby, and another man on the sidewalk in front of the tavern.

"May I introduce Thomas Worthington, owner of the sloop Majestic," Captain Darby said.

Everyone shook hands.

"I must warn you," Captain Darby said, "the ship is a little rough for wear, but she's still sea worthy and quite capable of enduring the waves for many more years."

"Can you provide some history on the ship?" John asked, as everyone meandered toward the harbor.

Worthington cleared his throat. "Well, she served for a brief time in the West Indies ferrying cargo from one island to another. She was purchased for trade along the coast here. I ended up with her two years ago, but shortly after found one better suited to my needs. She does need to be careened and she could use a good scrubbing, but she's certainly capable."

"And the condition of the sails?" John asked.

"If you're expecting a long voyage, they need to be replaced."

They continued to chat until they finally stepped out on one of the eight wharfs. Worthington pointed to a small ship anchored two hundred yards out in the harbor.

"Can we see it up close?" Mason asked.

"Of course," Worthington said. He pointed to a jolly boat already manned with oarsmen.

Mason turned to Nathan. "You should probably meet up with Jeremy and let him know what we're doing. We'll be along as soon as possible."

Nathan nodded and headed off.

The five remaining boarded the jolly boat and made their way across to the sloop.

Dorothy waited in the boat with the two oarsmen while Mason, John, Captain Darby, and Worthington climbed aboard.

"May I present the sloop Majestic," Worthington said, as he stepped upon the deck.

Having never been aboard or even seen an eighteenth-century sloop, Mason didn't know what to expect. It was made of wood, had a mast, and lots of lines, but beyond that Mason didn't know if the ship would continue to float or sink. At the moment it was floating just fine, rolling with the harbor's gentle waves.

John proceeded to finger the lines, the rolled-up sails, and the hardware as he and Mason walked from bow to stern.

Captain Darby and Worthington waited at the spot they came aboard.

"What do you think?" Mason asked in a low tone.

John took in a deep breath, exhaled, and shrugged his shoulders. "I've, of course, never seen one of these. But it's a single masted sloop. Looks to be fifty feet with an eighteen foot or so beam. Gaff rigged with a main sail and jib, probably multiple jibs." He bent down and massaged the deck with one hand. "I'm guessing this is cedar, which is better than oak when it comes to wood destroying organisms."

Mason scanned the deck from the bow to the raised sterncastle which accommodated what he guessed was a single cabin spanning the width of the stern. It had to have a low ceiling given the height of the structure.

"Can you sail her?"

John scanned the length of the ship. "Not alone. This is a small ship, probably 25 tons or so, but labor intensive."

"Okay, can we sail her?"

"I think we should hire a couple of guys for a shakedown," John said.

Mason nodded. "Any idea what this thing is worth?"

"Don't have a clue."

Mason followed John to a raised, covered hatch, about four feet square, in the center of the deck just behind the mast. The two of them slid the cover back which revealed the hold with maybe five feet of head room. Mason followed John aft to a second, smaller raised hatch and ladder just in front of the wheel. Both were a few feet in front of the sterncastle.

Mason followed John down the ladder to the lower deck.

"This would be the hold," John said. "For cargo. Two decks, the one above and the hold. Below this would be the bilge. Definitely used for short-run cargo. Don't see any obvious water infiltration." He walked aft to a second cabin positioned directly below the sterncastle. He opened the wood slatted door and peered inside the completely empty room. "Crew quarters I would guess."

"This should work for our needs," Mason said. He motioned with his head for John to follow him back up to the main deck where they proceeded to examine the small aft cabin, the various lines in more detail, the wheel, the mast for cracks, and all other aspects of the ship.

"What do you think?" Worthington asked, as Mason and John returned to where he and Captain Darby were standing.

"I think she might do," Mason said. "How much?"

Both Worthington and Captain Darby raised their eyebrows.

Mason immediately realized his abruptness. Apparently, people in this age weren't so direct.

Worthington cleared his throat and gazed at Mason for several long seconds. "Two hundred quid."

According to what Dorothy had said when they found the treasure, a British pound was equal to about three Spanish silver dollars. Six hundred dollars more or less. While he was trying to figure out how to respond he saw Dorothy step onto the deck.

She walked over and ushered Mason away by the elbow.

"Offer four hundred dollars," she whispered. "If you accept full price, they'll think we're complete fools."

Mason turned back to Captain Darby and Worthington. "We can afford four hundred dollars."

"You have silver?" Worthington asked.

Mason nodded.

"Five hundred," Worthington said, as he thrust out his hand.

Mason grasped Worthington's hand and smiled.

Smiles grew across Worthington's and Captain Darby's faces.

"Plus, ten percent as my finder's fee," Captain Darby said, as he continued to smile.

"Of course," Mason said.

"Let's head back to shore," Worthington said, "and I'll get a bill-of-sale drawn up. Should have it ready first thing tomorrow."

"That sounds fine," Mason said.

"And could you point out a couple of able-bodied men for a shakedown cruise?" John asked.

"There are plenty of those around," Captain Darby said. "Let's say we meet at your tavern tomorrow morning at nine to wrap up this sale."

"Sounds fine," Mason said. "Would you mind if a couple of us spend the night aboard?"

"Don't mind at all," Worthington said.

◆◆◆

By noon the next day, with all the business out of the way and the bill-of-sale in hand, Mason, Dorothy, and the two extra hands identified by Captain Darby joined Nathan, Jeremy, Mato, and the two braves already on the sloop. The two hands had agreed to one shilling each for the day. Mason liked both men. They were quiet and seemed capable.

Mason immediately turned back to the gunwale and pulled on a length of rope, hand-over-hand, until a large copper cooking pot, an axe, and two shovels appeared, all tied to the end of the rope. Mason untied the items, sent the rope back down, and handed the pot, axe, and one of the shovels to Mato. "Thank you, my friend, for all that you have done for us."

Mato stared at the gifts. He finally took the items and gave a slight nod of his chin. Nothing needed to be said.

Mason turned back to the gunwale, pulled on the rope, and with Jeremy's help plopped three large bags over the railing. "Potatoes, carrots, and rice will go a long way toward making the venison and fish stews more palatable." Other items they brought aboard included two wooden pails, wooden bowls and spoons, two wooden ladles, table salt, and needles and thread. Some were suitable for sail repair.

With everything aboard, John climbed on deck and approached the two hands, Malcolm and Sean.

After a brief conversation, the two men immediately went about preparing the ship to get underway.

Everyone stood watching not sure what they should do as the two men secured the jolly boat to the stern, untied the ropes securing the main sailcloth, and hoisted the gaff with the throat and peak lines. With the sail slack in the slight wind they hoisted the anchor. Malcolm manned the wheel; Sean set the boom and rolled out the jib. They made it look easy.

Slowly the ship began to move.

"She'll be sluggish," John said, "until the barnacles are scraped from her hull. I'm guessing a ship like this could do twelve knots with a clean hull; probably just eight knots as she is."

They spent the rest of the afternoon taking the ship through various maneuvers just outside the mouth of Charles Town harbor. They adjusted the sails against down winds, up winds, and winds on the beam at various angles. All the survivors, including Dorothy, had a chance to man the wheel, lower, raise, and trim the sails, and manage the various lines and sheets.

"As long as we don't run into a hurricane, we should be good," John said to Mason, as the two of them watched Nathan and Jeremy hoist the sails.

"We can head out first light," Mason said.

"The others will be wondering what happened to us," John said.

Mason took the wheel from Dorothy as the boat began to move once more. "What's the draft on this thing?" he asked, looking at John.

"Probably five or six feet without the center board," John said.

"So, we can park her in the inlet near the camp?"

"Shouldn't be a problem," John said. "We'll need to pull her in using the jolly boat."

Mason turned his attention back to steering the boat. With the return to camp only one night away, he thought of Karen, Lisa, and the others. He thought about how taking things one day at a time had brought him and the others to this point. Settling in Charles Town seemed like the only logical option and buying the boat was the best way to get everyone to town. He wondered about leaving someone behind, probably Dorothy, with the rest of the Spanish dollars to secure a place for everyone to stay. With twenty people to worry about it would have to be sizable. But leaving her behind would be a giant risk, especially to her. Neither Jeremy nor Nathan was dressed well enough to stay behind with her. He decided that leaving her was not a good idea. Everyone would be returning to Myrtle Beach.

CHAPTER 18

With beam and broad reach winds, the sloop ran well along the coast. She was not equipped with a compass, but then one wasn't needed as long as they remained close to land. They could use the sun for direction.

John estimated they were clicking along at about seven knots which meant they could be pulling into the inlet at Myrtle Beach in about ten hours.

Mason stood at the bow and gazed at the open ocean to his right and the coastline to his left. He watched a couple of porpoises keep pace with the bow as it sliced through the water. He glanced back at the crew. John stood behind the wheel, Jeremy had just finished securing the main sail's boom, and the others, including Mato and his braves, were scattered about the main deck.

"You look like you're deep in thought," Dorothy said, as she walked up.

"I'm just wondering if we can house everyone aboard this ship when we return to Charles Town."

"There's plenty of room above and below," she said, "as long as no one is prone to seasickness."

Mason nodded.

"Is that it, we live the rest of our lives aboard this boat?" Dorothy asked.

"You're starting to sound like Nathan."

"He does have a point," Dorothy said.

Mason glanced at Nathan standing next to John at the wheel. "He does."

Dorothy cocked her head.

"I'm still taking things one day at a time," Mason said. "You're the anthropologist."

"Maybe we should think about buying some property while we have the funds. With twenty people to worry about—" she stared off at the coast line. "I don't know."

"You changed back into your buckskins. Cooler?"

"Much," Dorothy said.

He put a hand on Dorothy's shoulder as he took a step. "Your knowledge about this time period has been invaluable. Not sure where we would be without your input."

Dorothy gave a slight nod as Mason continued toward the aft cabin along the rolling deck.

Mason, standing next to John at the wheel, pointed to the inlet just north of the camp.

John nodded as he turned the wheel. He motioned for Jeremy to adjust the main sail boom for the downwind. Less than a hundred yards from shore, the sails were lowered. Soon the ship glided to an almost full stop and bobbed with the rollers.

Using the jolly boat manned by Mason, Nathan, Jeremy, and Mato, it took the next two hours to pull the ship into the inlet against the gentle outflow. They finally dropped the anchor in about fifteen feet of water fifty yards out from the fish trap.

Mason felt like he was home when he and the others stepped to the edge of camp.

Jeremy and Nathan lowered the bags of food from their shoulders to the sand.

Lisa, Karen, and Angie were busy at the central campfire. Manny, Travis, and Tito were at the smoking racks. Apparently hunting over the last week had gone well. And the others were in various states of recline around the camp or busy with menial chores.

Koji was the first to spot Mason and the others. He just pointed with his arm fully extended until his mother noticed.

A broad smile spread across Hana's face. "They're back."

Nearly everyone in unison turned their head toward the group and suddenly rushed forward.

"We actually didn't expect you back this soon," Karen said, as she hugged Mason.

"We found a better mode of transportation." Mason said, as he wrapped his arms around her.

At that point the entire camp fell into a loud chorus of questions all blended together into an indecipherable jumble of voices.

Mason finally held up his hand. "All in good time."

When the rumble died off, Mason turned to Mato and extended his hand. "Thank you again my friend."

The two men shook hands.

"You stay or go?" Mato asked.

"We need to explain everything to the camp," Mason said. "Then we'll decide. We'll be here for at least a couple of days. I'll let you know when we decide to leave."

Mato tightened his lips and nodded at his braves. The three of them started off carrying the various supplies they had accumulated.

When they were out of sight, Mason turned to Karen. "What's for dinner?"

After a bath in the stream behind the camp and dinner consisting of a venison and vegetable stew, Mason got everyone's attention. Sitting on the mat in front of his hut in his period clothing, he described in detail the trip, the town, Francois' shop, and the purchase of the sloop.

"There are pros and cons to relocating to Charles Town," Dorothy said from her seat to Mason's right. "We've been able to determine that the year is 1720. At this time in history, Charles Town is immersed in political turmoil. There is still the threat of attack from Spanish and French forces. History says none of those threats come to fruition, but we don't know what impact our arrival will have on the situation. And there are still threats of Indian uprisings, one in particular that I know of. The Waccamaw will attack the colonial trading post near Georgetown."

"Why doesn't Mato trade his furs there?" Jeremy asked. "It's much closer than Charles Town."

Dorothy turned to Jeremy. "The colonists were less than fair with regard to their treatment of the Indians, especially when it came to trade.

"Hence the coming attack on Georgetown," Mason said.

Dorothy nodded. "I suspect Mato feels he can get much more for his furs if he goes to the source. He's essentially cutting out the middleman."

"And the pros?" Mildred asked.

"Safer in numbers," Mason said. "Access to more goods and services."

"I have to tell you," Nathan said, "the place really stinks. Sanitation is nonexistent. It's crowded. I actually think we're better off here."

"First you want to go and now you want to stay," Mason said. "You really need to make up your mind."

Nathan smirked.

"During the Yemassee War years, people in the outlying areas moved closer to Charles Town," Dorothy said. "The fields went unattended and food was scarce. Droughts, like the one we're in now, didn't help things. But that is changing. Charles Town will continue to grow and prosper. With our knowledge and abilities, we could thrive, even prosper."

"We have the boat," Nathan said. "We could travel to Charles Town when needed. We could build better homes here now that we have access to tools. Cabins, even houses."

Mason saw several people nod and sensed Nathan was making headway with his argument. "Life won't be easy no matter what we decide. There are risks. Many of us won't survive either way. I just think we're better off closer to what little civilization there is. Eventually my ammunition will run out. The Lenape could return or some other not-so-friendly tribe."

"Many of the tribes in the east are being pushed out of their homelands by colonial expansion," Dorothy said. "There was lots of movement around this time. And that might explain why the Lenape, a mostly northern tribe, around Delaware, are branching into new areas."

"What if we can't come to a consensus?" Tom Green asked.

"I can't force anyone to do anything," Mason said. "I just think we'll be better off in Charles Town."

"So, what do we do now?" Nathan asked. "Vote?"

"If you want," Mason said. "I think we should all stay together, but there's nothing keeping us from splitting up."

"I take it you're headed for Charles Town," Nathan said.

"I think so," Mason responded. "We'll have a better chance for survival there, or near there. You're the one who suggested we buy a plantation."

Nathan didn't respond.

"We don't have to make the move all at once," Mason said. "Probably better if we don't. We have the ship. We can travel back and forth as Nathan said. Maybe insert ourselves slowly." Mason saw Nathan give a subtle nod. "But I think we should start the transition now."

"Let's sleep on it," Dorothy said.

With that, the meeting broke up, and everyone moved off as they continued to talk among themselves. Nathan, Toby, and surprisingly, Gail Thomas formed the core of one such smaller group.

"What do you think?" Karen asked, as she stepped closer to Mason and Dorothy.

Mason closed his eyes as he rubbed his beard. He opened his eyes. "I don't know."

"By the way," Karen said, "you're starting to look a little shaggy with that beard."

"Good thing I picked up a pair of scissors in Charles Town," he said. "I could use a hand with that."

Karen smiled and with a nod to Dorothy, the two of them moved off toward Mason's hut.

The next morning, John, Tito, and Travis along with Hana, Asumi, and Koji headed off to work on the ship. The decks needed a good cleaning and there were several spots in the sails that needed repair.

Lisa, Angie, and Jeremy tagged along but would be gathering whatever fish had accumulated in the trap. Jeremy would stay behind after the fishing to help with the ship's maintenance. Mason was sure Jeremy was more interested in Lisa than he was fishing or the ship.

Mason, back in his jeans and buckskin shirt, headed out with Manny, Tom Green, Dorothy, and Karen in the direction of Mato's village. Armed with bows and arrows, they planned to do some hunting along the way, but mainly Mason wanted to check in with Mato before he headed out again for Charles Town.

Nathan, Toby, and the others remained in camp.

At Mato's village, the elders apparently saw the advantage of having a friend with a boat and asked if they could transport more hides on the next trip. Mato suggested he and his braves start transporting hides to the ship that day. It would take a couple of trips considering the village's relative lack of manpower and the accumulation of skins over the previous months. Mato said they had a total of twenty stacks like the first three they had traded in Charles Town. Also, that many hides at one time gave him considerable bargaining power.

Mason agreed, of course, and suggested they could probably head out the day after next. That would give them plenty of time to get the ship ready, the hides loaded, and to figure out who would be going.

While at the village, Mato presented Mason with a new buckskin shirt and long pants. Mato explained they were made by the women in the village specifically for Mason. Mason was fairly sure it had to do with saving Mato from the Lenape warrior, wiping out the Lenape raiding party, or both. Mason accepted without hesitation or comment. He just nodded with gratitude and shook Mato's hand.

On the way back to camp, the group gave up all pretense of hunting as each was deep in thought on the coming days.

"I think we should transport all the remaining silver to Charles Town and exchange a good portion for property, either a building in town or some land outside of town," Karen said. "I think it's dangerous to keep that much loot around."

Mason nodded and glanced at Dorothy. "What is land going for these days?"

"Not sure about a working plantation, if one could even be found," Dorothy said. "Most bare land was acquired via land grant, but there were private sales as well. Twelve pounds or about thirty-six dollars was the price for a hundred acres for a long time. The price didn't fluctuate that much during this era."

"And for something in town?"

"From what I saw, there's not much available actually in town. Given the number of taverns, we might be able to wrangle one of those. Something like where we stayed would also provide the room to house those who want to move to Charles Town."

"It might be easier to build something just outside the walls," Mason said. "You said earlier that the walls would be coming down soon to make way for easier trade." He turned his head to Karen.

"Whatever's most practical and timely given the personalities involved," she said.

Mason realized she was talking about Nathan and his growing cadre of rebels. Seems like no matter what is to be done, there are always dissenters.

CHAPTER 19

Mason had made up his mind to establish a beachhead in Charles Town by implanting a contingent of the survivors. He had discussed the proposition with those he recommended for the first wave and all had agreed. He also spoke to those not included in the first wave and they had understood the logic. Those selected for the first contingent were Dorothy, Karen, Lisa, Jeremy, Tom Green, Mildred, and Lana.

As the only blacks among the survivors, Travis and Angie didn't want to chance getting caught up in the slave turmoil that existed in Charles Town. Their transition would be less risky once a home front was established. The same logic applied to Hana, Asumi, and Koji. There was no telling how the town would respond to Asians at this point. Manny would also be staying behind. Given his Spanish appearance and the tension between England and Spain, getting him into town would be a little tricky. Mason wasn't even sure Manny wanted to live in town. He seemed to have taken a liking to the hunting and camping. Gail, the nurse, was needed in camp until everyone who wanted to leave was gone.

Sandy and Toby would also be waiting for the second or third round.

Mason, Nathan, Tito, and John would man the ship for the trips back and forth.

At least that was the plan.

Early the morning they were to depart, all seemed ready. Those going were aboard along with Mato, five of his braves, all armed with flintlocks, and twenty-two stacks of deer skins. Also aboard was the chest of remaining Spanish dollars, around six thousand three hundred of them. Mason wasn't sure what they would do with the coins in town. Probably they would leave them on the ship and keep the ship well manned until they had a more permanent place.

Mason, Nathan, Tito, and Jeremy loaded themselves into the jolly boat and began the arduous chore of pulling the ship through the inlet. The outflow was in their favor this time so it was really just a matter of keeping the keel in the middle of the channel.

At the same time, the rest of those on board raised the main sail but left it slack in the light breeze until the ship was well offshore. At that point they secured the jolly boat, set the sails, and gave a final wave to Manny and the others as they passed the camp.

The trip to Charles Town took twelve hours. The sun was less than an hour off the horizon when they made the turn into the harbor. By the time they dropped anchor, a hundred yards out from the wharfs, it was well into dusk. They would wait until morning to maneuver the ship up to one of the wharfs so they could off load the deerskins. John thought it best to hire a couple of hands and another jolly boat for the task. For the night, everyone would sleep on board. Mato volunteered his braves to keep watch. Mason was up most of the night as well.

"Charles Town isn't ready for tight jeans," Mason said to Lisa, as they stood on the deck in the early morning. "I think Dorothy and I should first try to secure something for everyone to wear."

"Just make it quick so I can get off this boat," Lisa said.

Mason scrunched his face. "You do look a little pale."

Lisa exhaled. "Uh-huh."

"She could wear my buckskins," Dorothy said.

"And Jeremy could wear mine," Mason said. He turned to Karen standing beside him. "We should be able to get you into town later this afternoon."

Karen nodded.

They loaded one stack of the skins into the jolly boat and then Mato, one of his braves, Mason, Dorothy, Lisa, and Jeremy rowed to the wharf.

As they separated from Mato, who was off to negotiate for the skins, Mason's first stop was the clothier.

Mason and Dorothy left Jeremy and Lisa with Francois and headed off to survey the town. They were both dressed in their 'town' clothes, and Mason carried a buckskin pouch containing his Glock, the extra magazines, and enough of the Spanish dollars to take care of Francois and any other incidentals.

They visited the fourteen taverns in town, gauging each for its ability to house twenty people. There were only two with enough rooms and even then, they'd have to put four or five people in each.

"This is going to be a rough transition," Dorothy said, as they walked down Broad Street toward the wharf.

"An impossible transition I'm afraid," Mason responded. "Can you see Mildred and Lana living here, not to mention Travis and Angie."

Just as Mason and Dorothy turned down an alley in the direction of the clothier's shop, they came face to face with two large men. Both were dressed like many of those he had seen working on the docks. Both men stepped out of the way to let Dorothy and Mason pass. When Mason was slightly past the two men, he saw a blur of movement, heard a *whap*, and immediately felt a sharp pain on the back of his head. Suddenly everything went gray. He was seriously dazed but not unconscious.

He heard scuffling, a muffled scream, and then all went dark.

He regained consciousness a few seconds later. One of the men had Mason under the armpits and was dragging him down the alley. He blinked his eyes open and saw the marks in the gravel left by his heels all the way back to the street where the assault had occurred. He was still a bit dazed and the back of his head ached. He closed his eyes trying to regain his full senses.

Just when he was about to make a move, the man let go plopping Mason to the gravel on his back.

"Check the pouch," one of the men said in a gruff voice.

The pouch contained the Glock, Mason reminded himself. There was no way he could let that out of his control.

Mason heard the crunch of boots on the gravel near his head and felt a tug on the pouch strap. He blinked his eyes open and saw the man's ugly face bent over only a couple of feet above his own.

The man's eyes went wide at Mason's sudden consciousness.

Mason twisted his torso, raised his shoulders off the ground, and struck with his closed fist. Four knuckles caught the man square in the throat. The strike was not full force, but it was enough.

The man's eyes bulged as he clutched his throat with both hands and staggered back. He dropped to his knees as he tried to take a breath. The wispy sound of air indicated his throat was partially closed. It would get worse as the soft tissue swelled.

Mason knew the man would be out of action, possibly forever, so he immediately rolled to his knees and locked eyes on the other man.

The man had his right arm around Dorothy's waist. He reached behind with his left and whipped out a fixed blade knife.

Without saying a word, he lifted the knife to Dorothy's throat, locked eyes with Mason, and smiled.

Mason was fast, but he wasn't fast enough to reach the man's arm if he decided to slice. In his mind's eye he imagined Dorothy's throat opening up, blood gushing, and her sinking to the ground.

The man's eyes shot to his friend who was on the ground struggling to breathe.

Mason figured it was fifty-fifty whether he would survive.

The man with the knife must have come to the same conclusion. He took a step back dragging Dorothy with him. He stopped, eyed Mason's pouch, and motioned with his knife. "The pouch, toss it over here," he said. His accent was barely understandable.

Mason got to his feet and raised both hands, palms out, as if surrendering to the man's will.

The man smiled with black and missing teeth and motioned with the knife at the pouch.

Mason had a move in mind but it would risk Dorothy's tender, young throat. Or he could give up the pouch. Mason didn't care about the money, but he did care about the Glock. There was no telling what mayhem the man could cause with ninety-eight rounds of high pressure 9mm, but even worse, there was no telling what impact the gun would have on history. Maybe none, but maybe a lot. Still, was any of that worth risking Dorothy's life?

Mason took hold of the pouch as he searched Dorothy's face. He expected to see fear, but surprisingly there was none. He saw determined and angry eyes. That's when he realized that Dorothy wasn't a delicate flower with a head full of information. She was much more than that.

Mason lifted the pouch's strap over his head, gathered the strap and the pouch into a ball, and took a step forward.

The man took another step back and fully extended his knife arm as he shook his head back and forth.

Mason nodded, wadded the pouch a little more, and went to toss the pouch at the man's feet. Instead he gave it a little extra effort.

The pouch flew directly for the man's face.

The man did exactly what Mason hoped. He released his hold on Dorothy in order to catch the pouch.

Dorothy immediately dropped.

With the man's eyes on the pouch, Mason got to his knife hand at about the same time the man clutched the pouch in the other hand. Mason grabbed the man's wrist, locked down with as much pressure as he could muster, and twisted hard.

The knife flew into the air as the man bent over at the waist and screamed in agony.

Mason knew that a tad more pressure would snap the man's forearm, but he decided not to do that. Instead he kicked the man in the solar plexus. As all the air expelled from his lungs, Mason grabbed the man by the throat, lifted slightly, and slammed the man's back against the ground. He went limp.

Dorothy got to her feet and hurried over. She knelt. "Is he dead?" she asked, as she placed a hand on the man's chest.

"He'll live," Mason said. He stood up and gazed down at the other man, still struggling to breathe, but breathing nonetheless. He retrieved the pouch from the ground and lifted Dorothy by the arm. "We need to get out of here," he said, as he hurried her toward the other end of the alley. "We're just lucky no one came along."

"We're lucky we're not dead," Dorothy said.

Mason massaged the back of his head and felt a large lump.

As they approached the main street, Mason slowed their pace and released Dorothy. "Act as if we're simply out for a stroll."

Dorothy glanced over her shoulder.

Mason followed her gaze and saw the two men still on the ground about half way down the alley.

"I'm guessing the word has gotten out about our silver coins," Dorothy said.

"It would appear."

"What do we do now?" Dorothy asked, as she settled into a normal gait.

"We gather up Lisa and Jeremy, find Mato, and head back to the ship. We may need to rethink this whole idea."

They found Lisa and Jeremy still at the clothier's shop. Both were dressed in clothes very similar to those Mason and Dorothy wore.

Mason settled up with Francois, took the clothes altered for Nathan and John, and the four of them headed straight to the jolly boat.

"What's going on?" Jeremy asked.

"We were assaulted," Dorothy said, as they walked.

"The word is out about the silver we have," Mason said. "I'm not sure how safe any of us are in town." Mason increased his pace. "Right now, I just want to get back to the ship and make sure everything is okay."

CHAPTER 20

They arranged for a second rowboat to help pull the sloop to the dock, met up with Mato, and returned to the ship.

Karen met Mason as soon as he stepped aboard. "What's wrong?" she asked, reading the serious nature of Mason's expression.

"Everything okay on board?" he asked. "Anyone approach the ship?"

"Everything is fine," Karen said. "What happened?"

"Dorothy and I were assaulted in an alley."

"And?"

"He was clocked on the back of the head and was out for a few seconds," Dorothy said. "They wanted the pouch."

Karen felt the back of Mason's head. "You must have a headache from that."

"I think the word is out about the silver," Mason said.

John, within earshot, stepped closer. "Sure it wasn't random."

Mason thought for a moment. "Could have been I suppose."

"The two men didn't say anything about silver during the assault," Dorothy said.

Karen turned to Dorothy. "You okay?"

"I'm fine. Mason recovered and took out both men before anything serious happened."

Karen turned back to Mason. "They're dead?"

"No," Mason replied. "But they'll be sore for a few days."

"We should be extra vigilant just in case," Jeremy said. "Probably need a twenty-four-hour watch on the boat especially if we remain at the dock."

"Speaking of that," John said, as he saw two men in a dory approaching the sloop.

"I hired an extra tug," Mason said.

"Good idea," John said, "let's get them tied off and get the anchor up."

Mason, Nathan, Jeremy, and Tito manned their jolly boat, maneuvered around to the bow, and waited for John to toss them a line.

With the anchor up and the lines secured, the men in both boats began rowing until the sloop slowly began to move. An hour later the sloop was secured to the very last dock which was completely empty of any other ships.

Mato, his braves, Tito, and Jeremy began removing the deerskins and loading them on a hand-drawn cart.

"We might as well get you dressed," Mason said, as he extended his hand to Karen.

"Most men want the opposite," she said.

Mason raised an eyebrow and smiled.

Karen changed into Dorothy's buckskin dress and accompanied Mason and Dorothy to Francois' shop.

After leaving Karen in Francois' capable hands, Mason and Dorothy went in search of someone whom might be able to provide information about securing a piece of property. Someone like Captain Darby, Mister Worthington, or even Colonel Rhett would be ideal. But none of those individuals were about.

"Perhaps we should go straight to the source," Dorothy said.

Mason raised his chin.

"The surveyor general's office plats all properties," she said. "That office would certainly know what's available."

"Seems logical," Mason said. "Where do we find the surveyor general?"

Dorothy took in a deep breath and exhaled. "I don't know." She thought for a few moments. "Who's the only other person we know in this town?"

"Francois," Mason said.

They returned to the clothier's shop and found Karen draped with various garments as Francois inserted pins.

"Francois, where would we find the surveyor general's office?" Mason asked.

Francois removed several pins from his mouth. "At the end of Broad Street near the wharf."

"Thank you," Mason said, as he turned to leave.

"But it's closed," Francois continued.

Mason stopped and turned back.

"Been closed since December, by order of the lord's council."

"December of 19?" Dorothy asked.

"Yep."

"So, who conducts land surveys?" Dorothy asked.

"Oh, we still have surveyors, but we don't have a surveyor general," Francois replied.

"So, who do we see about buying some land?" Mason asked.

Francois stopped what he was doing and stood up straight. "Buy land? Why would you need to buy land?"

"In all the turmoil," Dorothy said, "a grant is not likely."

"True," Francois said, as he bent down to continue his work on Karen's petticoat. "I'd talk to John Bayly. He does most of the surveying in this area."

"Where do we find him?" Dorothy asked.

Francois stood up again. "This time of day, if he's in town, probably the O'Brady tavern down the street."

"Thank you, Francois," Mason said. He winked at Karen as he and Dorothy left.

"Why was he surprised by our desire to buy some land?" Mason asked, as they walked.

"Originally parcels of land were given away, granted by the lord proprietors through a cumbersome process. To encourage settlement. If I remember correctly, the proprietors lost control over the colony in 1719. The crown took provisional control in May 1721. At this point, the easiest way to acquire land would be to find someone who is willing to sell. We would need to have a bill of sale written up, pay the money, and have it recorded."

They entered the tavern down the street and found all the tables full of men, mostly from the ships in the harbor. They were all eating and drinking. Mostly the latter. One table stood out in particular because it was occupied by four tough-looking men all dressed slightly better than anyone else in the place.

While Dorothy waited by the door, Mason approached the table. "Would any of you gentlemen be John Bayly?"

One of the men, dressed in a long buckskin shirt with fringe at the bottom and matching buckskin pants, paused the spoon on its way to his mouth. He was probably in his late thirties, thin and wiry. "What can I do for you sir?"

"I'm interested in acquiring some land in this area," Mason said. "I thought you might know of some available for purchase."

"I might," Bayly said. "What's your name?"

"Stephen Mason. Friends call me Mason."

"What kind of land did you have in mind?"

"Something on the river with enough land to do some farming."

"Rice?"

"And food crops."

"I might know of a place. The owner lost her family to the Yemassee." Bayly thought for a moment. "Where can I reach you?"

"I'll be on the sloop tied up at the last dock or anchored in the harbor. If the ship's not there, I'll be back in a few days."

"Fair enough," Bayly said, as he stood and extended his hand. "I'll be in touch."

The two men shook and Mason and Dorothy departed.

"Should we hang around or return to the camp and pick up the others?" Dorothy asked, as they walked.

"I think we should hang for a couple of days," Mason said.

◆◆◆

The crew spent the rest of that day and the next two days around the ship. The harbor master paid a visit on the second day to determine their intentions. He advised that as long as there was empty space at the other docks Mason could keep the sloop tied up. It wasn't causing any harm. The crew spent the time outfitting themselves and the sloop. Everyone ended up with period clothing. The ship ended up with sleeping hammocks.

Having concluded his trading, Mato was anxious to return to his village, but he agreed to wait.

Drinking water was the biggest problem. The local water was brackish and probably contained all manner of parasites. There were several wells in town and Mason found one willing to supply all that Mason wanted for a price. The owner also allowed Mason to set up a cooking pot for boiling the water. After the water cooled it was placed in earthen jugs. The crew was able to process and store plenty of water.

Mason ensured everyone had a chance to spend time in town to get acclimated. The rank odors were tough at first, especially for Mildred and Lana, but eventually no one noticed, or, at least, didn't complain. Everyone was also able to take advantage of the one and only bath house in town. The two-bit price included warm water and soap.

On the evening of the third day, Mason and Karen sat on the deck in the bow with their backs against the gunwale. The nine other survivors and one brave had already gone below or into the aft cabin. Mato and the other brave stood the first watch at the wheel.

Overcast skies blocked the stars and blanketed everything in total darkness. Eventually all was quiet except for laughter in the distance from the nearest tavern.

Enjoying the relative quiet and the breeze, Mason relaxed with his eyes closed. After a few minutes he felt Karen stir beside him and felt her hand on his leg. He opened his eyes, but couldn't see much except the vague outline of Karen's head.

"Are you awake?" she whispered.

"Yes."

He felt her hand make its way up his leg to the buttoned crotch flap of his breeches. Mason was a little surprised at her direct approach since they had never been intimate.

Mason started to say something, but she quickly shushed him and continued manipulating the two buttons on the flap. He felt himself start to strain against the thin linen.

With the flap completely open, she pressed her hand against his hardness for a few seconds and then pulled his underwear down exposing the shaft. She massaged a few seconds until it was at its full glory.

Mason heard the rustling of clothing, saw the outline of Karen's form rise up, and felt her settle herself on top of him straddling his hips. She guided his member inside and began to gyrate against him.

Mason began to move his hips in rhythm, enjoying the sensation and the closeness.

Karen increased the rhythm and intensity as she pressed against him.

Mason could see her chin up and head back in silhouette against the sky. He kept pace with her rhythm until he heard her hold her breath and felt her tense. The sensation was suddenly more than he could endure. He tensed with her as he exploded forth.

Karen went limp in a cascade of aftershocks until finally she buried her head in the crux of Mason's neck and shoulder.

After a few moments the shudders stopped and Karen's body relaxed.

He gently lifted her chin and kissed her deeply. After a few long moments their lips separated and Mason felt her staring into his eyes. He felt her muscles tighten as she started to rise up.

Something he couldn't quite place made him suddenly grasp her waist with both hands to prevent her from rising. He held her weight.

She settled back down. "What?" she whispered.

"Not sure," he whispered back. Then he heard a scuff and a barely audible thump on the deck only a few feet from where Mason and Karen sat.

Karen apparently heard it too because she tensed.

Neither of them moved a muscle or made any sound.

At the sound of another scuff, Mason raised his chin and peered over Karen's shoulder. Against the slightly lighter background of the clouded sky he saw the outline of three men, the last of whom was just stepping over the gunwale. Any movement on Mason or Karen's part would give away their nearly invisible position in the darkness, so they were forced to maintain their union.

Mason peered at the wheel where Mato and the other brave had been but saw nothing in the darkness. Mato should have heard the men just as he had. Mason could not imagine why there had been no response. Perhaps the two natives had stepped inside the aft cabin or perhaps they had gone down the ladder for some reason. Perhaps they were aware of his and Karen's dalliance and had left to give them privacy. Whatever the reason there was no response to the invasion.

Mason thought of his buckskin pouch and the Glock within. He remembered hanging it in the aft cabin hours earlier while he helped tend to some chore. His separation from the pouch left him completely unarmed. The men who had just boarded the ship and were quietly making their way toward the cabin had to be armed, certainly with knives and quite probably with pistols as well. They were still after the silver. Mason's desire to purchase land had apparently brought out the rats.

As the men tiptoed toward the aft cabin, Mason lifted Karen by the waist and quietly set her to the side on her knees. He buttoned the flap on his breeches and as quietly as possible rolled to crouch. He paused for a moment to listen and then rose. He kept his torso as low as possible so as not to silhouette against the sky over the gunwale. The only things Mason had going for him was concealment and surprise. The men would hopefully not expect anyone from the bow. Of course, that all changed when Mason's foot bumped against a wooden bucket on his fourth step. The noise was slight, but apparently enough to give away his position.

All three of the men's nearly imperceptible dark hulks came to an immediate stop.

Mason froze. He couldn't see any details in the dark, but he imagined all three of their heads turned toward him. For a few moments nothing happened. But then he caught a glimpse of movement off toward the starboard side of the ship.

Instinctively, without directions from anyone, they were spreading out.

Mason had lost the element of surprise and, unarmed, he stood little chance against the three men. Only one move came to mind. He bent lower, felt for the bucket, and flung it hard to his right toward the dock side of the boat. At the same time, he dashed to his left in full gallop toward the man on the starboard side. He hoped the noise would distract the other two men and get Mato's attention. A second later he drove his shoulder into what turned out to be a man's midsection and dug with his feet like he did in football training many years earlier. His momentum and the power of his legs carried the man until his back crashed into the cabin bulkhead in a cacophony of grunts, gasps, and finally a loud *thump*. The man was much lighter than Mason expected, thin and wiry, but solid.

Mason's greatest fear was that the man held a knife, so he immediately pinned both of the man's arms against the cabin. With all his might he brought his knee up hard into the left side of the man's rib cage. A *snap* told him he had connected with at least one rib.

The man winced in a long exhale and went mostly limp.

Keeping the man's arms penned until the last moment, Mason suddenly took a step back as he grabbed the back of the man's head with both hands. In one smooth motion he pulled the man's torso down as he brought his knee up crashing into his face. Mason heard a *crunch* and felt the man go completely limp as a knife *clanged* to the deck.

A sudden light from below deck, from the only candle lantern on board, threw the shadows of arms and legs against the aft cabin bulkhead as people, probably Mato and his brave, scrambled up the ladder.

With his eyes at last able to penetrate the darkness, he saw two men scurry over the gunwale and run down the dock. He turned back to the unconscious man lying at his feet. A dark blotch of blood was smeared across the man's face, likely from a broken nose.

Mato and one brave, both armed with muskets, appeared at Mason's side. Mato reached down and picked up the knife. He bent lower to check the man's breathing.

Mason stepped to the port side and scanned the empty dock.

"Are you hurt?" Karen asked, as she hurried to Mason's side.

"I'm okay," he said, as he put a hand on her shoulder.

"I think they're getting more determined to get that silver," she said.

Mason nodded in the dim light and turned around at the sound of people coming on deck.

"What happened?" Jeremy asked.

"Marauders," Mason said. "The second attempt."

"Will they be back?" Lisa asked.

"Not tonight."

Soon everyone was up, walking about the deck, and mumbling amongst themselves.

"Look," Mason said in a slightly raised voice, as he addressed everyone. "I think we should go back to bed. The excitement is over for tonight."

"What about him?" Nathan asked, as he motioned to the still unconscious man.

Mason walked over and knelt. The man was breathing, and his nose had stopped bleeding. But he was still very much unconscious.

Mason had no interest in trying to explain what happened to the authorities. The Night Watch was notoriously suspicious, according to Francois, and they tended to lock everyone up while they investigated. Mason did not feel like spending time in some dank, suffocating, flea infested lockup. "We need to get this guy off the boat."

Mason bent over, placed the man's right arm over his shoulder, and motioned for Nathan to do the same.

Nathan bent down and took the man's other arm.

Together they carried him to the gunwale as his lifeless feet dragged over the deck.

Jeremy went over the gunwale first and helped transfer the man to the dock. "Where to?" he whispered.

"The foot of the dock," Mason said, as he glanced around the pitch dark.

Only a few flickers of light were visible through the opening in the wall and down the street farther in town.

They carried the man the length of the dock and deposited him at the wall. They left him reclined back against the bricks with his head cocked to one side. Just another drunk among many.

Mason took another look around before ushering Nathan and Jeremy back down the dock toward the sloop.

CHAPTER 21

The next morning, Mason rose early from his hammock in the aft cabin and immediately made his way on deck and over to the gunwale. His heart sank as he peered in the distance through the early dawn light at the man still reclined against the wall. He turned at the sound of cloth rustling and greeted Karen by putting his arm around her waist.

She peered down the dock. "That's not good."

Mason twisted his lips as he slowly shook his head and exhaled. "There'll be questions if he's dead."

Movement brought his attention back to the foot of the dock. He saw two men stop and kneel down next to the man. He hoped to see them pick the man up, which is what he would expect if he were alive and needed medical attention. Instead, they both just stood up and scanned the area. One of the men locked eyes with Mason. *Shit.*

"That's not good," Karen said.

"We need a story, something plausible and as close to the truth as possible." He followed Karen's gaze down to his knee. The blood stain stood prominent on the beige of his breeches leg.

◆◆◆

The man staring at Mason had intelligent, very penetrating eyes. He wore an olive-green coat, black waistcoat, a white puffy shirt, and a white cravat to match. A three-point, black hat hung on a peg behind him. He also wore a stern expression on his face. He struck Mason as a serious man in search of the truth.

Mason contemplated his own state of dress which included his rumpled, linen coat and Nathan's relatively baggy breeches.

He stood within the red-brick, single story Watch House, adjacent to the half-moon battery overlooking the Cooper River. The building was visible from all the docks and housed three partitioned sections that Mason had noted on his way inside. The largest section included cots that could accommodate, he estimated, up to thirty men. There were about half that many in the room; some were in various states of repose and some idled away with menial chores. A much smaller section was designated a holding area for those detained during the night. There were no bars; it was just a stall sort of affair with a straw-covered brick floor. At the time of Mason's entry into the building, the holding area was devoid of any prisoners. And the third area, also small, served as an office for the provost marshal and the commissioner of the Town Watch. The building's entire interior was dim—even during the day with the door and two small windows open. It was also damp, musky, and smelled of body odor and urine. It was not a pleasant place, but Mason figured now was not the time to express any kind of judgment. He thus wore the best non-confrontational expression he could muster.

The two watchmen who had summoned him were each to Mason's side as he stood before the provost marshal seated behind a small wooden desk.

Mason imagined himself with his hands and feet shackled, sitting in the straw of the putrid holding area among pirates, derelicts, and runaway slaves. He further imagined himself disheveled, thread bare, and emaciated from lack of food. The marshal's deep, middle-aged voice brought him out of his reverie.

"As I said, my name is Sanford Tennison. I'm the provost marshal for the Carolina Colony. My watchmen tell me you, or someone on your ship, may have witnessed a crime."

Mason, trying to remain as subdued as possible, raised both eyebrows. "A crime?"

"A man was found dead not forty feet from your ship. Your ship, and the people on it, is the closest occupied vessel to the scene of the crime."

Where they found him wasn't the scene of the crime, Mason thought to himself. "I saw the man against the wall at about the same time your watchmen came along."

Tennison, elbow resting on the desk, with his chin cupped in the palm of one hand, didn't change expressions or even blink. His dark brown eyes bore into Mason looking for a hint of untruthfulness.

Mason's statement was plausible and the truth, although minus everything that had happened during the night. His blood-stained breeches popped into his mind's eye.

"My watchmen passed by that spot in the early evening," Tennison said. "The man wasn't there."

"Must have happened later in the night," Mason said.

Tennison lifted his chin from his hand and gave an almost imperceptible nod. "So, you didn't see or hear anything during the night."

"Everyone aboard was in their hammocks shortly after dark. No one saw anything and I can vouch for everyone on board."

Tennison nodded. "And who exactly are you?"

"Stephen Mason. I'm here with a group of settlers in search of property we can farm."

Tennison nodded again and stared.

Mason was just starting to feel uncomfortable, more uncomfortable than before, when the man finally looked away.

"Okay Mister Mason, that will be all for now. You can go." He nodded to the two watchmen.

One of them motioned to the door with his chin.

Mason turned to leave.

"One other thing," Tennison said.

Mason stopped and faced the marshal.

"You didn't ask how the man died. That's curious to me."

Mason thought for a moment as he gazed into the marshal's eyes. "How did he die?"

Tennison stared at Mason for several moments and then jerked his chin in the direction of the door.

The watchman to Mason's right gave him a shove on the shoulder.

Mason turned and walked out.

At the sloop, Mason found John Bayly standing on deck talking to John, Jeremy, and Karen. Mason was hoping to get out of Nathan's breeches but that would have to wait.

Everyone turned to Mason as he stepped aboard.

"Everything okay?" Karen asked.

Mason nodded and turned to Bayly. "Mister Bayly, has anyone offered you something to drink?"

"I just arrived a few moments ago," Bayly said.

"I believe we have some ale on board and some biscuits from town," Mason said. He ushered Bayly to step under a canvas tarp erected in front of the aft cabin to block the sun. Mason motioned to a wood bench for Bayly. Mason sat on a stool as did John and Jeremy.

Karen disappeared into the cabin.

Bayly took out a handkerchief and mopped the sweat from his forehead. "It's a hot one." He lifted his eyes to the tarp cover. "This helps."

"It does," Mason agreed.

Karen returned with mugs and a platter of biscuits obtained just that morning from a shop near the harbor.

Bayly took the mug offered, one of the biscuits, and promptly took a gulp of the ale. He sat the mug on the bench beside him and took a bite of the biscuit. He held it up and paused his chewing to smile.

Mason smiled as he raised his mug and took a drink. At the realization that his mug contained water, he glanced at Karen.

She smiled.

"About that farm land," Bayly said, "I do know of a parcel owned by a widower. She lost her husband and both sons to the Catawba during the war."

Mason gazed over Bayly's shoulder at Mato and two of his braves talking to Tito in the bow.

"How many acres?" Jeremy asked.

"Only a thousand, some marsh, but there's still plenty for vegetables."

"And the owner wants to sell?" Mason asked.

"She does. Paid her a visit yesterday on my way in."

"What is included?" John asked.

"The fields, a modest house, fifty slaves and their quarters," Bayly said. "Along with ten horses, two cows, chickens, and sundry items of equipment.

"Slaves?" Karen asked.

"Of course," Bayly said. He took another gulp of the ale.

Karen didn't comment.

"Seven miles up the Ashley," Bayly said. "West bank. Close but not too close."

Mason nodded. "We'd like to see it."

"Easiest way would be by boat," Bayly said. He glanced around the sloop's deck. "This will make it up that far. Or we can paddle. Canoe would be fastest."

They made arrangements to meet at the town's west gate early the next morning. They would hike to the peninsula's west side and take canoes from there.

While they finished their ale and biscuits, Bayly talked about the Indian war.

"Hard to imagine it's been two years," Bayly said. "There was some fierce fighting on the outskirts. They almost made it to the walls. The Catawba were especially murderous. Bloodthirsty." He glanced over his shoulder at Mato but didn't comment further.

"I guess all of that has ceased," Jeremy said.

"Mostly. Still get some skirmishes from time to time. Most tribes have come to see the advantages of trade."

They chatted a while longer until finally Bayly drained the mug, sat it on the bench beside him, and stood. "First thing in the morning," he said, as he extended his hand to Mason.

Mason stood and shook. "First thing."

◆◆◆

Mason, Dorothy, Jeremy, and Tito met Bayly at the west gate a half hour after sunrise. Mason wore his town clothes minus the blood stain on the knee thanks to Karen.

Bayly carried a flintlock and a pouch presumably containing paper cartridges.

They exited the gate, crossed the bridge over the moat, and followed a rough gravel path to a wide, well-worn trail. This would be the King's Highway that Dorothy mentioned. It would ultimately be transformed into an actual road from Charles Town to Boston by order of the King of England. It was already used as a major postal route in the north.

They turned south and followed the trail to a landing on the bank of the Ashley River. It consisted of a simple, one-room, three-walled log structure, open to the river. Five canoes were beached in front of the structure. Three of the canoes were dugouts made from the entire tree trunk; two were much lighter made from some kind of tree bark over a wood frame. This was apparently an established location from which to cross the river. Three men, sitting on stools next to the structure, watched as Bayly directed Mason and his group to the two bark canoes. Bayly and Jeremy would paddle in one, and Mason, Dorothy, and Tito would occupy the other.

As they set out, it became obvious that Tito had never paddled a canoe, but he faked it well. Soon he was in rhythm with Mason, and they were able to keep up with Bayly.

Mason kept his head on a swivel, sweeping both banks. He was attentive to anything that might constitute a threat, man or beast, but he was also amazed at the unspoiled splendor of the lightly touched vista. They hugged the west bank which was mostly wide expanses of marsh and muck. It wasn't that different from the condition of the river in modern times. Farther up, as the banks narrowed, it became less marshy in spots. Soon they came upon a field of planted rice. The field paralleled the river for at least two miles and ran inland for another mile or so. Slaves dotted the landscape. They continued on.

Mason thought of the fifty slaves that came with the plantation he hoped to purchase. No one in his group of survivors would tolerate any kind of forced servitude, but just freeing them came with its own set of complexities. Slavery was basically the law around here, and the locals would be up in arms if they found out fifty of them had been freed. Plus, there was the problem of working the fields. Mason couldn't imagine anyone in his group working that hard. They would have to figure something out because owning slaves was not an option.

Bayly pointed with his paddle to an open grassy area and a two-story house. A vast field of crops, dotted with workers, ran north of the open field along the river as far as Mason could see.

Bayly began paddling toward a rough wood dock that extended thirty feet into the river. Mason's canoe bumped against the dock as Bayly and Jeremy, already out, walked to meet an approaching woman. Mason stepped out and helped Dorothy and Tito up to the wood planks.

Bayly introduced Wilma Stewart, the owner. Mason could tell she had been quite attractive at one time, but now she carried a weathered appearance with deep creases in her face, probably a combination of hard work, age, worry, and despair. She was very cordial, but she smiled little.

In a matter-of-fact manner, she proceeded to guide the group around the property pointing out and explaining its various aspects. The property included a total of one thousand acres arranged between the river and a dirt road that fronted the main house. Five hundred acres were cultivated with rice with another ninety acres devoted to food crops. The remaining property included a section of unusable muck along the river, and about two hundred acres of thick forest. She did in fact have a total of fifty slaves. All but five were devoted to the planting, harvesting, and processing of the crops. The other five took care of the house.

"What kind of yield on the rice?" Dorothy asked.

"The good years it has run about a thousand pounds per acre," she said. "This year will be less given the drought. As you can see, we will be harvesting soon." The owner gazed at Dorothy a few moments.

Mason too could see the wheels turning in Dorothy's head.

"If you're wondering, we average about six thousand dollars on rice and another thousand on the food crops we don't eat," Mrs. Stewart said. "It's a small operation compared to some, but we make do."

The owner continued her tour. The slave quarters consisted of five small cabins about a hundred yards from the main house. The main house included a separate kitchen—a small wood structure a few yards from the main house—along with a well near the kitchen for fresh water, and another separate structure that housed the horses and various items of equipment.

The house itself was frame with ten separate rooms and three fire places. It had been well maintained with no signs of leaking. Of course, given that it hadn't rained in weeks, Mason couldn't be sure about the leaking.

Basically, if the survivors had to remain in this time period, this property was a near perfect solution to their survival needs.

Mason thanked Mrs. Stewart for the tour, promised to give it serious thought, and make a decision within a day or so. Everyone bid their farewells, and the group returned to the dock.

At the dock Mason paused before stepping into the canoe. "I wonder if we can get the sloop up this far?"

Bayly shrugged his shoulders. "Others have gone farther in bigger. You have the wind to your back on the way up and the current with you on the way back. You'll need some long poles."

CHAPTER 22

"The property is the best we could hope for," Mason said, as he stood before everyone on the deck of the sloop in the late afternoon. "Size is manageable, and the location is near perfect."

"Shouldn't we discuss this with the rest of our people?" Mildred asked.

"I agree with that," Nathan said.

"I'd like to do just that," Mason said, "but the word is out that Mrs. Stewart wants to sell. She's anxious so the price will probably be commensurate with her desire to leave. Plantations in the area will want to scarf up the property. I think we have to move quickly."

"What's the price?" Tom Green asked.

Mason looked to Dorothy for an answer.

"We're just estimating based on my understanding of the economy at this time," she said. She paused and contemplated the sky for a moment. "The slaves alone are likely worth around seventy-five hundred. The land, probably twelve fifty. The house, I really have no idea, but figure a thousand for the sake of argument. Another three fifty or so for the animals and equipment."

"And up to seven thousand for the rice and food crops that will be ready for harvest in a few weeks," Mason added.

"That's seventeen thousand," Lana said. "We don't have seventeen thousand."

"That's true, which is another reason we need to act fast," Mason said. "Other's in the area might have more buying power than we do. We'll need to offer most of what we have left up front and make payments over time."

"The surveyor told us she plans on moving to New York," Dorothy said.

John cleared his throat. "After we're finished ferrying everyone around, I think we should use the sloop to carry cargo up and down the coast. Periodic stops in New York would be no problem."

"Why don't we just move to New York?" Nathan asked.

Several nodded in agreement, probably thinking about the amount of work required to run a plantation.

"There's nothing stopping anyone from doing anything they want," Mason said. "But this plantation offers a readymade solution to our long-term survival. Yes, it will take some work. But life won't be easy where ever you go."

"Anyone who does decide to leave would always have a place to come back to," Dorothy said. "I think we should do it."

"If she takes the offer," Jeremy said.

Mason nodded.

"What will be the offer?" Mildred asked.

"We offer fifteen thousand, go to twenty if we have to," he said. "Five thousand now, the balance in yearly payments from the crop proceeds until the balance is paid. That would leave us about thirteen hundred for incidentals."

"We do have one thing in our favor," Dorothy said.

Everyone raised their eyes to Dorothy.

"Not many people have five thousand in silver on hand."

The next morning, Mason, Dorothy, Jeremy, and Tito returned to the plantation with Bayly.

Mrs. Stewart invited them to join her on the portico covered porch facing the river.

One of the house maids served hot tea from a silver tea service poured into small, elegant, porcelain cups with saucers. They were more of a bowl really since the cups didn't have handles.

"I like to take tea here on the porch before the heat is up," Mrs. Stewart said. She took a sip and then lowered the cup and saucer to her knee. She looked at Mason expectantly.

"First of all," Mason said, "We were very sorry to hear about your trouble here during the war."

Mrs. Stewart gave a subtle nod. Her lip tightened slightly as she stared with piercing blue eyes.

"And you have a lovely place here; you've obviously worked very hard."

Barely perceptible, Mrs. Stewart raised her chin.

Mason paused. Rather than making an offer that might be completely offensive, he decided to take a different approach. "Can I ask what kind of price you had in mind?"

Mrs. Stewart took another sip of tea and placed the cup and saucer on a small side table. "I think twenty thousand dollars would be a very fair price."

"We were thinking more along the lines of fifteen thousand," Mason countered.

"You have that in silver?" She glanced at Bayly.

"Five thousand in silver, half the proceeds from the crops each year until the balance is paid. We can deliver the payments to you in New York."

Mrs. Stewart glanced at Bayly. She stood, stepped to the edge of the porch, and stared out at the river for a full minute. She finally turned around and stared at Mason. "I like you Mr. Mason. You're different from most." She turned back to the river. "Seventeen five. Five thousand at signing, first payment immediately after this harvest. I'll even throw in the furniture."

Mason stood up. "You have a deal."

She turned her head to Bayly. "Can you have Arthur draw up the agreement? All the particulars about the property are on record."

"Yes Ma'am," Bayly said, as he stood.

Mason and Mrs. Stewart shook hands.

"How much time do you need?" Mrs. Stewart asked.

"As soon as the agreement is ready," Mason said.

"We'll meet back here in a week then."

"Perfect." Mason said.

They all sat and continued to discuss the details. Bayly would be paid one hundred dollars, fifty from Mrs. Stewart and fifty from Mason. All fees associated with the sale, for recording and such, would be split. Mrs. Stewart introduced Mason, Dorothy, Jeremy, and Tito to Sylvester, an older gentleman, the head slave, and the main point of contact between Mrs. Stewart and the field hands.

"By the way," Bayly said looking at Mason, "I need a name for the agreement and the deed. I presume you will be the buyer."

Mason smoothed his beard with one hand while he thought. "Let me confer with my associates," he finally said, and led Dorothy, Jeremy, and Tito to the far end of the porch.

"I'm fine with your name on the deed," Dorothy said.

"Ditto," Jeremy agreed.

"With the sloop to operate, I'm not sure how much time I'll be spending at the property." Mason thought for a moment. "A husband and wife would be nice," he said, as he turned his attention to Jeremy.

"What?" Jeremy asked.

"How about Mister and Misses Jeremy Jackson?"

"Who's the misses?" Tito asked.

"We all see how much time you spend with Lisa," Mason said.

"She's married," Jeremy objected.

"Not for another three hundred years," Dorothy countered.

Jeremy opened his mouth to object, but Mason had already turned back to Bayly and Mrs. Stewart.

"Jeremy and Lisa Jackson," Mason said. "Mister and Misses."

"Who's going to tell Lisa?" Jeremy whispered to Dorothy loud enough for Mason to hear.

◆◆◆

Lisa agreed as soon as Jeremy posed the question. That was the easy part. The hard part was actually getting them married. Since neither Jeremy nor Lisa was a member of a church, none of the several churches in town, or meeting places as they were called, would agree to conduct a service. Even if they had agreed, most of the churches performed services recognized only by that particular church. Only the English Church, the official church of the colony, could perform an official wedding. St. Philips, the English Church, had apparently been badly damaged during a hurricane some years earlier, and a new church had been under construction ever since. It still hadn't been completed. The church's commissary, the rector, was not inclined to go out of his way for anyone, especially a non-member, until his church was fully restored. To make matters worse, no wedding could be performed until a license was granted, and only the governor could grant a license. Since the governor, a James Moore, didn't know the parties to be married, he wasn't inclined to expedite the process.

Mason finally employed Arthur Sills to arrange the marriage. He was one of only two barristers in town and the fellow who would be handling the sale of Mrs. Stewart's property. With the license finally secured, Jeremy and Lisa were married on board the sloop by a local small denominational minister found at one of the taverns. Mister Sills assured everyone that the marriage would be official enough.

The next day, eight days after the verbal agreement, Mason and the survivors maneuvered the sloop up the Ashley with Bayly and Arthur Sills aboard. They anchored as near the Stewart plantation dock as possible. All was finally coming together nicely until Mrs. Stewart saw Mato and his braves on the deck of the sloop.

"I'll not sell my property to anyone associated with those heathens," Mrs. Stewart said, as she stood on the dock facing Mason, Jeremy, Lisa, Bayly, and Arthur Sills.

"I can assure you Mrs. Stewart, Mato was not involved with the war," Mason said. "He's my friend, and we've had several discussions about his situation."

"He's a Catawba, isn't he?"

"Well yes," Mason said, "but he, along with two elders, and a small group of his people separated from the main tribe just prior to the start of hostilities. Apparently, there was great contention among his people on whether to join the Yemassee. Many believed it would disrupt trade and that the mistreatment by some traders could be worked out without going to war." Mason motioned to Mato. "He and his small group established a new village much closer to the coast, well away from the fighting."

Dorothy approached the group. "Mato was the first person we met when we arrived in this area, and from that first day he has gone out of his way to help us."

"We've gone this far with the sale," Arthur said. "Might as well finish it so you can be off to join your sister in New York."

Mrs. Stewart stared at Mato for several long seconds. Finally, she shook her head. "Fine."

Jeremy, Lisa, and Mrs. Stewart walked to the house where they would sign the necessary papers while Mason, Nathan, and Tito transferred the chest of silver

Spanish dollars from the sloop. "I'm actually relieved to have this out of our hands," Mason whispered, as he lowered his end of the chest to the floor. They joined the others in the parlor where the signing had just wrapped up.

"All that's left is to have these recorded," Arthur said, as he stuffed the documents into a leather satchel. He turned and shook hands with Jeremy, Lisa, and Mason in turn. "The property now belongs to you," he said, as he stared at Jeremy. He turned and shook hands with Mrs. Stewart. "Thank you. We'll miss you in these parts."

Mrs. Stewart gave a weak smile as she perused the interior of the room like she had never seen it before. "I'll miss it here as well."

"Is there anything we can help you with?" Mason asked. "We'd be happy to transport you to town on the sloop."

"No," she said, as she dipped her chin. "My sister and her husband will be here tomorrow. I should be out of the house the day after."

"That's fine," Mason said. "Do you mind if Jeremy and Lisa stay behind to get acclimated with the property?"

"It's their property now," she said.

Mason raised both eyebrows in agreement. "I guess we'll be off then."

Lisa remained behind with Mrs. Steward while Jeremy walked everyone to the dock.

"We'll return to Myrtle Beach and pick up the others," Mason said, as he lagged behind with Jeremy. "Should be back here in two or three days."

"What do we do in the mean time?"

"Get to know the place. Let the slaves do what they normally do. We'll sort that out when we all return."

Jeremy glanced back at the porch, at Lisa and Mrs. Stewart, and at the sloop and the people watching from the deck. "Why don't you ask Karen to stay? Lisa and I would appreciate her company. And you'll be back in a couple of days."

Mason immediately understood that it wasn't her company they would appreciate so much, it was her confidence. Mason smiled. "I'll ask."

As it turned out, Karen was all too happy to remain behind. It would give her a head start on getting organized. If this was where they would spend the rest of their lives, she meant to make the most of it.

The two of them stood embraced on the dock.

"Two days at the most, maybe three," Mason said. "I'll be back here as soon as possible."

"I know," Karen said. She reached up and pulled his head down to her. Their lips met, in a peck at first, but then deeply for several moments. They finally parted, and with a final wink, Mason hopped in the jolly boat and rowed to the sloop. He watched Jeremy and Lisa join Karen at the dock.

With the anchor up and the sloop pointed in the right direction, John unfurled a portion of the jib as Mason, Tom, and Nathan manned long poles in case they neared shallow water.

Mason gave a final wave to Karen, Jeremy, and Lisa still standing on the dock. He kept Karen in sight until she disappeared around a bend. He would be back as soon as possible. He had never felt so strongly about anything in his life.

After settling up with Bayly and Arthur, Mason rowed them to the canoe landing on the Ashley side of the peninsula. Mason told them he would likely be in Charles Town often since he planned to start hauling cargo up and down the coast. With that they parted, and Mason returned to the sloop. They set sail for Myrtle Beach even though they would arrive after dark. A full moon and cloudless skies were expected that night.

CHAPTER 23

Mason stood at the bow and gazed back at the crew.

Everyone was on deck engaged in everything from minor chores to nothing at all. And everyone was dressed in period clothing. He felt like he was visiting the tourist attraction at Colonial Williamsburg in his own time. It was still hard to believe that somehow, they had been transported three hundred years into the past and were actually living as they did in that time. There was, of course, one major difference. They knew the future. Most had only a vague understanding of history, just the main events like the Revolutionary War. But Dorothy knew the details. Such knowledge could be very useful; it could also be very dangerous. Mason didn't know if it was even possible to change the course of history, but just in case it was, they had to be careful.

Mason watched the sun beginning to set over the stern. He turned to the shoreline in the distance and tried to determine their location in the dimming light.

Dorothy lit the candle lantern and hung it on a peg to the side of the aft cabin door. The dim light sent dancing shadows along the deck.

Mason made his way back to John standing behind the wheel. "What do you think?"

"I wish we had more light," he said, as he glanced at the sky.

Mason nodded and then joined Dorothy standing at the gunwale. She stared at the shoreline. They both stood silent for several long moments.

"This is a time of transition for Charles Town," Dorothy said.

"How so?"

"The Lords Proprietors give up their control of the colony. In a few weeks the first royal governor will be appointed: Sir Francis Nicholson. He succeeds James Moore. Nicholson doesn't actually arrive until May of next year. They've already started dismantling the wall to make it easier to transfer goods to and from the town."

"Pirates?"

"The bad ones have already been rounded up and killed. There's still a few around, but nothing like it used to be." She paused a few moments as she stared into space. "This is a good time to own a plantation. The economy here and up and down the coast will swell with trade. If I remember correctly, there's a slave revolt in thirty-nine, a short battle with the Spanish in forty-two, and a hurricane or two. For the most part, the next major threat, the British and the Revolution, are years away." She turned to face Mason. "Have you given any more thought to how we got here and our chances of finding a way back?"

"I've thought about it."

Dorothy gazed at his face for several moments and finally turned away.

"One day at a time," Mason said.

"What about the slaves?"

"All I know is it's wrong. We can't be a party to it. But we also need the manpower necessary to operate the plantation. Do you have any thoughts?"

"When the slaves were eventually freed after the Civil War, the vast majority had nowhere to go. They ended up continuing to work as they had. We could simply free Mrs. Stewart's fifty slaves; most will probably remain where they are. We could offer them their own plots of land."

"What about some kind of wage?"

"Probably not a good idea," Dorothy said. "It would lead to thefts and conflicts within the compound."

"So, we free them and ask them to stay in exchange for a plot of land?"

"I don't know," Dorothy said, "better living conditions. Like I said, most have nowhere to go."

Mason smoothed his beard.

"You need to understand," Dorothy said, "the economy grew, and the area prospered because of the slaves. Blacks greatly outnumber the whites. None of the plantations that exist now would have made it without the slaves." Dorothy glanced back at the others on deck. "Can you see Nathan or Tito or Tom Green working the fields?"

"No," Mason said.

"It's the same for the English that settled here. They just weren't willing to work that hard, to endure the heat, the bugs, and the diseases which are even more prevalent in the fields."

"A cooperative," Mason said.

"What?"

"We form a cooperative with everyone owning a portion that will accumulate value. For the next three years or so a large segment of the proceeds will go to paying the balance. After that, everyone benefits."

"There are no banks here," Dorothy said. "Wealth at this time was a matter of property and stuff, not so much a matter of currency. You can't really hand someone a chair when they are ready to move on. About all you can really offer is a better way of life."

"Okay," Mason said. "We offer them a better way of life if they agree to stay."

"It might work," Dorothy said.

"How will the other plantation owners feel about us freeing our slaves?"

"They'll be up in arms," Dorothy said, "if they know about it."

"Keeping it quiet will have to be part of the deal," Mason said.

Dorothy nodded. "That might work for a while."

Mildred emerged from the aft cabin and approached Mason. "I've been watching a light in the distance out of the back window."

"On shore?" Mason asked.

"No, out on the water," she said, "a ship's lantern I suppose."

Mason, with Dorothy and Mildred, entered the cabin and peered through the single window.

A very dim light, probably in the far distance, was visible. "There are plenty of trading vessels about," he finally said.

"May be nothing," Mildred said. "I just thought you should know."

Mason nodded. "We'll keep an eye on it."

With the moon up and everyone back on deck, they each searched the coast. The long, unbroken white-sand curve of the shoreline in the distance put them in the right area. It was just a matter of spotting the inlet.

"I think that's it," Tito said, as he pointed.

Mason followed Tito's gaze and focused. "I think you're right."

John turned to starboard putting the ship into the wind.

With instructions not necessary, Mason, Tito, and Nathan immediately lowered the mainsail when it went slack.

John turned the wheel to port and let the jib pull the bow back around in line with the dark area on the shoreline. He let the sloop creep along until it was a hundred yards off shore.

Mason and Nathan furled the jib while Tito and Tom brought the jolly boat alongside. Two hours of rowing and maneuvering put the sloop well inside the inlet where they had anchored before.

"Any idea of the time?" Mason asked, as he glanced at the non-existent watch on his wrist.

"Has to be eleven or so," John said.

"We might as well sleep here and enter camp in the morning," Mason said.

Early the next morning, they used the Jolly boat to ferry everyone except John and Tom to shore. The two of them would remain aboard.

Mason and Tito helped Mato and his braves with their provisions. Negotiations this time had netted them significant goods—mostly camp utensils, more muskets, powder, shot, some cloth, and bags of rice. Mato also picked up an extra axe and shovel. Everything was bound together into bundles. It would take more than one trip to get it all to the village.

Just as everyone going ashore was ashore, Angie and Travis showed up to gather the day's catch. Angie, especially, was giddy at seeing the ship and the others.

"We thought you had gotten lost at sea," Angie said.

"Took longer than we expected, but we accomplished a lot," Dorothy said. "We now own a plantation."

At the camp, everyone crowded around the arrivals.

Manny extended his hand to Mason. "Glad you're back."

"Anything exciting while we were gone?"

"Nope, same old-same old," he said.

"We own a plantation," Angie announced. Her face suddenly turned serious. "What does that mean for Travis and me?"

Mason proceeded to describe the plantation in detail, the crops, and the potential for long term survival. Lastly, he explained about the fifty slaves, the need for manpower to work the land, and the plan he and Dorothy had discussed to improve the lifestyle for those who agreed to stay after they were freed.

"That's about all we can do," Dorothy said. "We now live in a time that is much different from our own. We will try to apply our values as much as possible. But our goal is to survive."

While the rest of the camp continued to discuss the prospects of living on a plantation, Mason pulled Angie and Travis aside.

"You have my solemn promise that I'll do everything in my power to ensure no harm comes to you two," Mason said.

Travis took hold of Angie's hand. "We'll do whatever we have to," he said.

"You may have to play a role at times," Mason said, "but we'll survive, maybe even prosper."

Angie and Travis nodded and walked off together.

Mason walked back to the center of camp and raised his hand to get everyone's attention. "There's nothing keeping us here. We have a house and we have the means to subsist. I suggest we pack up what we need or want, load ourselves on the ship, and head out. We can work out the details once were at the plantation."

"Where's Jeremy and Lisa?" Manny asked, as he scanned the camp. "And Karen."

"The three of them remained behind at the plantation. As of today, we are the owners."

"Well actually Jeremy and Lisa," Dorothy said. "Their names are on the papers."

"For appearances," Mason said. "We all own the property and we all have a place to live. If anyone decides to head out, they'll always have a place to come back to."

"Jeremy and Lisa are married," Dorothy said.

"What?" Gail asked.

"Oh yeah," Mason said. "I forgot that part. The two of them were getting close anyhow, and we thought a married couple on the deed would look better to the town's people. So, they got married."

"We'll explain more about the plantation and work out all the details of who does what later," Dorothy said. "For now, we should just get moving."

Everyone except Manny meandered off in various directions.

He stood in the center of camp and slowly turned in a circle. He finally glanced at Mason standing nearby. "I've gotten used to this place."

Mason tightened his lips and nodded. "You'll get used to the new place. We're going to need your skills."

Manny remained quiet as he continued to look around the camp. He finally nodded, turned, and walked off.

CHAPTER 24

By the time Mato, his braves, along with Mason and Manny had finished ferrying the Indian's goods to their village, it was too late in the day for the survivors to head out. It was just as well. They needed to process some drinking water for the trip.

Late in the day, Angie and Travis made their final visit to the fish trap. Mason tagged along, mainly because he had nothing else to do and it would take his mind off the coming transition. They walked the length of the beach like always.

While Travis and Angie gathered what fish there was and dismantled the trap, Mason checked in with John and Tom. They would remain on the ship for the night. All was well. John had mended a couple of new holes in the mainsail and there were several other minor issues he wanted to tackle before they headed out the next morning.

Mason returned to camp with Travis and Angie, and the day's catch. They roasted the fish for dinner, and everyone sat around the camp's fire for the last time to eat and talk. Even Nathan seemed like he was in a good mood.

After dinner, Mason carried the leftover fish, wrapped in palm fronds, down to John and Tom. He sat on the deck with them while they ate.

"I like the idea of running cargo up and down the coast," Mason said. "We can supplement the income from the plantation and get it paid off that much faster."

"It's an interesting life these people had," John said. "Simple. I like simple. I'm not sure I would go back to our time even if we could."

"It's a tough life, but satisfying," Tom said. "And a little smelly." Tom stared at Mason.

Mason didn't get his meaning at first until he considered his linen coat and breeches.

Tom cocked his head.

Mason tried to remember the last time he had a bath. It had been a while, just before his encounter with Karen on the boat. He glanced at his clothes again. There were several stains and suddenly he was aware of his own stench. He needed a bath. Mason nodded. "I should probably visit the stream in back of the camp before it gets completely dark."

Tom raised an eyebrow and nodded.

John smiled. "Wouldn't hurt."

As the sun began to set, Mason made his way back to camp. Having left his buckskins on the ship, he retrieved his jeans and t-shirt from the hut, and walked down to the stream.

All the others in camp had already turned in except Dorothy and Manny. They sat around the camp fire talking.

Mason stripped down, waded into the stream and dunked himself under the water. He scrubbed at his hair and beard with his fingers and rinsed. He next grabbed a handful of bottom sand and used its coarseness to scrub every inch of his skin. It wasn't the same as soap, but it was the best he could do under the circumstances. With a final dunk to remove all the sand, he took a few moments to let the cool water ease the tension from his muscles. This had been home for a while. He thought back over the days since they had arrived. He recalled the plane crash, their quest for food and water, meeting Mato, the huts, the many meals around the campfire, and the people. In his mind's eye he saw Karen scurrying around camp. He saw her with that frustrated expression on her face, and he saw her laugh. He tried to remember when he first felt the attraction. He saw himself walking up to the gate at the airport. It was then. The first minute they had met. He had no idea what the future held for the survivors, but he intended to spend as much time as possible with Karen.

Finally, Mason dunked under the surface a final time, stood in a shower of droplets, and used his fingers to comb his hair back. He shuffled his feet along the sandy bottom to the water's edge and quickly slipped into his jeans, t-shirt, and boots. He rolled his dirty linens into a ball and walked back into camp. He nodded at Dorothy and Manny still talking around the fire, entered his hut, and curled up on the mat envisioning Karen lying beside him. He fell asleep to the loud rackety hum of the crickets.

◆◆◆

The next morning Mason was up early. He could see a glow on the eastern horizon which told him sunup would be in about thirty minutes. Wanting to get an early start, he slipped into his shoulder rig, holstered the Glock, and went about rousting everyone from their slumber.

Reluctantly, everyone was up and ready just as the sun broke free. They all grabbed what they were taking and headed for the beach.

Mason took one final glance around the camp, kicked a little extra sand on the smoldering camp fire, and walked off to catch up with the others.

As soon as he broke through the tree line at the beach, he came to an abrupt stop behind everyone else. They were all staring out across the water.

There, in the dim light of early morning, stood a large sailing ship. Two masts. Sails down. A bit of jib was visible. It just stood there about a mile or so off shore with its port side facing the land. There didn't appear to be any activity on deck, but a black flag with a speck of red tossed in the breeze from the stern. It was too far away to see what emblem was on the flag.

"What are they doing?" Nathan finally asked.

"Waiting," Dorothy said.

"For what?"

"For us," Manny replied.

Mason nodded. "Yep."

Dorothy turned around and locked on Mason's eyes. "The ship we saw in the dark."

Mason shrugged his shoulders.

Manny turned around to face Mason. "Now what?"

"We head for the sloop," he said. "Maybe they're sleeping."

"Somehow I doubt that," Dorothy said.

The group began hurrying down the beach with everyone's head facing the sailing ship.

The hulk continued to undulate, like a skeleton standing on the water. Its masts rocked gently back and forth.

Mason caught up to Dorothy. "The black flag?"

"It's a pirate's vessel," she said. "Each pirate had their own emblem, almost always on a field of black. Sight of the flag alone often brought the prey to their knees, to just give up without a fight."

"Maybe we should do that," Nathan said.

"Most people didn't fair very well when they came in contact with a pirate," Dorothy said, "whether they gave up or not. The only thing that gave most pirates cause for alarm was a large British ship of the line."

Mason scanned the horizon. "I think we're fresh out of ships of the line."

Somehow the sloop seemed smaller than before when Mason came around the bend and could see it in full view. John and Tom already had the jolly boat brought around. Tom was climbing in to row it to shore.

It took two trips to get the fifteen survivors on board. No one spoke and they rowed as quietly as possible. John secured the jolly boat to the stern and removed the lashings from the mainsail.

The pirate ship remained unstirred during the entire process.

"What are they doing?" Manny asked, standing next to Mason on the deck.

Everyone, except John and Tom, watched the ship in the distance.

"They're trying to scare us," Mason replied. "And I'd say it's working."

Mason, followed by Manny, stepped to where John and Tom were working the sheets to hoist the mainsail. He glanced at Mason. "Let's see if the current will ease us out. The tide is up and we have plenty of water under the keel. As soon as we clear the sandbar, we raise the sail and make a run for it."

"Can we outrun that ship?" Manny asked.

"If we had a clean hull, maybe," John replied.

Manny looked at Mason. "Did you guys clean the hull while you were gone?"

Mason tightened his lips and shook his head.

As the sloop started to move with the current, Mason spotted activity on the pirate ship. He gestured in the direction of the hulk. "They're up."

Mason watched the crewmen, tiny in the distance, scurry about the deck, climb the rat lines, and begin hoisting the sails. Within minutes, the large ship was moving.

"They'll have to turn out, into the wind, to come about," John said. "Maybe we can slip past them on the inside, but we'll need all the sail we have including both jibs."

Mason nodded, motioned to Manny to follow, and then dashed off toward the bow.

Just past the opening to the inlet, only a few yards past the sandbar, John turned the wheel and motioned for Tom and Nathan to hoist the main.

Mason and Manny began to unfurl the jibs.

The men pulled with all their might to raise the sails as quickly as possible.

As the boat came around to starboard, the main and both jibs filled with close reach air. The craft leaned to starboard as it picked up speed and gradually pulled away from the coast.

The pirate ship was nearly full circle with its crew still releasing sail when the sloop passed its bow with three hundred yards between them.

Mason watched as the sloop increased its lead, but each agonizing yard seemed to take forever. Within minutes, with the big ship at full sail, the separation began to fade. Mason tightened his fists as he stood at the gunwale and subtly shook his head. *Helplessness is a terrible thing*, he thought. He felt the muscles in his neck tighten and the hairs stand up signaling that sense of anxiety when control is slipping away. He turned to face John at the helm; they locked eyes. Mason saw John's chin move subtly back and forth.

Mason gazed up at the full and perfectly trimmed sail. He glanced at the jibs, also trimmed perfectly in the morning's breeze, at least according to his meager understanding of sailing. He stepped across the slightly pitched deck to the helm. "Anything we can do to increase speed?"

"If we turn more into the wind to gain ocean, we'll lose speed. And we obviously can't turn into the coast. We're doing the best we can."

"It's not enough," Mason said, as he glanced at the big ship off their port quarter.

"I know," John said. "We're dragging a boat load of barnacles."

"How many guns on that thing?" Mason asked.

"It's a large schooner. Ten guns in total."

Mason scanned the sloop's deck. Everyone stood at the gunwale watching the big ship match their pace. The expression on everyone face told the story. Scared would be an understatement.

Mason thought of throwing a few rounds of 9mm at the big ship, but at three hundred yards on a moving deck, he doubted he could even hit the thing. There was literally nothing he could do, except what everyone else was doing. Watch.

After an hour at their best speed, the sloop was about two miles off shore. The pirate's ship was still three hundred yards off, but it had pulled abreast of the sloop. The pirate captain could open his doors and fire a broadside anytime he wanted. Mason was sure the pirate would have done just that if there was any chance the sloop could outpace the bigger ship. Mason wondered if the captain intended to take the sloop undamaged. *Not likely*, he thought. The sloop was probably too small for their purposes, and worse, it had no armament. More likely he was just trying to terrorize the people on the sloop, like a cat playing with a mouse.

"Prepare to come about," John yelled. He turned his head to Mason. "This sloop, even with the extra drag, has two advantages over that schooner."

"I'm listening," Mason said.

"We can turn tighter and we can probably head into the wind faster," John said. "We come about to starboard, continue almost full circle, and head due south into the wind across her stern."

"Tell me what to do," Mason said.

John gave Mason, Nathan, Tito, and Tom precise instructions on what to do and when. With everyone in position he turned the wheel.

The sloop immediately turned downwind, toward the shore, and continued the circle until it was headed almost due south, close hauled against the wind.

Mason and the others did their part to trim the sail and jibs precisely as John had instructed.

Just as expected the sloop cut across the schooner's course line two hundred yard to aft.

Mason saw a scurry of activity on the schooner's deck as the ship began to turn to port, directly into the wind away from the coast.

The sloop's maneuver alone put an extra hundred yards between the two vessels, and for the first time since they started out that morning Mason thought they might have a chance. The only bad part was they were now headed directly out to sea away from Charles Town.

CHAPTER 25

As the schooner's bow came around, there were a few moments when the big ship's broadside was directly lined up with the sloop's starboard quarter.

Mason noted that the gun doors on their port side were already open. "They're going to fire," he yelled. "Get down!"

A beat later a loud *boom* echoed across the water followed by four more in rapid succession. Thick smoke bellowed from the schooner's side.

The first cannonball splashed fifty yards in front of the sloop. The next hit the water twenty-five yards in front and skipped across the surface. The third put a cannonball sized hole, more of a split, in the sloop's mainsail. The other two balls fell harmlessly to stern.

Mason raised his head above the gunwale. The schooner's bow had come around which meant they would not be able to fire again. At this point it was a race against the wind. Mason peered at the hole in the sail and made his way to the helm. "Any other tricks up your sleeve?"

"If we can maintain a lead until dark, we might have a chance," John said.

"That's eleven or twelve hours," Mason reminded him.

"All we can do now is hope that hole doesn't get any bigger."

After two hours of maintaining the optimal angle on the wind, Mason gauged that the gap between the two vessels had actually widened.

"They must be dragging some barnacles too," John said. "And they're having to tack a little with those square top sails."

After five hours the gap had widened even more. The schooner was still there and still coming on strong, but it was being out paced by the sloop's lighter hull and sleek lines. Barring a catastrophe, the sloop would be well ahead by dark.

With Tom at the helm, Mason and John stood in the shadow of the mainsail and sipped water.

Dorothy and Manny joined them.

"This might work," Manny said, as he glanced at the schooner in the distance.

John nodded his chin up and down. "We might get lucky at that." He glanced up at the sail and suddenly the optimistic expression disappeared from his face.

Mason looked up. The split had grown longer, not by much but definitely longer. "Can we climb up there and put in a couple of stitches?"

"Not under sail," John said. "We'd have to heave to for that."

"We have a pretty good lead," Manny said.

"Not enough," John said. "We keep going and hope we run out of daylight before that hole gets much bigger."

"Would it help to tack?" Mason asked.

"We don't want to put a sudden strain on the cloth," John said. "We've gone this long without a significant change in speed; let's hope she can stay together a bit longer."

"That's a lot of hoping," Dorothy said.

John lifted his chin in agreement.

Manny turned in a circle scanning the open ocean in all directions. "Can you find your way back? I have no idea which way is land."

"North," John said. "We can use the North Star at night or wait for the sun tomorrow."

"You don't seem all that worried," Manny said.

"It is what it is," John said. "All we can do is our best. Beyond that, it's out of our hands."

Mason clapped John on the shoulder. "I'm just glad you survived that plane crash."

"God, that seems so long ago," John said.

Mason nodded. He left the others as he made his way along the rolling deck. He stopped at each person or group of people to reassure them, let them know the plan, and to answer their questions.

He found Mildred, her dog, and Lana inside the aft cabin.

"I've got a bad feeling about his," Mildred said. Her face was pale, and she didn't look so good.

"You might feel better out on deck," Mason said.

"With cannonballs flying around, I'll stay right here," she said.

Mason glanced at Lana.

"We'll be fine here," she said.

Mason stepped over to the stern window. He saw the schooner still behind them with no sign of them giving up. He wondered what kind of captain commanded the vessel. He turned to Mildred and Lana. "Did either of you see what kind of emblem was on that ship's flag."

"A full-length skeleton in red," Lana said.

Mason nodded as he turned back to the window. He didn't know what that meant, but Dorothy mentioned every pirate had a distinct flag. He gazed at the schooner in the distance a few moments more and turned to leave. "If you start feeling worse, it will help to be on deck," he said to Mildred.

Mildred sat on the deck with her back reclined against a bulkhead and her eyes closed. She didn't bother to answer.

Lana smiled.

Mason exited the cabin and joined Manny and Dorothy at the bow. "Full length red skeleton," Mason said, "any idea whose flag that would be."

Dorothy snorted. "There were only so many pirates in this area at this time. That would be Edward Low. Ned to his friends. I wrote a paper on him."

"Anything we need to know?" Mason asked.

"He was ruthless, tortured his victims," Dorothy said. "He normally operated farther north, New York and Boston."

"Why is he after us?" Manny asked.

"It wouldn't be for this sloop or its potential cargo," Dorothy said. "I can think of only one reason."

"That was his silver," Mason said.

Dorothy nodded.

"At least two crewmen steal the chest and scurry away in the night on the jolly boat," Mason said. "They die at sea, and the boat washes up on our shore."

"Lucky us," Manny said.

"Sounds reasonable," Dorothy agreed. "Probably heard about us spending Spanish dollars in Charles Town."

"His Spanish dollars," Manny said.

Mason nodded. "So, he's pissed and ruthless."

"We've got a problem," John yelled. He pointed to the mainsail.

The rip had grown. And then, as Mason watched, the rip tripled in size. Mason rushed aft and peered over the gunwale to the rear. The large schooner was still in sight but just barely. He turned to John at the helm. "Are we slowing?"

"Yep," he said, "we've lost our advantage in speed. The schooner will be on us in two or three hours at this rate."

"So, we heave to and fix the sail," Mason said. "We can be underway again in half an hour."

"We don't have that much thread," John said. "And even if we did, it wouldn't hold."

"So, we're helpless," Manny said, as he stepped closer.

"Pretty much," John said.

"How many crew on that ship?" Mason asked, as Dorothy arrived at the helm.

"Forty or so," Dorothy said.

Mason nodded his chin up and down. "As I see it, we have to stand and fight. We drop the sails to eliminate any reason for them to fire at us, let them approach, and bam." He patted the Glock in its holster.

"Forty men, with muskets, swords, and daggers," Manny said. "And we have one pistol."

"One pistol with ninety-eight rounds that fire very quickly," Mason said. "It's all we have."

Manny tightened his lips and nodded. "Let's heave to."

The sloop bobbed on a nearly flat ocean. The moderate wind was enough to fill a sail, but it wasn't enough to stir up significant waves.

The survivors watched and waited at the port gunwale, broadside on the approaching schooner.

Two hundred yards out the schooner's crew began reducing sail as the big ship continued forward. It was moving much too fast to stop anywhere near the sloop.

Mason glanced at John standing next to him. "Either the captain intends to veer off at the last minute or—"

"—ram us," John said. "Given his reputation, according to Dorothy, I'm guessing the latter."

Mason swiveled his head. Everyone except Mildred, Lana, Koji, Asumi, and Hana were on deck. "You'll be safer in the cabin or down below," Mason said in a raised voice.

Everyone except John and Manny began moving.

"There's nothing you two can do up here."

"Just the same, I'm staying," Manny said.

Mason looked at John. "We might need you later."

John took in a deep breath and exhaled. He tightened his lips, turned, and started off toward the cabin.

Mason glanced at Manny. "Stay with me," he said, as he dashed off toward the bow.

The two of them ducked low as they slid into the tight spot.

"Better angle from here," Mason said, as he lifted his head enough to see over the gunwale. He pulled the Glock, removed the magazine and slammed it back home. He extended both arms over the top of the railing.

The big ship was within a hundred yards when it began turning to port bringing the first of its guns to bear.

"This is an unarmed vessel," Manny said. "They must know that."

"If they fire, it will be to teach us a lesson."

At that very moment Mason heard the loud *boom* of one of the schooner's guns and immediately felt the entire boat shudder from the impact of a ball against the hull amid ship. He stuck his head up and saw a large cloud of smoke bellow across the water and engulf the sloop. Multiple *cracks* of musket fire followed. The balls splintered the surrounding wood.

Suddenly Manny jumped up and began running toward the cabin. It appeared he was running away from the fire, but knowing Manny the way Mason did, Mason knew exactly what he was doing. Drawing fire away from the bow so Mason could get some rounds off.

Just as intended, the musket balls followed Manny. Mason heard them *thump* into the deck. Mason had to take advantage of the diversion and tore his eyes away from Manny, still devoid of any musket ball holes.

Mason brought his attention back to the schooner and immediately acquired several targets visible on its upper deck. Mason took aim and squeezed as he rapidly moved from one target to the next. He saw several men fall in the wake of his gunfire.

Mason caught sight of the man whom had to be the captain. He wore a bright blue coat and a matching three-point hat with a feather. He stood aft near the helm. Two other men stood next to him.

Mason took careful aim, squeezed the trigger, and saw the man closest to the captain fall.

The captain glanced at the downed man.

Mason ducked while he changed magazines. He felt the man's eyes bore into the spot where Mason was hunched behind the gunwale. He heard another loud *boom* and glanced back just in time to see two cannonballs connected by a chain fly through the air almost in slow motion. The chain-shot sliced through Manny's torso in a cascade of blood and tissue and then tore into the aft cabin in an explosion of fragmented wood.

Mason could only imagine the damage it had done to those hiding inside. He turned his head back to the schooner as musket fire raked the wood above and around him. He raised up and fired all fifteen rounds in rapid succession. He didn't wait to see if he had hit anyone before he ducked back below the top rail. *It's time to move.*

He changed magazines and crawled across the deck dragging his rucksack behind him. Musket balls *thumped* into the wood as he moved. Being careful to keep himself concealed as much as possible, he got to a kneeling position behind the thick wood base of the mast. Musket balls landed against the wood in a dull *thud*. It was then that he heard the crying and moaning from the aft cabin. And it was then that he realized his efforts were futile. He would die here, on the deck of an eighteenth-century sloop three hundred years in the past. But not before he exhausted all of his ammunition. He thought of Karen and how he had promised to return soon. It appeared he wouldn't be keeping that promise. And the worst part was she would likely never know what became of him and the other survivors. He closed his eyes for several moments. He felt the moisture accumulate in the corners and felt the tears roll down his cheek. He glanced back at the shredded wood of the aft cabin and saw Dorothy prone on the deck in the open doorway. A mass of blood had soaked through the layers of fabric and pooled on her back. He shook his head and lowered his chin as the tears continued to roll.

After several long moments he wiped both cheeks with the sleeves of his t-shirt and then tried to focus on the schooner. The moisture in his eyes clouded his vision. He wiped both cheeks again, refocused, and brought the Glock up. He extended his arms around the mast while keeping most of his body concealed. He jerked his head over to take aim looking for the captain.

Before he could find his target, he heard another loud *boom* and immediately felt the boat shudder violently. The thick mast before him exploded in a shower of wood. Mason felt himself being lifted into the air and flung backwards as the world before him began to darken. The colors muted into gray. Somewhere in his consciousness he felt the wet and coolness of water. The sounds of battle—explosions, men yelling, screams of terror, moans of agony—slowly diminished, as though being separated by a great distance, until all was finally quiet. Time became indistinguishable as his mind swam in a pool of dark confusion. At intermittent intervals he climbed to the edge of consciousness and a sense of drifting only to sink rapidly back into the dark void. Deep, somewhere in his mind, he saw a synaptic spark of blue among vague, constantly changing, colorless shapes. And then all went completely dark.

CHAPTER 26

Mason heard voices. They were muffled and far away. He struggled to understand the words but all his mind could discern was a mass of unintelligible sounds. He felt pressure on his left bicep. He fought to open his eyes, clawing his way up. Before he reached the surface, the sounds faded, the pressure on his arm subsided, and he fell back into darkness.

His mind stirred. Images flashed. An explosion of wood and smoke, submerged in water, cradled by the cool water. He drifted below flashes of orange and red. And then darkness.

"Mister Mason, you need to wake up now."

The words were distant and vague, like they were being shouted from the next mountain. He struggled to clear his mind. He felt the weight of his eyelids, grogginess, and a dull pain in his head.

"Mister Mason, I need you to wake up."

He felt something prod against his shoulder and felt pressure against his cheek. He saw a flash of white light, as bright as he had ever seen.

"Mister Mason, you're almost there. Wake up."

Mason opened both eyes and winced at the brightness. He snapped his eyes shut.

"It's okay, you're safe. I need you to open your eyes."

Mason opened his eyes and saw a blurry image—a man hunched over him. He blinked to clear his vision and slowly the man came into focus.

"Welcome back, Mister Mason," the man said.

Mason struggled in his mind to put words together. He licked his lips. "Where am I?" he mumbled almost incoherently.

"You're in a hospital," the voice said. "I'm Doctor Turner."

Mason focused on the man's face. Finally, the details began to register—thin, white hair, clean shaven, metal framed glasses, and a white smock.

"What happened?" Mason asked.

"You were in an accident," Turner said. "But you'll be fine."

Mason became aware of the tubes protruding from his arm. He felt some discomfort in his groin and reached down.

Turner caught Mason's arm before his hand reached the source of discomfort.

"You're on an IV, and you have a catheter," Turner said. "Don't touch it. We'll be removing it soon."

"What about the others?" Mason mumbled.

"The others?"

"On the boat," Mason said in a slightly raised voice.

"I don't know anything about that, but there are some gentlemen anxious to speak to you," Turner said. "Give us a little while to make you more comfortable and we'll let them in. For now, just lie back and relax."

Mason lifted his hand and touched his forehead. He felt a gauze bandage that encircled his head.

"You sustained a nasty bump on the head. You have a concussion, but you'll be fine. We've conducted numerous scans. There's no permanent damage."

Mason felt a squeeze on his shoulder.

"Just rest."

Mason felt pressure building around his bicep. He reached for it.

"It's just a blood pressure cuff," Turner said. "We need to keep that in place for a while."

Mason felt the pressure release. He blinked a couple of times, inhaled deeply, and closed his eyes. He tried to relax, but suddenly Karen's face flashed in his mind. He opened his eyes.

The doctor was gone, but a nurse was next to the bed straightening his covers.

"What city am I in?" he asked.

"Jacksonville, Florida," the nurse replied. "But you need to lie back and rest. I'm sure all your questions will be answered soon."

Mason nodded and rested his head back against the pillow. He closed his eyes. He tried to remember the sequence of events that brought him to this place. He remembered leaving Karen at the plantation, and he remembered himself with the others on the sloop. The rest of it was just bits and pieces of jumbled images that became more confused the more he tried to remember. He tried to clear his mind. Slowly, he felt the tension at his temples begin to release.

He felt a discomfort in his groin and a stinging in his penis. He opened his eyes and focused on two nurses.

One of them smiled. She was young and pretty. "We're taking the catheter out. You'll feel much better in a few minutes."

The pressure he felt was replaced by an intense stinging. He put his head back and closed his eyes.

"Doctor Turner will be in to see you in a little while," the nurse said.

"He was just here," Mason mumbled.

"That was yesterday," the nurse said. "Don't worry, you'll be up and about in nothing flat." She tidied the covers over his legs. "We'll be back in a little while." Both nurses left the room.

Mason immediately reached down and massaged his penis. It began to feel better. He gazed through the window at the tops of trees and buildings. He surveyed the room. It was sparse, with only one chair in the corner, and a bedside retractable table with a pitcher of water and a glass. Electrical instruments and monitors lined the wall behind him. He tried to remember how long he had been there but finally gave up with no earthly idea.

After a few minutes there was a knock on the door. It swung open.

Doctor Turner walked in with the pretty nurse. "How are we today?" He turned to the nurse. "Is the catheter out?"

"Yes, a few minutes ago," she said.

He continued until he stood at Mason's bedside. "Do you remember anything?"

"Yes," Mason said.

"Do you remember being on an airplane?"

"Yes."

"Do you remember how you got in the water?"

"Mostly," Mason said.

"So, you remember the crash?"

"We didn't crash," Mason said. "We ditched."

Turner paused for several moments. He took out a small flashlight and shined it into each eye. He stuck the flashlight back in his pocket and stared at Mason for several moments. "Okay, do you remember what you were doing before you got on the plane?"

"I was hurrying to the gate."

"Good." Turner studied Mason's face for a few moments. "Do you feel up to visitors? There're some men who would like to ask you about the airliner and what happened."

"No problem," Mason said, as he reached for the glass of water. He took a sip through a straw. "When does the IV come out?"

"Probably later today, after we get you up and walking."

Mason nodded.

"The gentlemen will be in shortly," Turner said, as he headed for the door. "I'll check in later." He turned and exited.

"Is there anything you need?" the nurse asked, as she moved the bedside table closer. "Do you need the bed pan?"

"No, I'm fine for now," Mason said. He glanced at the needle in his arm and the tube running up to a bag of clear liquid on a metal hanger. "Can you take this out now?"

"Soon, Mister Mason. I'm sure we'll have it out before this evening."

Mason took in a deep breath and exhaled. He didn't like being sick, and he didn't like waiting, but it appeared he didn't have a choice. "Okay."

The nurse went to the door and pulled it open revealing two men in suits. One was Mike Reeves. The nurse left and the two men entered.

"Hey, Mase, you're looking a lot better than I last saw you," Reeves said.

Reeves was just as Mason remembered him. He always wore a suit and tie. He had a slight pouch, but was otherwise in excellent shape for a man of fifty. He still wore his dark hair short. He said it showed less of the gray patches.

"This is Dan Miller with FAA," Reeves said.

The man was also dressed in a gray suit. He was much younger, medium height and weight. He was ordinary but with a serious expression.

"We have a few questions," Reeves continued. "Do you feel up to it?"

"I'm fine," Mason said. "A bit of a headache."

"We won't take too much of your time," Miller said. "We just want to get some preliminary information. We can work on the details later as needed."

Mason nodded.

Miller scanned the room, apparently for a chair, and ended up leaning against the window sill.

Reeves stood at the foot of the bed.

Both men took out a pen and a pad.

Miller produced a small recorder and placed it on the bedside table. "We need to record all questioning," Miller said.

"No problem," Mason said, as he adjusted himself in bed to raise his torso against the pillows. "Shoot."

Miller switched on the recorder. "Interview of Stephen Mason. The date is June twenty third, twenty nineteen, University of Florida Hospital, Jacksonville,

Florida. The time is ten fifteen AM. Those present are myself, Daniel Miller, FAA, Mike Reeves, Federal Air Marshal's Service, and Stephen Mason, Federal Air Marshal's Service."

They both made notations on their pad.

"What can you remember about the flight?" His voice was direct, even toned, almost fatherly.

Mason had listened to everything the man said, but not much registered after *June twenty third, twenty nineteen*. That was only four days after he boarded the plane to Charlotte. Mason did not let his expression change as he tried to wrap his mind around that single concept. Obviously, he had returned to his own time period within days of the event even though he had been gone for months.

"Mister Mason."

Mason raised his chin.

Reeves smiled. "He's been through a lot. Give him a moment."

Miller relaxed the pen in his hand and nodded. "When you're ready."

"The flight," Mason finally said. "It was normal out of Miami."

"Yes, and?" Reeves asked.

Mason's mind spun. If he told the truth, they would think he had completely lost his mind. He could make things easier and say he couldn't remember. He was in his seat on the plane and the next thing he knew he was in the water. In reality, today's reality, that was the truth. But it wasn't his truth.

"Mister Mason?" Miller prompted.

Mason adjusted his pillows. "Everything was fine until we were about an hour out of Charlotte." He explained how Karen had informed him of the loss of nav instruments and his visit to the cockpit where the captain confirmed the loss of all navigation except the Inertial Reference System. He repeated Captain Anderson's description of the sudden loss of all contact from the outside including the radio.

Miller tapped his pad with his pen as he considered the information.

"Did the captain have any idea as to why?" Reeves asked.

"Not really," Mason said. "We passed through a storm, but otherwise it all just went out."

"And all other systems on the plane were working correctly?" Miller asked.

"According to the captain and first officer, they were. Only nav and the radio were affected. Basically, they weren't receiving any kind of signals from the outside."

"So, what caused the plane to crash?" Miller asked.

The point of no return, Mason thought. Crossing this threshold with the truth meant he'd be labeled a lunatic. He thought of Karen, Lisa, and Jeremy at the plantation, and he thought of all those who had apparently perished on the sloop at the hands of Edward Low, a pirate—an eighteenth-century pirate who died three hundred years ago. Even Mason found it hard to believe.

What the hell, in for a penny in for a pound. "We didn't crash. We ditched."

"The captain ditched." Miller stated rhetorically.

Miller cocked his head, as did Reeves, the two of them almost in unison.

"Flight controls are working fine, you have fuel, any one of a number of airports is a few minutes away, and he ditched," Miller said.

Mason nodded his head up and down. "Actually, we had no fuel and there were no airports. We had no place to put her down."

"I don't understand," Miller said.

"We continued on the route, flew over Charlotte, flew over Savannah, Hilton Head, Columbia, Charleston, and Wilmington. Where once there were sprawling cities, there were only trees. No airports, no runways. We flew around until we were nearly out of fuel. We finally ditched just off the coast of what would be Myrtle Beach."

"What do you mean by *what would be*?" Miller asked.

Mason took a deep breath and exhaled. He proceeded to tell them the entire story. He went through the sequence of events on the plane and the ditching. He talked about how the survivors washed up on a deserted and desolate Myrtle Beach, their efforts to find food and water, the death of Captain Anderson, their encounter with the Catawba Indians, the chest of Spanish silver dollars, their trip to early Charles Town, the sloop, the plantation, and the battle with Edward Low. He described everything in detail including the plantation's location, the house, number of rooms, the property, the fields, and the people, including the surveyor, the barrister, Mrs. Stewart, and the slaves. And, of course, he described how Karen, Lisa, and Jeremy came to remain behind.

When Mason finally stopped talking Miller walked over and flipped the recorder off. He glanced at Reeves.

"All of this is clear in your mind, there's no fogginess?" Reeves asked.

"It's clear," Mason said. "It happened. Look, I know my story is impossible to believe, I hardly believe it." Mason pinched between his eyes and reengaged Miller. "Did you find any wreckage from the plane? Any bodies besides mine?"

"No," Miller said. "When we lost contact with the plane, we initiated the regular protocol. A search was up and running within an hour. You were found floating in the water unconscious, draped over a piece of wood, eighteen hours after we lost contact. You were fished out of the water and brought here. The search was, still is, being managed from here, Jacksonville."

"Where was I found?" Mason asked.

"You were eighty miles off the coast, north of where the plane was when we lost contact. We presumed the plane went down close to where you were found. We've concentrated our search around that area. We're still searching, but so far there are no signs of anything. Just you. And you've been unconscious since they brought you in three days ago."

"How did you find me in all that water?"

"Some fishermen spotted you, pulled you on deck, and called it in," Reeves said.

"Pings off the black box?"

"No," Miller said. "We never got any pings. We've concentrated our search around where you were found. So far, we have zip. Except you."

"How do you explain that?" Mason asked.

"Plane may have slipped off the continental shelf," Miller said. "We don't know."

"That's two hundred miles out," Mason said.

"We won't have the answers until we find the plane," Miller said.

Reeves nodded. "Let's give him some more time to rest. What do you say we return here tomorrow? Okay with you Mase?"

"Sure, but my story won't change. What about all the people's names I know? How could I know their names?"

Miller cocked his head. "You sat next to Lisa, you talked to Karen and Angie, you had an encounter with

Nathan, Dorothy was in first class with you, along with Travis. You had contact on the plane with most of the prominent characters in your story. For the others, maybe you reviewed the flight manifest and forgot." He shrugged his shoulders.

Mason shook his head but said nothing.

"We'll be back tomorrow," Reeves said.

The two men said their goodbyes, shook hands with Mason, and left.

Mason rested his head back against the pillows. *I wouldn't believe it either.*

CHAPTER 27

Including the three days Mason was unconscious, he spent a total of ten days in the hospital. He was subjected to five more interviews during that time. His story did not change. Upon his release, he returned to Miami and sequestered himself inside his condo, except for a few follow-ups with local doctors and two more interviews, one by FAA and one by his own agency. He stuck to his story.

After a month of rest and recuperation, the TSA concluded that Mason could not be returned to active duty as long as he continued to show signs of mental distress. A month after that, Mason resigned his position as a Federal Air Marshal. Reeves tried to intervene. He tried to convince Mason to give it more time, but Mason was adamant that time would not wipe away the memories. They were not dreams or hallucinations; they were memories.

Mason was fully aware that it didn't have to play out the way it did. He could have told them enough of the truth to make them happy and claim he couldn't remember anything else. He could have lied. He could have described a crash in the ocean never knowing the cause and not knowing how he ended up on that piece of wood. But somehow, to do that, would have denied the memory of Karen, Jeremy and Lisa, Manny, Dorothy, and the others. Even Nathan. Those people followed his lead. They trusted him for guidance. He could not pretend their lives in Charles Town did not happen. It did. Three hundred years ago.

A couple of weeks later Reeves stopped by Mason's condo and tried again to convince him to give it more time.

Mason remained adamant.

As Mason walked Reeves to the door, Reeves handed him a small package.

"What's this?"

"Something to remember us by," Reeves said.

Mason opened the box, lifted the folds of white paper, and stared at the contents.

"It's a replica of your badge. A retirement badge."

"I didn't retire," he said, staring at Reeves.

"I pulled a few strings. You deserve it."

Mason tightened his jaw and extended his hand. "Thank you, Mike."

"I just wish it had worked out differently," Reeves said.

Mason opened the door.

"You take care," Reeves said, as he stepped out. "Call if you need anything."

"I will," Mason said. "Thanks."

A month later, Mason put the condo up for sale. It sold almost immediately, and he closed within thirty days. On the morning of closing, the Salvation Army picked up most of his belongings. He loaded his Prius with a few essentials and headed north on Interstate 95. He didn't know where he would end up; he only knew he needed a new start.

He drove without the radio, eyes fixed on the road, but deep in thought. He contemplated the many scans, the prods, the pokes, the lab exams, the neurologists, sessions with the psychologists, and their conclusions. He had suffered a serious blow to the head. There had been some bleeding in the brain around the hippocampus near the medial temporal lobe. This was the area responsible for memories. What Mason thought he remembered were really just aberrations of the mind created to fill gaps in his memory. Basically, he imagined the whole thing. After all, time travel was impossible.

Their logic was solid. Time travel was impossible. These were experts, and they had seen this sort of thing before. Maybe they were right. But Mason's mind kept coming back to the details and the vividness of those details. He replayed each encounter with Karen through his mind, the kisses, the hugs, and especially their romantic encounter on the boat. He thought about the strong emotion he felt toward her, still felt. Would that be possible with a dream? These were not like dreams which tended to be vague around the edges. To him, it was all real.

After several hours of driving and thinking, Mason's mind was weary and his head hurt. He popped a couple of Tylenols, suggested by the neurologist for his headaches, and washed them down with water from a plastic bottle. He flipped the radio on and searched the channels for something that would take his mind off the past. He came across a talk radio channel and sat back to listen. He tried to focus on what they were saying. The host was discussing the various political happenings in Washington. It was the same type stuff everyone had been talking about when Mason boarded the plane. The president did this, and the president didn't do that. It was as though only a few days had passed, which was exactly what the doctors were trying to get Mason to understand. For the first time since he woke up in the hospital, a sliver of doubt entered his mind.

Forty miles past Savannah he saw the sign for Charleston. It was funny that since waking up in the hospital he had not even thought of visiting the source of his memories. At the last moment he veered into the exit lane and merged onto Highway 17. He made a quick stop for gas and then continued. The sign read sixty-three miles. He was tired, but he had no intention of stopping. He could drive another hour.

It was early evening when he crossed the bridge over the Ashley River, took the first exit toward the visitor's center, and ended up on Bee Street. Of course, the city looked nothing like it did during his latest encounter, but for the most part, the streets were still laid out in a nice grid pattern. There were just a lot more of them.

He drove around making turns at major intersections, first on Rutledge and then on Calhoun, generally where his instinct for direction told him. There were three streets he remembered from old Charles Town: Bay, Meeting, and Broad. As he drove down Calhoun Street, he came upon Meeting Street first. Waiting for the light at the intersection, he spotted a hotel on the southeast corner and decided he had done enough driving for the day. He continued across Meeting Street and pulled into the hotel's drive.

It appeared to be a nice place, probably expensive. But he didn't care what it cost. He just needed a pillow to rest his now throbbing head.

As it turned out, being a Thursday, they had a vacancy. But only for the one night. They were booked for the weekend. That was fine with him. If he decided to stay longer, he'd find something cheaper.

Mason checked in, moved his car to the lot behind the hotel, and found his room. He wasn't hungry, just tired. So, he took a shower, closed the drapes, and fell into bed.

The next morning, he was up early. His head felt much better, and he definitely had an appetite. He ordered a hearty breakfast in the hotel restaurant. While waiting for his food, he took out the new iPhone he had acquired shortly after he arrived back in Miami. He did a search for the oldest homes and structures in Charleston. He was surprised to learn there were several built prior to 1720 that still existed. Colonel William Rhett's home was among them at 54 Hasell Street, just as Dorothy had said. It was built in 1712 according to the article. Another was the Powder Magazine, built in 1713, on Cumberland. He remembered the Powder Magazine; he had walked past it a time or two, but on neither occasion did he pay it much attention. He also learned from the article that the walls that surrounded Charles Town in the early eighteenth century ran along what were now Meeting, Bay, Cumberland, and Water streets. He therefore wouldn't have walked past Colonel Rhett's home. Hasell Street was outside the walls of old Charles Town and he didn't stray outside the walls except on the east side when he followed the surveyor to the canoe landing.

Since it was still early after he finished his meal, he decided to take a walk. He had plenty of time before the twelve o'clock check out, so he left his belongings in the room, stepped out onto the street, and walked to the corner. The old part of the original town was to the south, so he started walking in that direction.

Charleston was a busy, metropolitan city with lots of buildings, people, and cars. The cobblestoned streets that remained of old Charleston didn't even exist at the time he was there last. The streets he walked were all gravel, dirt, and oyster shells.

He continued walking until he came to Hasell Street. Deciding he'd take a look at the Colonel's house, he turned east. He stood in front of the large, three-story dwelling and perused the double entrances. As he suspected, nothing clicked. He had never seen anything like that house before. And even if he had seen it in 1720, a lot had probably changed.

He walked back to Meeting Street and continued south. He soon crossed over Market Street, already starting to get busy, and continued another block to Cumberland. He turned east and within a few yards he stopped in front of the Powder Magazine.

The building was a lot like he remembered. The roof was different, and, of course, the surroundings were much different, but the building was basically the same. Still, a lot had changed. A multi-story parking garage stood where the earthen wall once was. The bastion with cannons pointing to the north that once existed just outside the magazine was now an asphalt road. His version of the magazine, with the wall and cannons, did nothing to support his memories since no one in modern times really knew how the property around the magazine was laid out three hundred years ago. His version really meant nothing. It could be a fabrication of his dreams, or hallucinations, or whatever they were.

He continued along Cumberland, turned on Bay Street, and soon found himself standing in front of the Old Exchange and Provost Dungeon building at the end of Broad Street. This was where he had been called to the Night Watch to answer questions about the dead body on the wharf. But nothing about the building was the same. The original building, tiny in comparison, was gone and, of course, the entire wall was gone. Nothing rang any bells.

He began to think his visit to Charleston had been a stupid idea. What did he hope to prove? Even if it really happened, that was then, and this was now.

He made his way back over to Meeting Street and began walking toward the hotel. Within a block of Calhoun, he saw a sign for the Charleston Museum. He decided that as long as he was in town he might as well take a look.

The museum had just opened when he stepped up to the doors and entered. He paid his fee at the desk where he was handed a map of the various exhibits. He walked around the exhibits but found that except for a few Native American displays, there were almost no artifacts back to 1720 or before. A lot about the old town had been destroyed during the Revolutionary and Civil Wars. Charleston was an impressive place, he concluded, with a lot of history, but none of that helped his cause. He wasn't even sure what his cause was, or why he was walking around Charleston. Doing so just made him question himself even more. Curiosity was rapidly turning into depression. It was time to leave.

On his way out through the lobby a stack of magazines in a chair caught his eye. The colorful cover depicted an artist's rendition of a Native American village. He flipped the pages and began to read the cover article. Apparently, archaeologist had discovered the remains of what they thought was a Native American village in the area of Myrtle Beach. Their dig had produced arrow heads, pottery shards, wood fragments, partial skeletons, and even the remains of a smooth-bore musket. The scientists had no way of knowing which tribe had lived at the site, but they speculated it pretty much had to be one of the several coastal tribes. The bone had been carbon dated to the late seventeenth or early eighteenth centuries.

Mason gazed at photos of the various artifacts and read their captions. He wondered about Mato's village. Was that the one they had found? There were others in the area; it was hard to tell. He flipped the page and immediately froze. His eyes locked on one particular artifact, mostly rust colored with a single spot of silver. The hair stood up on the back of his neck. He focused on the image. There were several engraved letters, barely visible. He could just make out an *82* and the letters *DOM* at the end of an unreadable section. The full inscription immediately came to mind—*Steve Brown, USA, 82nd Airborne, Operation Iraqi Freedom*. It was the bracelet Mason had given to Mato only months earlier.

Mason read the short caption which basically said the scientists had found it next to a skeleton and they had no explanation for its existence at that site, especially given the depth and context. It was a mystery.

At last he knew for sure. His memories were not aberrations of the mind; he lived them. He slowly closed the magazine, returned it to the stack, and closed his eyes. He knew where he had to go next.

CHAPTER 28

Mason checked out of the hotel and headed west back across the Ashley River. Just past the west bank he veered onto State Road 61 and drove northwest. About seven miles up the two-lane road, he turned off onto an asphalt drive. Thick trees and brush lined the drive up to an aluminum gate and beyond. An elderly man, probably in his seventies, had just closed the gate and stood watching as Mason pulled up. The man's pickup truck was parked, still running, just beyond the gate.

Mason stuck his head out the window. "Excuse me."

The man raised his chin.

"I'm doing research for a book about South Carolina plantations. I saw your property on Google Maps and was wondering if I could ask you a few questions."

The man rubbed his clean-shaven chin. He checked the watch on his arm. "I have a couple of minutes."

Mason stepped out of the Prius and approached. "Thank you; I won't take much of your time." He stuck out his hand and stepped closer to the gate. "I'm Stephen."

The man reached over the gate and took Mason's hand. "Fred."

"You have a beautiful piece of property," Mason said. "Google Maps indicates plenty of open fields. This must have been one of the bigger plantations back in the day."

"Started out with rice in the flatlands along the river; food crops on higher ground," Fred said. "It's been in my family for three hundred years."

"The house as well?"

"No that was burned down twice, Revolution and Civil Wars. The core of the current house was built in 1875. We've been adding on ever since."

Mason turned in a three-sixty and scanned the surrounding forests. The house was not visible through the trees.

"We don't get many visitors," Fred said. "Put the gate up to keep the kids from driving through."

"It must be something."

Fred nodded. "You look like a nice-enough fellow, would you like to see the property close up?"

"I would," Mason said. "Thank you."

Fred opened the gate wide. "Just pull your car up behind the truck."

Mason returned to the Prius, pulled slowly through the gate, and followed the pickup down a winding drive. After seventy-five yards the trees gave way to a broad open area of mostly grass with a few large, sparsely placed oaks. The house stood in the distance. It was nothing like the original. The new house was all red brick. It was large but not massive. Five white-framed windows on the top floor and two on each side of the front door overlooked a circle drive. A large garage, and probably a work shop, also of red brick, stood separate off to the left side of the house.

Fred stopped his truck on the circle drive in front of the door.

Mason stopped behind the truck, got out, and met Fred standing next to his truck.

Fred waved his arm in a wide arc. "Started out a thousand acres. Grew to three thousand at one time. It's now only five hundred."

"It's beautiful," Mason said, as he scanned the property. He turned to the house. "Backs to the river."

"It does," Fred said. "We have a wide porch on the back side." He faced Mason. "I didn't get your last name."

Mason paused for a moment to think. "Johnson. Steve Johnson."

"Fred Mason," Fred said.

Mason's expression did not change, having learned the name of the owner from the Internet on his phone before he drove out. "Three hundred years. That would put this property very close to the start of Charleston. It's been in your family from the very beginning then?"

Fred rubbed his chin. "You say you're writing a book."

"Yes sir. Just gathering data for now."

Fred nodded. "What kind of book?"

"Historical," Mason said. "I plan to showcase a number of plantations, talk about how they got started."

"Well, to answer your question, no it didn't start out in my family," Fred said. He took a handkerchief from his pocket and wiped his forehead. He glanced back as the front door opened.

A young woman, middle twenties, dressed in jean shorts, a white button-down shirt, and barefooted, stood in the open doorway. Her hair was pitch black, cut short.

The image of Karen leaped into Mason's mind. The resemblance was uncanny.

"Are you going to stand in the sun all day?" the woman asked. Her attention turned to Mason.

"This is my granddaughter, Emily," Fred said. "We're just talking."

"Well why don't you come around to the porch," she said. "Get out of the sun. I'll bring you two some tea." She stared at Mason.

"This is Steve Johnson," Fred said. "He's a writer; writing a book on plantations in the area. I agreed to answer some of his questions."

Fred turned to Mason. "Want some iced tea?"

"Sure," Mason said. He looked at Emily. "Thank you. You look a lot like someone I used to know."

Emily smiled, gazed at Mason for several moments, and then went back inside. The door closed behind her.

Mason followed Fred around the side along a red brick walk to the back of the house and up on the porch. The view of the river was spectacular, same as before, although the property was much more manicured now. The river itself had barely changed. Crop fields stretched off on both sides of the green grass between the house and the river.

Fred took a seat in a metal porch chair and motioned for Mason to do the same. "What was that you asked me?"

Emily popped out the back door and sat two glasses of iced tea on a metal table. The outside of the glasses was covered with condensation. She smiled at Mason.

Mason smiled back.

"I'll be inside," she said, as she shut the door behind her.

"In your family from the very beginning?"

"Yes and no," Fred said. "Jeremy and Lisa Jackson bought it in 1720. I always thought Lisa was a rather modern name for the early eighteenth century."

"I agree," Mason said.

Fred continued. "Anyhow, Jeremy died two years later, probably from one of those swamp diseases. According to a rumor handed down generation to generation, he worked in the field right along with the slaves, mostly rice. But I don't see how that would be likely. It just wasn't done back then."

Mason nodded. "Probably not. So, they had slaves."

Fred smiled and snorted. "That was another rumor handed down. Supposedly, the Jackson's freed all the slaves and worked out some kind of deal for them to continue working the land. But that's not likely either."

"So how did the property get into the Mason name?"

"Jeremy and Lisa never had children," Fred said. "But there was an aunt or a sister, friend or something, not sure of the relation, also living in the house. She gave birth to one son. Named him Stephen." He looked long at Mason. "Like you."

Mason stared off in the distance for several moments as he took in a deep breath and exhaled. He finally turned back to Fred. "And her name was Mason?"

"Yeah, Karen Mason," Fred said. "Another rather modern name for that time."

"So, Lisa willed the house to Stephen Mason," Mason said.

"And the rest is history."

"What about Karen's husband?" Mason asked.

"That was never real clear," Fred said. "She obviously had a man in her life, but the details didn't make it through time."

Mason nodded. "How many children do you have?"

"Three sons, four grandchildren, three boys and Emily. Emily has lived here with me ever since my wife died a few years ago."

"And this is still a working farm?"

"It is," Fred said. "Much reduced from what it was once, only three hundred acres under cultivation. One of my sons manages the farming part; the others went off to school. One's a doctor, the other's an attorney."

"Sounds like a nice family," Mason said.

"I'm a very lucky man," Fred said.

They both stared at the river without saying anything for a full minute. Finally, Fred turned to Mason.

"There's a painting you might like to see," Fred said. "It's pretty much the only thing that has survived the destruction during the wars."

"I'd love to see it," Mason said.

Fred stood. "Follow me."

Mason followed him through the house to the front sitting room.

Fred pointed to a painting hanging over the brick fireplace. "That's Lisa and Karen."

Mason gazed at the painting. It was a little dark and dingy but the likenesses of Lisa and Karen were unmistakable. Mason's heart beat so hard he was sure

Fred could hear it. His eyes moistened. He cleared his throat. "Two lovely women."

"Strong women," Fred said. "Had to be back then."

"I don't doubt you for a second," Mason said, as he continued to gaze at the painting. His eyes fixated on the boy standing in front of Karen, about ten years old with thick dark hair. "The boy?"

"That was Stephen, the first male Mason in the line. He would be my great, great grandfather. Not sure how many extra greats come in front of that."

The two of them stared at the painting.

Mason could see that both Karen and Lisa had aged some, mostly from hard work he was sure, but they were both still beautiful.

"I'm sorry," Fred said, "I don't have any documents that far back. Either lost in the fires or just disintegrated with the heat and humidity around here."

"That's okay," Mason said. "I believe I have the information I wanted." He checked the new stainless dive watch on his wrist. "I've probably taken up enough of your time."

"Well, if you have more questions, you know where to find me," Fred said.

Fred walked with Mason out the front door. The two of them stood next to Mason's Prius. Fred stuck out his hand. "I'm glad you stopped by Mister Johnson."

They shook.

"You have no idea how much I feel the same," Mason said. "It was very nice to meet you Mister Mason."

Fred lifted his chin and smiled.

Mason got in his car and drove off with a final wave out his window. He drove through the still open gate and stopped at the state road. He looked both ways. There was no traffic in either direction, but Mason didn't pull out. He sat there staring out of his windshield. He knew what he had to do; he just didn't know how to do it.

He finally pulled out on the highway and headed back toward Charleston.

Mason pulled into the parking lot of a small restaurant on the north side of the old part of Charleston. He ordered a large salad for lunch and took out his iPhone. By the time his salad arrived, he had found two good room rental prospects in Mount Pleasant across the Cooper River east of Charleston. Both were available for viewing that afternoon.

As he munched on the salad, he continued to search the Internet. There were several items he wanted to get, but the actual ordering would have to wait until he had an address for receiving shipments.

After lunch he drove directly to the first rental, a two-story house in a residential community. The neighborhood was rather distressed and obviously unregulated by an association. That didn't really matter to him. It turned out to be a room and bath on the top floor with a separate entrance. The woman Mason spoke with had a lease agreement for the entire house and was hoping to offset part of her rent. There would be no rental agreement for him since technically, subleases were not allowed. That wasn't what turned him off about the place. It was her four rambunctious kids. One in particular seemed especially devious, so he decided rather quickly to move on.

The next prospect was a small furnished cottage in back of the main house in a quiet neighborhood. It included a designated place to park, one bedroom, bath, kitchen, and a small living room. It even came with a television. The owner was an elderly woman living alone. They clicked immediately. Mason paid her six months in advance. The best thing about the place was that it was only two miles from the Mount Pleasant Regional Airport.

He spent the rest of the afternoon picking up a few things he would need for the cottage. A nearby Walmart provided almost everything: a few linens, eating utensils, a bowl, a plate, a mug, a pot, and a few items of food including slow-cook oatmeal and fresh fruit which he liked for breakfast. He didn't know how long he would be in the area, so he didn't go overboard with his purchases. He wished he had kept such items from his condo in Miami, but he had no way of knowing then that he would need them so soon. He considered getting a cheap laptop computer, but decided the phone would suffice.

On his way back to the cottage, he stopped by Whole Foods Market for takeout. It was expensive, but he liked the variety. Some of it was even wholesome. He spent the first evening settling into his new home, temporary as it may be. He even watched some television before turning in.

CHAPTER 29

The next morning, he ordered a rucksack to replace the one he lost during the battle with the pirate Edward Low. Online he found one in a premium vintage canvas designed without zippers. He also ordered a couple of knives, both fixed blades with premium steel and a full tang. One was a four-inch spear-point, good for finer work and slicing. The other was much longer, more of a machete with some weight. Both came with fine leather sheaths. In addition, he ordered the components he would need for a small survival kit including fire starting implements, fishing line and hooks, mil spec cordage, and everything else he could think of that might be useful in a survival situation. To that he added a mini water filter, stainless water bottles, foldable camp shovel, and a medium-sized first aid bag, complete with several suture kits. He also ordered a cleaning kit to go along with the new Glock 19 and ten boxes of 9mm ammunition he bought in Miami before he resigned from law enforcement.

He placed a call to a doctor friend back in Miami, explained he would be roughing it in the wilderness for a while, and talked him into a prescription for a wide spectrum, long shelf life antibiotic.

Doing the research for what he wanted and placing the orders took most of the day with a brief stop for lunch from the fridge. By early evening he'd had enough of staring at the tiny screen. He ate dinner and turned in early.

He awoke before the sun. He tried to sleep longer but to no avail. So, he lay there thinking in the dark. His intent was obvious. He had traveled through time twice, so it was apparent that such travel was possible. He didn't know how it worked; he just knew that it did. If it could be done twice, logic dictated it could be done a third. That was his intent, to at least try to return to eighteenth century Charles Town, to Karen, and their son. He owed it to them to at least try. He had an idea about how to go about it, but had no idea if it would work. Still, if he was able to accomplish the impossible, he further intended to be much more prepared than the first time. Hence the accumulation of stuff. In addition to what he had already ordered, he would need a few items of period clothing.

After lying in bed an extra full hour, he finally rose, padded to the kitchen, and made a bowl of his usual porridge and a cup of coffee. As he munched and sipped at the small kitchen table, he made notes on a pad of paper.

Reenactments in the Charleston area were a common occurrence. There had to be someone around capable of making such garments. He checked the Internet on his phone and found two potential shops. He wrote down their contact info.

He turned his attention to the specific items to be ordered. He figured two suits, one a little more formal than the other, but both would include a coat, waistcoat, breeches, stockings, a cravat, and a three-point hat. He noted the particulars on the paper.

As he spooned more porridge into his mouth and munched, he stared down at his bare feet. Shoes. He would need period shoes. No, not shoes, boots. Like the high top variety he ordered from Francois but never picked up. He made a note to research custom boot makers. He already knew there were several in the United States. He was sure that an extra fee could make his order a priority.

Next, he thought of the shoulder holster he wore during his time in Charles Town. He would need another. But this time it would be a custom job without any elastic. Just leather. He made a note.

By the time he finished eating and scribbling, the page was full of notes and drawings. One of those drawings was a small, single-engine airplane. That's what his current license allowed. Riding on an airplane into a cloud—that's how it worked the first time, maybe it would work again. He thought back to the airliner and all the people who had perished during the ditching. This time there would only be one person at risk.

Mason studied the page of notes. Even if he were never able to find a way back, most of the items on his list would come in handy no matter where he ended up.

Dressed and with the dishes washed, he took a seat to wait the few extra minutes until nine o'clock. He had found two potential custom boot makers on the Internet, one in Maine and one in Wisconsin. There were others, but they seemed to specialize in lace-up or cowboy type boots.

On the dot he phoned the one in Maine and spoke to a nice young lady. She passed him on to the production manager. Mason described what he wanted and explained it would be for reenactments, so it had to look the part.

The manager explained that he had fielded several such calls over the years, but except in a couple of cases, most people couldn't afford what it would cost. He would have to pull someone off the line for several days to cut and hand stitch much of the leather.

Mason said he wanted a quality boot that would hold up over time, and he was willing to pay whatever was necessary. He also wanted a rush on the job.

The manager said that the instructions for measuring his feet were on the website and that Mason should print out the forms, follow the instructions precisely, and send them in to the company. The manager would consider the job and let Mason know the cost after he received the forms.

Mason got a similar story from the boot maker in Wisconsin. The only difference was that he got an estimated quote immediately from the second company. A custom pair of boots like Mason wanted would cost a minimum of two thousand dollars.

Mason made a note to stop by the nearest Office Depot so they could print the forms on full size paper. Apparently, drawing a line around his feet on the form was part of the process.

Since it appeared the boots would take the longest, the office store was his first stop that morning. He filled out the necessary forms, including the diagrams of his feet, right there in the store and had them overnight the packages to both companies. He wasn't sure if he would pick the maker based on price, or just order both pair of boots and decide which he liked better.

His next stop was what sounded like the more experienced of the clothiers capable of making period garments. This particular shop actually specialized in historical garments of all kinds and often received orders from around the country.

Mason explained what he had in mind to the owner, a middle-aged gentleman. A little gruff, but he seemed to know his stuff. Mason always told himself he would take superior abilities with a lousy bedside manner over the less experienced but nice any day of the week. It applied to doctors and apparently it applied to tailors.

The owner took Mason's measurements, suggested several fabrics, colors, and ornamentation, and said he could have it all done within two weeks. The owner also suggested a heavier overcoat since it did get cold in South Carolina. Mason agreed. He also asked for a pair of full-length pants and an over-shirt in buckskin. The owner said he could do it. He asked for a rush on the job, but the owner was insistent on the two weeks. It might even take three.

Mason finally relented and paid the man half up front. The price was exorbitant, but the owner promised first rate work and a tailored fit.

By mid-afternoon his head throbbed. Skipping lunch was probably a contributing factor. He picked up some takeout from an Italian place, returned to the cottage where he ate and relaxed for the rest of the day. By early evening he had thought of some other stuff he needed to order, including a couple of heavy-duty waterproof bags. He ordered the items from Amazon. He sat back and contemplated all that he had accomplished in just one day. He realized he was going about this like it was a sure thing. It was far from anything of the sort. The chances of him making it back to Karen were so miniscule it barely registered on the scale of possibilities. Still, he had to try.

The next morning, with all the ordering done, it was time to think about the elephant in the room. A means to the end. An airplane.

Mason sat reclined on the small sofa, feet up on the table, and a mug of coffee on his lap. He visualized his flying lessons four years earlier, the classroom, and his time in an actual airplane. He learned to fly and soloed in a Cessna 172. He also had time in a friend's Cessna TTx, basically an improved Columbia 400. He had more hours in the former, but he really liked the latter. Plus, the TTx had more range, greater speed, and a higher ceiling. The higher ceiling—twenty-five thousand feet—might come into play.

He pulled out his phone and searched a few sites. It quickly became apparent that he couldn't afford to buy one, even one used. Most of the used Cessna TTx 400's were priced well over three hundred thousand, some were four and five. The sale of his condo had netted him a couple of a hundred thousand, plus he had another two hundred thousand stashed away in a retirement account, and another eighty thousand in readily available funds. But he couldn't afford to spend all of it on an airplane. There wouldn't be enough left to buy fuel. And what if this entire endeavor was a bust? That left one option. He'd have to rent an airplane. He didn't like the idea of ditching someone else's plane, even if it was insured, but there was really no other way.

He turned back to his phone. There were plenty of planes for rent in the area, but most didn't fit the bill. They were too slow and their altitude was limited.

Mason dropped his phone on the sofa and laid his head back. Maybe this was a pipe dream, and impossible dream. It could end up taking nearly every cent he had to even make the attempt. What if it didn't work? What if he couldn't find that black cloud with the blue haze? What if he did and, heaven forbid, he ended up in the Stone Age? He was willing to take risks, but everything depended on finding that cloud. After all, there were thousands of flights every day and his flight, Miami to Charlotte, was apparently the first to encounter that dark cloud with the blue haze. He had a thought. Maybe his flight wasn't the first.

He picked up his phone, did some searching, and found there had been two flights, plus his for three, that had gone missing over the Atlantic without a trace in the past fifty years. All were off the east coast. Three planes over fifty years did not provide very good odds of finding that cloud again. But at least the odds were better than zero.

◆◆◆

Mason ended up finding a 2008 Cessna 400 TT Corvalis Turbocharged available for rent at the Charleston airport. The owner had several planes and was amenable to a six-month lease. The plane had four hundred hours on the engine and superior electronics. The owner was also open to selling the plane, but the price was beyond Mason's budget. They agreed on fifty thousand for the six months. Mason considered that a bargain since hourly rental for a plane like that was over two hundred dollars. Three flights a week, five hours per flight, for six months at the hourly rate would run over seventy-eight thousand. And Mason planned to fly as much as weather permitted. The owner also agreed to move the plane to Mount Pleasant as long as Mason paid for the parking.

Even though it had recently gone through its annual inspection, Mason hired a mechanic to go over the plane. There were no major problems found.

The owner wanted three check rides in varying weather condition which they accomplished over the following ten days.

Mason ended up ordering the boots from both companies and within three weeks he had them in hand along with all the other stuff he had ordered. Both pair of boots fit fine and were of high quality. Both could be resoled with leather without modern adhesives.

Mason also converted several thousand dollars into silver ingots with no markings, each about an ounce in weight.

He carefully packed everything into the two waterproof bags, included plenty of food—jerky and protein bars—and loaded them in the plane along with a small rubber inflatable raft and a paddle. He was finally ready. He had the equipment, the means, and the desire. The rest was up to fate.

CHAPTER 30

On what Mason called day one, he parked his car at the airport and walked out to the plane sitting all nice and shiny on the apron. The tank was full, the plane was loaded, and the sky was clear. Wearing jeans, t-shirt, a light Patagonia puffy jacket, and lace up service boots, he climbed into the cockpit.

He immediately went into his preflight. He checked the breakers, selected the fuel mixture to full rich, adjusted the prop to full power, and flipped the strobe on. With the master on, he primed for four seconds, and turned the key to start the engine. The plane vibrated as the prop spun and fired. He changed the mixture to lean, checked the speed brakes, checked the alternators, and checked audio and the frequency. He checked the weather on the Garmin G100 glass display and noted the wind and freeze zones. Ready for taxi, he announced his approach to the runway as a precaution even though this airfield did not have a tower. He released the brake, increased the throttle, and felt the plane begin to roll. Just short of the runway he stopped the plane and performed an engine run up at full rich. He noted a slight RPM drop during the check, so he switched the mixture to lean, waited twenty seconds, and performed the RPM check again. All was normal. He cycled the prop, checked the idle, and checked all the gauges. Everything appeared ready for flight. He let the plane roll out onto the runway, made his turn, and announced his departure to the Charleston tower as he throttled forward. The plane's acceleration pressed his torso back against the seat as the speed increased. The airspeed indicator came alive and at seventy-five knots he rotated the stick.

The plane lofted into the air and climbed at what seemed like slow motion as the earth dropped away. On a due south heading, the wide expanse of the blue ocean quickly came into view. He notified Charleston of his course, speed, and intended altitude.

Mason turned off the backup fuel pump, retracted the flaps, adjusted the mixture for optimum speed and fuel consumption, and let the plane continue to climb. He gazed at the city of Charleston out his right window until it disappeared under the wing.

At fifteen thousand feet he leveled off and continued his due south heading. He intended to fly a pattern off the coast from Savannah and gradually extend his distance south. At optimum fuel consumption, he could stay in the air for five hours or so. He could fly all the way to Miami if he wanted, he had plenty of range, but he wouldn't be going that far south. He would run patterns closer to the shore, down to about even with Jacksonville, maybe Daytona Beach.

The first day of flying the pattern was uneventful. He saw a lot of puffy white clouds but nothing like the dark formation he remembered from the airliner's window.

He landed the plane at Mount Pleasant, refueled, and parked it in its designated spot. He grabbed some takeout on his way back to the cottage, ate, watched television, slept, and went through the same process the very next day. And the day after that.

He didn't meet many people with this routine, a few, mostly while food shopping or doing laundry. There were even a couple of attractive women who expressed some obvious interest, one in produce and the other on the cereal aisle. Was he tempted? Maybe somewhere deep inside. But Karen's face popped in his mind each time to pull him back from the dark side.

After the first week he backed off the daily flights. The fuel charges were starting to add up much faster than he expected. So, weather permitting, he took on a three-flight per week schedule. The actual days varied, but three days a week was his goal.

After thirty days, even that routine was starting to wear on him. More than ever before, he began to question his sanity. He had no doubt that Karen was back there, wondering what had happened, but the idea of returning to that time was growing doubtful to the point of dread.

He saw dark clouds, even got bounced around when he flew into a couple of fairly hefty storms, but nothing like the one he remembered. He kept his eyes peeled for the blue haze, arcs of light really, but so far, he had seen nothing like that.

Around day sixty he began to feel the pangs of anxiety even when he wasn't flying. But it was worse in the air. It's weird to feel bored and anxious at the same time. But that's exactly how he felt sitting in that cockpit, hour after hour, day after day. To say doubt was a big part of his life would be an understatement. His mind would drift to other things he could be doing and probably should be doing, like finding a job. He could go back to Miami, declare himself cured, give them the answers they wanted to hear, and resume the life he had before he stepped foot on that airliner. It was an option.

The Cessna's engine droned on as he sat there idly in the cockpit. The airplane pretty much flew itself which was good and bad. Good because he only had to keep one eye on the instruments and one eye out the windows. It was bad because the monotony was beginning to dull his senses. If he kept this up the entire six months, he really would be insane.

In the beginning the high point of each flight was lifting off from the runway, but now the high point was when it was time to head home. Mason knew this wasn't good. There was no way he could continue this way much longer. The prospect of coming across another portal was small to begin with, but now, Mason realized, it was actually the size of an electron. Realistically there was no chance at all.

On day ninety-three, as he turned the key to start the engine, he was convinced this would be his last flight. One more time and that was it. He smirked and shook his head when he realized he had told himself the same thing every flight day for the last month. But this time he was sure he meant it.

On a first name basis now with all the Charleston tower controllers, he announced his departure, accelerated, and lifted off into space. By now he had flown in every kind of weather, from clear skies to some serious thunderstorms. On a couple of occasions, the tower warned him that flying was too dangerous. This was one of those days. At least the thunder and lightning would break up the monotony. He had become so accustomed to the plane he began to think of it as his. He ensured all the routine maintenance was performed, per the agreement with the owner, and he kept it neat and clean. There wasn't much else to do when he wasn't flying.

Rather than leveling out at fifteen thousand like usual, he headed up to twenty-three after getting clearance from Jacksonville. That was just two thousand short of the top ceiling for the Cessna, but high enough to get him over most of the rough air that had moved in over the Atlantic. Mason had been up that high in the Cessna only once before. The turbocharger kept the air-to-fuel mixture in sync, and the onboard oxygen kept him from developing a headache.

Usually he followed his regular route south, but this time he turned more easterly which would take him farther out over the Atlantic away from Florida and hopefully away from the storm. In the beginning, flying out over the ocean in a single-engine plane had been a little nerve racking. But after so many flights he didn't worry about it anymore even with the dark clouds looming ahead.

As he suspected, just before reaching altitude, he broke out of the clouds and entered clear and much smoother air. He continued on.

When the weather screen indicated a break in the system below, Mason decided to make his turn early. He received clearance from Jacksonville of the new direction and a lower altitude.

He leveled out at twenty-thousand which was considerably more turbulent. He checked his gauges and continued to survey his surroundings. There were fat, dark clouds in the distance to the east and west, but just as indicated on the weather screen, the route directly ahead was relatively clear, just a few clouds and a little rain.

As he cruised along thinking of nothing in particular, out of nowhere the plane pitched and suddenly dropped. He felt the force of the wind and the plane's rapid descent. It was cause for concern, but he knew he had plenty of altitude and the plane was running fine. As expected, the plane's descent abated nearly as quickly as it started, and he was once again at level flight. Looking up from his instruments, he saw the wall of clouds on both sides closing in ahead. This was unexpected. The two banks were actually merging into a flurry of swirling mist, mostly dark gray and black. He checked the weather and found that the top of the system was above his ceiling; below, the winds were even worse. That's the moment he wished he had heeded the tower's warning. He should have stayed home.

The air became more turbulent, the plane bucked, and the engine coughed but quickly regained its footing.

All he could do was hold on, keep going, and have faith. That's when the lightning struck in a flash of blinding light and the thunder *boomed*. The plane dipped and recovered. He found himself gripping the stick so hard his knuckles had turned pure white. The muscles in his neck and shoulders were nearly to the point of spasm when he consciously forced himself to relax.

The wall of clouds ahead had turned pitch black with frequent arcs of static electricity all swirling in a funnel shaped mass. There was no going around, above, or below.

He suddenly realized he had been holding his breath, so he consciously relaxed his shoulders and neck again, inhaled deeply, and exhaled. He resumed normal breathing and pressed on.

Just before he entered the wall of darkness, lightning struck again, this time up close and personal. The white-hot streak vaporized the air in front of him in a cloud of misty blue. The plane bucked, coughed once, and regained its composure. And then the darkness closed in around him. Lights from the instrument displays became brighter in the relative darkness of the clouds. The plane dropped from wind shear and nearly as quickly regained altitude. It jerked from side-to-side and at times vibrated to the point that Mason was sure everything was about to short out. But the little plane chugged on.

Fourteen knuckle-white minutes later the plane emerged from the storm just as the instruments finally gave up the ghost.

Mason flipped some switches and cycled through the various displays, but basically just got a steady green glow with an occasional blip. The thing was dead. Obviously, the vibration and static electricity had been too much.

It didn't matter; Mason knew generally where he was and kept the nose heading north. He'd meet the coast at some point and limp back to Mount Pleasant. He looked to the left and right at the dark clouds gaining distance behind him, wiped some sweat from his forehead with the back of his hand, and flew in the direction of home.

CHAPTER 31

Ted Wilson stepped inside the open door to Mike Reeves' office. "Hey."

Reeves looked up from the papers on his desk. "Hey."

"You remember Steve Mason?"

"Of course," Reeves said. "What of him?"

"Apparently he's been doing a lot of flying out of Mount Pleasant South Carolina."

Reeves expressed bewilderment. "Yeah?"

"His plane is missing."

Reeves cocked his head. "When?"

"Just got an FAA notice. About two hours ago. They lost contact when he flew into a storm. His transponder dropped off as well."

Reeves stood up and walked to a map of the southeast United States covering most of one wall. "Where?"

Ted walked over and put a finger on the map. "Southeast of Savannah, about two hundred miles."

"What in the hell was he doing out there?"

"Don't know."

Reeves turned to Ted. "What are they doing about it?"

"Waiting for the storm to clear. Visibility is near zero on the deck."

"That son-of-a-bitch," Reeves said. He returned to his desk and picked up the phone. "He just wouldn't let it go." Reeves flicked his hand motioning for Ted to leave and dialed the phone.

◆◆◆

The next morning Mike Reeves and Dan Miller stood in the Jacksonville office of the US Coast Guard. The office was bustling with the sights and sounds of people busy behind various screens and displays, except for the man in a commander's uniform standing in front of Reeves and Miller.

"The storm cleared late last night," the commander said. "We had planes and water craft out at sunup." He looked at his watch. "That was four hours ago. It's a big ocean and it will take some time."

"I understand," Reeves said. "Can I get a ride on the next flight out?"

"No," the commander said. "Don't have the room and you'd just be in the way. Let us do our job."

"Fine," Reeves said.

"They're doing everything possible," Miller said. He turned to the commander. "Nothing from an emergency beacon?"

"Not so far," the commander said. "But we have to be in range to receive the signal, especially if it's submerged."

Reeves snorted and turned away.

"You'll have to excuse me," the commander said. He turned and walked toward a group of people crowded around a computer screen.

"I should have locked that bastard in a room," Reeves said. "This is as much my fault as it is his."

"Not true," Miller said. "You did everything you could."

"Obviously, not everything."

Two days later, Reeves was wide awake before the sun, but still in bed. He rose up, twisted, punched his pillow to make it flatter, and then lowered his head as he rolled to his side. He hated hotel room pillows. They were either too hard or too soft.

In his mind, he played back Mason's report of everything he encountered after the airliner went down. The recording of what he said had been reduced to a written report which Mason signed.

Reeves recalled the details of what Mason had said. Of course, flying through a cloud and being thrust back in time was ridiculous, and obviously he imagined or hallucinated his purported time in eighteenth century Charles Town. It didn't happen. Still, his account was detailed and vivid. But that's often the case with hallucinations or whatever it was Mason experienced in his mind. When he didn't improve over the weeks and months after leaving the hospital, Reeves should have done more. The poor bastard died trying to prove what he imagined was true. And that was on Reeves, at least partially.

A knock on the door brought Reeves from his thoughts. He rose, padded to the door, and swung it wide. Miller stood at the threshold fully dressed. Reeves motioned for Miller to enter.

"They've terminated the search," Miller said.

Reeves nodded without looking back. "Want some coffee?"

"Sure," Miller said. "Get dressed and we'll go down for breakfast."

"I can make some here," Reeves said, as he ambled over to the plastic coffee pot next to the television. He fumbled with the various parts and then just stopped. He lowered his hands to the counter.

"I don't need any coffee," Miller said.

Reeves nodded without looking up.

"We might as well head back to Miami this morning," Miller said.

Reeves turned to face Miller. "You should go back. I need to take care of Mason's personal effects."

"They found his car at the Mount Pleasant Regional Airport."

"I'll start there," Reeves said.

Miller nodded. "I can tag along if you want."

Reeves pursed his lips as he considered the offer. "That's okay," he finally said, "you head back. I should be back in the office in a couple of days."

"Okay Mike," he said, as he started to turn. "You're okay, right?"

Reeves turned, faced Miller directly, and smiled. "I'm fine. Just need to take care of some stuff for a buddy."

Miller tightened his lips, raised his chin, and closed the door behind him.

Reeves stared at the closed door.

Reeves drove his rental sedan onto the Mount Pleasant Regional Airport grounds and pulled to a stop next to a white Prius. He exited the rental and approached Mason's car.

Local law enforcement had run the tags and confirmed it was Mason's car, but Reeves recognized it from Miami. He always thought it was weird that a tough, special forces operator would drive such a mild-mannered car. The search had been called off early that morning, so the car had not yet been searched.

Reeves checked all the doors but found them locked. He peered in the windows and found it empty except for a single cardboard Amazon box on the back seat. The delivery address on the box was clearly visible. He made a note.

He walked over to two men standing next to a Piper Malibu Mirage. "Nice plane," he said, as he approached.

Both men nodded.

Reeves pointed at the Prius. "I'm wondering about the owner of that car."

"Belongs to Mason, Steve Mason I think," one of the men said.

"He's here practically every day," the other man said.

"When was the last time either of you saw him?"

The first man cocked his head. "Can I ask who you are?"

Reeves pulled out his badge and flipped open the case. "He's a former employee."

The man stepped closer and peered at the badge. "Federal Air Marshal." He stepped back. "Well let's see."

"I think it was three days ago," the second man said, "Monday. He was here early and departed as usual."

"As usual?"

"Yeah," the first man said. "He flies several times a week sometimes. Always gone about five hours, which is about the range on the Cessna he flew."

Reeves gazed around the field. "Is that plane here?"

Both men glanced, but already knew. "No," they both said in unison.

"What's this about?" the first man asked.

"He went missing two days ago, out over the Atlantic," Reeves said.

"That's too bad," the first man said. "He kept to himself, but he seemed like a nice guy."

"He was," Reeves said. He thanked the two men, peered in the windows of the Prius again, and returned to the rental car.

Reeves used the GPS in his car to find the address listed on the box, and he soon pulled up in front of the house. He knocked on the door and was greeted by an elderly lady.

"Hi, my name is Mike Reeves," he said to the woman. "I'm a friend of Steve Mason's."

"Mason," the woman said. "He rents a cottage from me. In the back."

"There's been an accident, and it appears he may have gone down in the plane over the ocean," Reeves said.

Shock replaced the woman's kind expression. "That's terrible. What happened?"

"Not sure," Reeves said. He pulled out his badge and opened the case. "He's a former air marshal, a federal law enforcement official. I'm here to try to figure out what happened."

The woman glanced at the badge. "What can I do?"

"I'd like to get access to the cottage. There might be something there that will help us piece it together."

"Wait just a moment," she said, as she turned back into the house. She returned a few moments later with a key in her hand. "It's around this way."

Reeves followed the woman down a stone walkway to the cottage in back.

The woman opened the door and stepped inside. She held the door for Reeves. "It's simple, but Mister Mason didn't seem to mind."

She stood in the light of the open door while Reeves stepped into the interior.

There wasn't much to see. There were a few items of clothing in the bedroom, some food in the fridge and on the counter, the covers on the bed were tossed, and there was a pad and some papers on the small kitchen table.

Reeves examined the papers. There were receipts for a number of items. Reeves found the one for the two pair of leather high-top boots, and the one for several items of clothing from a local tailor. He read the description for the clothing. When it registered, he let the receipts drop to the table as he lowered his arms to his sides. He stared at the ceiling. After several moments, he dropped his chin and picked up the pad. A list of various items was scribbled on several pages, along with a lot of doodling, and an address. It was a house number on Ashley River Road, Charleston, SC. He made a note of the address. Based on the receipts, the notes, and the items he had purchased, it appeared Mason was planning a trip into the bush. Camping maybe. That would be a good explanation except for the period clothing he had bought.

Reeves turned to the woman. "Thank you." He surveyed the room again. "I think that's all I need."

The woman led Reeves to the door and stood to the side as he stepped out. "Is he coming back?"

Reeves stopped and turned. His jaw tightened for a moment. "I don't think so."

"What do I do with his stuff?"

"I think it's safe to donate anything usable to Goodwill," Reeves said.

The woman nodded.

Reeves returned to his car, set the GPS for the address he found on the pad of paper, and drove away. It was late afternoon, but he felt he had time even with the traffic in Charleston.

He drove west, crossed over the Cooper River on the Ravenel Bridge, through the city on Highway 17, across the Ashley River, and north on Highway 61. He soon pulled into a driveway indicated as his destination on the GPS. Before him stood a high, wrought-iron gate attached to arms that would open the gate electrically. In front of the gate on the driver's side stood a concrete pillar with a key pad and a camera. A small placard said to push the number 3 for service. Reeves pushed the number 3.

The loud speaker squawked with a man's voice. "Yes?"

"Hi, I'm following up on a missing person. I found this address written on a pad in the man's effects."

"Are you law enforcement?" the man asked. He sounded middle-aged, forties maybe.

"I am," Reeves said.

"Hold your badge up to the camera."

Reeves did as instructed. He saw the lens in the camera change focus. A few seconds later the gates swung open.

"Drive up to the house," the man said.

Reeves pulled up and stopped at the top of the circle drive.

A man in probably his late forties, wearing jeans and a white t-shirt, was standing in the open doorway. He approached when Reeves opened the car door and stepped out. It was warm for a March day.

"What is this about?" the man asked. "And please excuse my appearance. I was working in the back yard. Came in for some water and heard your buzz from the gate.

"I'm looking into a missing person," Reeves said.

"And you think it has something to do with me?" the man asked.

"Well, this address. As I mentioned, I found the address scribbled on a pad in the house he was renting. He went missing a couple of days ago."

"Can I see that badge again?"

Reeves pulled the badge and extended his hand.

"Federal Air Marshal," the man said, as he lifted his chin.

"He was a colleague. His plane when down over the ocean a couple of days ago."

"I see," the man said. "And who was this man?"

Reeves pulled a four by six color photo from his inside coat pocket.

The man perused the photo for several seconds. "He does look familiar somehow, but I don't think I've ever met him. Sorry."

"You're sure?"

The man looked at the photo again. "Nope, never met him."

"And you're the owner of this property?" Reeves asked.

"I am, along with my three brothers, as of last year when our dad died."

Reeves turned in a circle. "It's a beautiful place."

"Been in the family for three hundred years," the man said.

Reeves turned back to the man. "Well I guess I've taken up enough of your time." He turned to leave but then stopped. "By the way, any chance I could get a glass of that water?"

"Sure, the man said," as he turned and stepped off. "Follow me."

Reeves followed the man through the open door and into a large sitting room with a fireplace.

The man continued through the room and into an adjoining kitchen. He placed a glass up to the refrigerator's water dispenser and let the glass fill. "Filtered water."

Reeves smiled and nodded. He took the glass from the man when offered and took a long drink. He looked around the kitchen. "The house really is beautiful. How old?"

"This version was built in 1872 to replace the one burned down during the Civil War. The one before was burned down during the Revolutionary War so this is the third iteration."

Reeves finished the water and handed the glass to the man.

He placed the glass on the counter.

"Well, I guess that's all I need," Reeves said. He turned. "This way?"

"Yep," the man said. He led Reeves back into the sitting room and toward the front door.

Reeves paused in the middle of the solid wood floor and gazed around the room. His eyes fell on a painting hanging over the fireplace. He pointed. "Original owners?"

The man stopped and turned back. "First in the family."

Reeves focused on the five people: two men, two women, and a boy. All wore clothing from the early eighteenth century. He stepped closer to the painting and squinted at their faces. He tightened his jaw. One of the faces he recognized. The resemblance was unmistakable. "Who are they?"

The man stepped closer. "That's Jeremy and Lisa Jackson on the left and Karen and Stephen Mason on the right. That's their son, Michael, there in front. The first owners in my family."

Reeves gazed at Mason's likeness in the painting. He glanced back at the man. "What did you say your name was?"

"Michael Mason. I was named after the boy in the painting." He smiled as he peered at the boy.

"And the four of them owned the property?"

"Well, started out in the Jackson name, but apparently the wife wasn't able to have children. The property was willed to Michael there."

"And the Mason's only had the one child."

"Yep. With so many childhood deaths back then, most families had a parcel of kids hoping at least some would survive."

"But they had just the one," Reeves said.

"Not sure why they didn't have more, maybe the wife wasn't able."

"Or maybe he didn't want to mess up history," Reeves said.

"What?"

"Nothing," Reeves said, as he stepped closer to the painting and squinted. "What's that in Mister Mason's right hand?" he asked, already knowing the answer.

Michael stepped closer. "None of us in the family could ever figure that out. Looks like something gold. His fingers are closed around most of it. Hard to tell, especially with the age of this painting. It's pretty much the only thing here that goes back to the very beginning, except their graves. They're all buried on the property."

"Like a badge," Reeves said.

"Yeah, now that you mention it, like a badge." He leaned closer to the spot of gold in the painting and then peered at Reeves. "Like your badge."

Reeves nodded and turned to Michael. "Where are your brothers?"

"Two doctors and a lawyer," Michael said. "Too busy to worry about this place. That's my job."

Reeves extended his hand. "It was very nice to meet you Mister Mason.

Michael took his hand. "You too Mister—"

"Reeves, Mike Reeves."

Michael escorted Reeves to the door. "I can't imagine why this address was written on the pad, but I hope you find your missing man."

"I have a very good idea where he is," Reeves said.

Michael smiled, they shook hands again, and Reeves returned to his car.

He drove away with thoughts of what it would be like to live in eighteenth-century Charles Town.

A REQUEST FROM THE AUTHOR

Thank you for reading *A Ripple In Time*. I hope you enjoyed the story as much as I enjoyed writing it. I do have one request. I ask that you please take a few moments to enter a product review on your Amazon Orders page. Independent authors depend on reviews to get their books noticed. And reviews also help make my future books better. A few moments of your time would be much appreciated. I look forward to reading your thoughts. —**Victor Zugg**

ABOUT THE AUTHOR

Victor Zugg is a former US Air Force officer and OSI special agent who served and lived all over the world. Given his extensive travels and opportunities to settle anywhere, it is ironic that he now resides in Florida, only a few miles from his hometown of Orlando. He credits the warm temperatures for that decision.

Check out the author's other novels—*Solar Plexus (1)*, *Near Total Eclipse (Solar Plexus 2)*, *Surrounded By The Blue*, and *From Near Extinction*.